I0527424

Dipped

Stripped and

Dead

Elise Hyatt

Goldport Press

Copyright © 2018 by Sarah A. Hoyt

Cover Copyright © 2018 by Jack Wylder

Cover Design by Jack Wylder

All rights reserved.

No portion of this book may be reproduced in any form without written permission from the publisher or author, except as permitted by U.S. copyright law.

CONTENTS

ONE WOMAN'S TRASH

W HEN I WAS LITTLE, I was going to be a ballerina. This was a strange ambition for a five-year-old who could trip over both feet at the same time while standing still. As soon as that tragic fact dawned on me, I settled on the more attainable ambition of becoming a lion tamer. This, at least, seemed perfectly within my reach, because my cat always did exactly what I wanted her to—well, except when she balked at jumping through the lighted hoop. Which is just as well, because Mom didn't exactly approve of my setting fire to her quilting frame. With the quilt in it.

In the aftermath of the fire-in-the-living-room incident and subsequent grounding, I'd regretfully dropped the lion-taming ambition—probably good, because Fluffy wouldn't come near me anymore, though her fur did grow back—and with it all my hopes of a career in the performing arts.

A failure at age six, my ego crushed, I'd actually been weak enough to consider Dad's lifelong ambition of having me grow up to become a private eye. Except that I wasn't absolutely sure what a private eye was—it seemed to me you'd have to go around with your hands over your eyes to prevent anyone from seeing them and . . .

Well, that also didn't go well. And my *Little Investigator's Kit*, which Dad bought me, didn't provide me with many clues. I spread the fingerprint powder over the cat, finger-painted with the ink pad, and used the magnifying glass to start a fire in the leaf pile in the backyard.

After the fire department had been by and we'd found Fluffy cowering under the azalea bushes at the far end, I thought that this private eye thing was by far too hazardous.

And this is how I never quite figured out what to be when I grew up.

Which probably explained why, at age twenty-nine, I had parked at the edge of the Goldport College campus and was rummaging through a Dumpster.

Okay, it wasn't exactly as dire as Mom had always said it would be. I wasn't living on the streets. I still had all my teeth—even if there had been some doubt about that when I went flying from my bike at age eight, after riding down Suicide Hill with no hands—and I wasn't looking for food.

Well, at least I wasn't *exactly* looking for food, only for the stuff that allowed me to make a living. Because, after waffling through two years as an English major (until the word *postmodernism* could put me to sleep like a hypnotic suggestion) and a year as a teaching major (before I remembered that another name for hell was *schoolroom full of kids*) and a year in pre-law (before I realized I just didn't have the required forked tongue), I'd left college with an MRS degree.

And when *that* exploded in my face—worse than the quilting frame—I'd found myself as at a loss for what I wanted to do with my life as I had been at six, when my hopes of lion-taming had been so cruelly dashed.

Only no longer was it a career, or a matter of keeping myself amused, or even feeling like a productive member of society. No. My marriage to Alex—All-ex, completely ex, he couldn't be more ex if I killed him, something I was tempted to do twice a week and four times on Sundays or whenever we had any interaction—Mahr, though otherwise completely unproductive, had left me with a child.

Enoch (his father had chosen the name because he thought it sounded solid; I called him E because I hoped to save on therapy bills when he grew up) had been one year old when his father and I got divorced. His primary interests in life had been attempting to stuff all his fingers in his mouth at once and finding ever more interesting bugs to eat.

He was still interested in gastronomic entomology at two and a half. But he didn't look at all like All-ex—or like me, though he had the blond hair and blue eyes I'd had till age three, before both had turned pitch-black—and he showed some signs, through some amazing genetic mutation, of growing up to be someone worthwhile. Which would be thwarted if I let him starve to death or even—forbid the thought—if I allowed his father full custody.

My working retail would have supported us—sort of—but I'd have had to leave E with someone. Mom and Dad weren't an option. They worked all day in Remembered Murder, the mystery bookstore they owned, where Fluffy—who I believed remained alive on the hopes I'd die first—was store cat. And Fluffy started twitching whenever she saw me or E.

This left me with the one skill I'd more or less inadvertently picked up while furnishing my first home. I'd taken a course in furniture restoration and refinishing at the community college. Back then I'd done it to fit furnishing a house within the scant budget All-ex would allot to it.

On my own—after some experimentation—I found that picking up old beat-up and abused furniture, refinishing it or fixing it or giving it a total makeover, and selling it—under the business name of Daring Finds—made just about enough money to keep me and E in three meals a day with a roof over our heads.

Said roof was rented and in an area of town that made my friend Ben cringe, and the meals might run to pancakes a lot, but it beat the alternative. Homeless shelters struck me as a terrible place to take a kid who liked to sample bugs.

And so I was at the corner of the college, on a bright Saturday in late May, looking at a bulky green Dumpster.

You see, although real antiques go for exorbitant sums in Colorado, they sell at those prices *because* they are hard to get. Very few people have an attic full of pieces like Grandmama's breakfront dresser or Great-Great-Grandmama's Duncan Phyfe dining set that they would be willing to sell at a garage sale for mere pennies and that could be made radiant by a simple wiping with oil.

No. I heard of such things from other people who came from places out east, but I figured that most people on the way to Colorado by covered wagon had ditched Grandma's carved walnut chairs halfway across Kansas, possibly with Grandma still clinging to them.

What could be gotten—in various states of disrepair—were twentieth-century knockoffs and good, solid furniture of forties and fifties vintage, made in factories, but capable of looking quite good once one had scraped off the twenty coats of paint, including the two inevitable metallic coats applied in the sixties by someone who had found truly interesting mushrooms.

Oh, sometimes, rarely, in a thrift shop or at a garage sale, I'd come across a good piece, which I refinished and took to Denver to leave for consignment at Shabby Chic. But for the most part, I cleaned and fixed and varnished, then put the pieces up at the local flea market, where they made a modest profit just barely enough for our daily pancakes.

Which brought me to cost cutting.

"Bah, bah, bah, bah!" E said from the strapped-in safety of his child seat in the back of my fifth-hand blue Volvo station wagon. I looked over to see him glaring at me, his face scrunched intently, as he clutched the top of the half-lowered window with his chubby spit-covered fingers. "Bah!"

Because he could say quite a few words and even the occasional sentence, I assumed "Bah" was his view of the situation.

I looked over to the Dumpster, overflowing with black trash bags. Though it was still too early in the morning for it to be really hot, there was a distinct smell of spoiled meat coming off the container. "Undoubtedly," I told E. "On the other hand, look—there's something that looks like a gracefully curved table leg. Painted white, but a table leg."

"Bah!" E said.

Which was probably true. I frowned up at the maybe-table-leg.

Yeah, it was definitely wood and it looked gracefully curved. But the way my luck was running lately, it was probably just the leg, which some student had broken off the long-discarded table and used for years as an ersatz remote control to turn the TV on and off without getting up.

On the other hand, I'd learned in my year and a half in this business that end of term at the college was the absolutely best time to pick up real antiques—the type of thing I could restore and sell for enough to keep me in rent and food for a month. I figured parents back east gave the kids whatever had been kicking around the family for a few decades, and the kids—not really caring for it—discarded it when they graduated. So it was worth a try. Though I would admit, the way things were piled in that Dumpster, it was likely to all collapse on me as I tried to look through it.

Well, I thought, dubiously, as I shoved my hands in the pocket of my denim coveralls, donned for the occasion. If that happened, I would just have to remove the coveralls and shove them in the trunk of my car to wash when I got back home. "Tell you what," I told E. "I'll give it a quick look, and if there's no sign of anything interesting, we'll go back home and have some nice pancakes."

E looked offended, probably because we had eaten pancakes for the last three meals in a row, and said, "Bah!"

"Okay, fine. Just a quick look." As I spoke, I pulled out the extra-thick, chemical-resistant gloves I kept in the pocket of the coveralls and slipped them on. I'd added the gloves to my getup about six months ago, when I'd put my hand on something so disgusting even E wouldn't put it in his mouth. I started climbing up the side of the metal container.

There is a technique to climbing Dumpsters. I'm as sure of it as I'm sure there is a technique to lion taming. Unfortunately, I don't know either.

What I did was to try to clamber up the little metal ridge on the side of the Dumpster, the one where the claws of the trash truck grab when they tip it, and try to touch the piled-up bags as little as humanly possible, while I took a look at the contents. If justified, I would then map my acquisition of the pieces that were worth getting.

A hand here, a hand there, a hand on the plastic bag, and another hand reaching up for the table leg. So far, so good. To be honest, my greatest fear when doing this was that I'd get my hand stuck on a used needle. I didn't think the gloves would hold up to it.

Precariously perched on the mass of trash, I grabbed at the table leg and pulled. It was held up on something, which meant that it just might be an intact table. Also, from the look of it, up closer, it deserved investigation. You can tell real wood because it's lighter, and the edges of any carving are sharper—even under multiple layers of paint—than pressed conglomerate board.

Of course, this wasn't a guarantee that the rest of the piece was an-tique or even real wood. Because legs are hard to make of pressboard, they are usually real wood—often cheap pine—even in trash modern pieces.

I pulled at it again. It didn't feel heavy enough to be pressboard, but it was definitely caught on something.

One more pull, and it came loose. And then I did. There was that moment of confusion that comes before any accident—the moment before you go flying off your bike and mouth meets ground, at the bottom of Suicide Hill. The moment you will replay over and over again in your mind, thinking if only you'd done something, if only you'd reacted in some specific way, you could have averted the whole mess.

The truth was, it was already too late.

As I pulled, the table gave—the whole thing coming loose and leaving me to overbalance and fall backward, landing with a thud on the asphalt of the parking lot, while bags of trash, a chair, and what looked like a piece of a drawer rained all around me.

As soon as my brain stopped rattling in my head, I thought some-thing had made the Dumpster explode. But as I blinked and looked around, I realized nothing had been fragmented as such.

Now, I don't have much experience with explosions. The closest I ever came was when I had filled a flask with gasoline and thrown it at the garden shed. I was twelve and I'd just read about this in a book.

Look, *nothing* would have happened, if Mom hadn't been warming up the grill at the time and if I weren't such a bad shot.

But the fragments of the grill—and the oak tree, bits of which had somehow managed to end up embedded in our back door—hadn't looked as whole as these bags did.

The bags must have been holding the tabletop down, and I'd pulled hard enough to bring down all the bags atop the overloaded Dumpster. I groaned, realizing that now I would have to pick up each one and throw them back in. At least the table seemed to be a real prize—the top too thin to be any kind of pressboard, and the little downturn on the edge speaking of at least reasonable quality, if not age.

"Oooh oh," E said from the car, his face contracting into a distasteful frown. "Phew."

The *phew* was justified. I realized that the miasma of rotting meat had grown exponentially stronger. Presumably the rotting burgers were in one of the bags. "Yeah, ew," I told E, as I opened the back of the car and put the table in, before looking back at the bags. "Right, I'll put them back in, and then we'll go home, okay?"

"Yay."

It was universal. Okay. There might be other furniture in the Dumpster, but I didn't feel looking. Not with that smell Nope. I was going to put the bags back and go home.

So I grabbed the nearest couple of bags, which felt quite light, as though they were filled with clothes, and headed for the Dumpster. I'd taken the whole accumulation of bags off the top, and I could probably fling these into the Dumpster without climbing it. Except that with my luck they'd fall on my head again.

I looked over my shoulder and saw E looking intently at me, like he expected me to do something interesting. Right. I wasn't in the mood to gratify his expectations. I'd climb the side of the Dumpster and *put* the bags on top.

Joining action to thought, I climbed up the side of the Dumpster again, carefully balancing with a bag in each hand. At the top, I stretched out my hand to put the first bag inside.

And then I made a terrible mistake. I looked in the Dumpster. I swallowed hard—my body reacting to the stench before I could figure out what I was looking at.

What looked like another chair that matched the one that had fallen off lay at cross angles to what appeared to have been—once—a lovely little dresser, possibly of French restoration vintage or a good imitation. But in the middle of it there was . . .

At first I thought it was a plastic mannequin that someone had put in the fire that had partially melted. An art project? But why did it smell like that? Not like melting plastic . . . like rotting meat.

I stared at the distorted, gelatinous-looking facial features, which led down to a distorted, gelatinous body, and I swallowed hard. My stomach, sending burning bile up to my throat, was trying to tell me something I was simply not ready to accept.

And then I realized that the mannequin had . . . well, the top of it, from the forehead up, was undeniably the top of a very human forehead, and there was blond hair cut short, frosted and coiffed into those little peaks I always wandered how people managed. It wasn't melted, and it wasn't—had never been—a plastic mannequin.

I felt like I'd been looking at one of those weird pictures, with an area in black and one in white, that look like one thing, until you blink and they look like another completely different thing.

Realizing that the . . . thing had been human made me see that it was a body. Torso, two legs, arms. All of it distorted as if it had been turned into wax and held up to heat till it melted. Or perhaps it had been thrown into acid. I didn't know what could make a human look like that, and I didn't want to know.

Some places, like the nearest knee, shining wetly, were still a recognizable shape, but the rest of the body was such a taffy-pulled shape that I couldn't even tell what gender the person might have been.

I felt the bags I'd been holding fall from nerveless hands, while my stomach clutched and did a flip-flop and the smell rose worse, more penetrating, as though it were entering not just through my nostrils, but through my eyes and ears and my all-too-porous skin.

Slowly, very slowly, afraid that I was going to fall, I stepped down, climbing my way down from the Dumpster to the asphalt of the parking lot.

There was a buzzing in my ears, like the sound of the sea or the sound of an accelerating fan. Through it, I vaguely heard E say, "Mom?"

I shook my head at him, wanting to get in the car and drive him away from all this. Drive him away fast.

But this was real life, and I was no longer six years old. One didn't run and hide when something went wrong, and one didn't drive away from an accident, much less from something like this.

An inner voice encouraged me to just run. After all, it said, I *was* wearing gloves. There would be no fingerprints.

But someone might have seen the car. And besides, I watched TV. I knew the police had ways of figuring out things these days, even without fingerprints.

7

Right. I swallowed hard, because some bitter fluid was trying to make its way up from my throat.

I opened my car door deliberately, as though each movement might cause an explosion. Which it very well might. It might cause me to throw up and that would be explosion enough.

With relief I dropped to sitting in the driver's seat and reached over to the floor on the passenger side, where I'd left my purse. I grabbed my cell phone and turned it on, and realized that Ben had called me twice without my answering. This would lead to a lecture about actually carrying your cell phone on your person at all times. Right at that moment, I'd welcome a lecture from Ben. But I was not twelve, and I would not call Ben to come and save me from the scary discovery.

I swallowed again, and instead of dialing him back, I dialed 911. I heard my own voice, thickened and strange, "Police," I said. "I want to report a murder."

A Table in Hand

T HEY GAVE ME COFFEE from a thermos. Hot, strong, and sugary, poured into a paper cup and pressed into my hand. A woman officer had come and asked me questions. I had no clue what I'd told her, save for one thing—I had not told her about the table in the back of the car.

In retrospect, this seems completely insane—and probably was—but all I could think about was that if I was going to find a corpse, and have to sit here, with E quiet and sullen in his seat, I was going to get a table out of it, damn it. It was, I think, my attempt at preserving a bare shred of rationality, as irrational as it might be. I had gone through this to get a table, and I was going to get that table.

After the officer left, I sat in my car, the door open and my legs hanging out, my feet in dirty tennis shoes resting on the black asphalt. E had gone very quiet except for the occasional, outraged "Phew."

I sipped my refilled cup of coffee, trying to stretch it out before it became all cold and gross, because I'd rather smell the coffee than the body. I watched the officer who had interrogated me, because the most threatening thing she was carrying was a clipboard. She wasn't going near the body, and she wasn't carrying any weird instruments.

Other people were doing scarier things—I was vaguely aware of them around the Dumpster. They were taking pictures and tagging all the trash. And two had climbed nimbly into the Dumpster, looking like they had gotten the secret handbook of Dumpster climbing that no one had bothered to share with me.

The officer who'd talked to me now approached the people near the Dumpster and presumably called to one of the men there, who took the clipboard from her. He was tall—as tall as Ben (which was saying

9

a lot, because Ben was six-three easy), though, at least from this far, of a completely different type: dark haired, golden skinned. He wasn't wearing a uniform, either, just a pair of jeans and a blue T-shirt. From the back, I thought, as I sipped my coffee and tried to breathe only the smell of coffee and not the smell of death all around, he didn't look at all bad. Broad shoulders narrowing down the length of a well-muscled body to a nicely trim waist. Long legs, which—though one thing had nothing to do with another—made me think he might be a runner.

He gestured broadly, and though I couldn't quite hear what he said, I gathered the impression that he was giving orders to the swarm of people who were doing something I refused to look at out by the Dumpster. He nodded, which I thought was to the officer who'd interviewed me. I caught only the tail end of his words, carried on a sudden bit of breeze blowing my way: "Right there."

But then he walked away toward a parked van at the end of the vast agglomerate of police vehicles on the other side of the parking lot from the Dumpster, which I took to mean that the *right there* he would presumably be right at was some distance away and required driving.

I watched the woman officer walk away from the Dumpster and go to another van and retrieve a couple of heavy bags, presumably filled with equipment. I wondered when I'd be allowed to leave. Which didn't at all prepare me for a silky smooth voice coming from my left. "Ms. Dare?"

I looked to the side. He was undeniably the guy I'd seen from the back before. From the front . . . my first reaction was that he was absolutely the ugliest man I'd ever seen. Not that there was anything exactly wrong with his looks. His face was well shaped, with strongly marked cheekbones and a square chin. His nose was aquiline and straight. His eyes, under dark eyebrows, were a stormy-sky gray, of the kind that looked like clouds might move across it at any minute. And though his mouth might be slightly too broad, it was not in any way misshapen or shapeless. It was more, I thought as I looked up at him, that his features didn't seem to work together, like each was slightly at odds with the others.

And in that moment, as I thought that, something happened. In between one blink and the other, one breath and the next, the man I was looking at went from being the ugliest man I'd ever seen to being the best-looking.

Overwhelmingly handsome—beautiful really, with an almost inhuman beauty that couldn't help but cause a reaction—just looking at him was kind of like being hit on the head with a mallet. All thought stopped, your mouth dropped open, and you couldn't quite remember how to speak. A sentence that I thought was from the Bible, which Grandma used to read now and then, ran through my head: *beautiful and terrible like an army arrayed for combat*. I felt a blush climb up from under my T-shirt and coveralls and up my flaming cheeks in a tide of warmth. *The features don't work together because each of them is so perfect*, I thought. At least I hope I thought it and didn't say it, not that at that moment I could really have said much more than inarticulate syllables. I was reduced to cavewoman thinking. *Big man take me to cave and bring much mammoth?* Only, truth be told, I hadn't gotten as far as the mammoth.

He cleared his throat and looked slightly amused, and the heat on my face was in serious danger of causing my complete self-combustion. In confusion I looked at his T-shirt, which was just a little too tight—not as though it didn't fit him, but as if it were the sort of clothes one wears around the house or while doing laundry. In paler blue, on the chest, it said, *Tell the Law Everything*.

On this I found my footing, because I'd be damned if I'd tell him about the table. Let him imagine I'd gotten it elsewhere, and it just happened to be in the back of the car. I sat up straight and looked back at him, and realized he was looking behind me at E, who in turn was sitting in his car seat, bending slightly forward.

"Your son?" he asked.

"Yes," I said. "That's E."

"He?"

"No, E. It's his initial. It's what I call him."

He raised his eyebrows at me, but didn't say anything. Instead, he turned to E. "Hey, E, would you like a Sprite?" he asked, in a soft voice but not, I noted with relief, the sort of voice that people who don't know kids normally use.

I waited to see if his approach had worked, but it hadn't. E remained silent, though his eyes were riveted to the Sprite can in the man's right hand.

"He won't talk," I said, tiredly. Right then explaining E's foibles seemed like rolling a particularly heavy stone uphill.

"He can't talk yet?"

I shrugged. "He talks to me, but no one else. To me he even says sentences."

This brought a delighted chuckle from the man, and at what must have been my look of total, bewildered surprise, he explained. "I did that to my mom till I was three. People thought she was crazy. She recorded me speaking, and Dad said it was her doing voices."

I groaned. I could imagine E doing this to me for another six months or more.

"Can he have the Sprite?"

"Sure," I said, and he opened the can and gave it to E. Considering that E and I had mostly been drinking water with our pancakes, a Sprite was a rare treat and if E didn't say thank you, he graced the policeman with a broad grin.

"So, you're Ms. Dare?" he said, turning to me, after a final smile at my son.

"Dyce Dare," I said.

"Like . . . playing dice?"

"No, like *Candyce*. With a *Y*. I was . . ." I was not about to tell a total stranger the story of my birth. "I was born in a candy store. Unexpected. Mom went into labor." I wasn't about to explain that Mom and Dad had had such a huge fight after the ultrasound showing I was a girl that Mom had left Dad and they were meeting in the candy store to discuss making up. Nor that the fight had been about names, because Mom wanted to call me Agatha and Dad wanted to call me Sherlockia. Nor would I, even under torture, reveal that my middle name was Chocolat. Only Ben knew that, and only because my mom had told him. "So Mom wanted to call me Candy, but Dad added the *C* and the *E*, and I go by Dyce."

He made a face, half grimace, half grin. "My father called me Castor. I go by Cas." He offered me a massive, square hand. "Cas Wolfe. I'm one of two senior serious-crimes investigators in Goldport." He nodded toward the Dumpster. "We don't get many of these. Not this bad."

I shook his hand. It was hard and firm and squeezed enough to let me know he could crush my hand—without his actually doing it. "It is . . . ," I said. "It is a murder, then?"

He shrugged. "I don't know," he said. "It may very well be just inappropriate disposal of a corpse, but when people go to this kind of trouble . . ." He shrugged.

I nodded. "Like those corpses thrown into the shark aquarium last year," I said.

"Exactly like that," he said.

"Turned out some woman was pushing guys she seduced into the tank, didn't it?" I asked, dimly remembering the solution of the case that had kept the pages of the local paper full of lurid and unlikely pictures. I confess I always skimmed murder news, mostly because Mom and Dad discussed every case from the moment the first signs of crime were discovered. Normally I was tired of the whole thing long before the murderer was caught.

"Something like that," Officer Wolfe said, with a sin-inducing grin. "Though my team wasn't on that case."

I became aware that he was almost bent over to talk to me—to keep his head at a level with mine. I gestured vaguely toward the passenger seat. "If you want to sit down."

Once more I was graced with the expressive, mobile grin that made the blush start again, upward, on a path from my belly button to my cheeks. *Oh, pipe down, Dyce,* I told myself. *Man like that will be drowning in college girls every weekend—and maybe during the week, too. What would he want with the almost-thirty-year-old, divorced mother of one who is the queen of pancakes?*

By the time I'd talked myself down—or a convincing counterfeit thereof—he had walked around the car, opened the passenger door, and gotten in. "Thank you," he said. "Not that I have much more to go over." He looked over the clipboard. "Officer Giles seems to have asked you all the relevant questions. You were . . . looking for furniture?" he said.

"It's not illegal," I said, defensively. "I refinish it. It's what I do for a living."

He shrugged. "I'm sure if I dug through the books I'd find some ordinance against looking through Dumpsters for discarded furniture. Probably a public health measure. But the thing is that I have no interest in that. People rescue stuff out of Dumpsters, so much the better for . . . for landfills and all. You were . . . climbing the Dumpster?"

"Yeah," I said, and was glad I was blushing anyway. I looked away. "I put my hand on a bag, and the whole thing fell." I took a deep breath, which was a bad idea, because I got a big noseful of the smell. I swallowed hard and said, "And then I went to put them back and I saw . . . I saw . . ."

I became aware that my voice was shaking. He nodded. "The first one is always bad." He shrugged. "Weirdly, this one is not *that* bad, because it doesn't really look human. Or not at first glance."

"No," I said. I rubbed my nose because I felt like I was about to cry. "I thought it was a mannequin. I only knew it was human by the hair. And the top of the forehead, you know?"

He nodded. "Well, that's about it," he said. "You didn't do anything else we need to know about, right? Removed something, or put something extra in the Dumpster?"

I shook my head. I was *not* going to tell him about the table, even if this had started to have the feel of when I went to explore the construction site without telling my parents. It was impossible that the table had anything to do with the body. The corpse hadn't been bludgeoned with a table, and I was not about to lose my find for the sake of bureaucracy.

"And you gave us your address," he said. "You'll be at two-sixteen Quicksilver today?"

"I'm always there," I said. "Well, unless I'm out, you know, delivering furniture or . . ." I shrugged. "You have my cell phone."

"Right. And I'll get back to you on this. Sorry you had such a shock. Try to take it easy today, okay? Have a quiet day with the munchkin back there. Don't think about any of this."

A likely idea. First, the quiet day with the munchkin would get cut short, as I had to hand him back to All-ex tonight to stay till Tuesday evening at his dad's place. Second . . . second—I thought of Ben's messages on my phone, as yet unlistened to—this was not shaping up to be a quiet anything.

"Do you have any idea who she was?" I asked.

At first I got back a slight stare, then an intent frown. "She?" he asked.

"The . . . corpse . . ."

Suddenly the very hot guy with the laid-back manner was replaced by the eagle eye of the law. His eyebrows seemed to struggle to go up, while he kept them stubbornly on a level, and he spoke in a voice that was too deceptively calm. "How do you know if it's a woman?"

"The hairstyle," I said. "I've seen that short, blond, frosted hairstyle in magazines. Must be very expensive." I sighed. "I could never afford it, and there's no way I could do it to myself. The one time I tried to cut my hair . . ." I was not going to tell my life story to a stranger. "It didn't end well."

He looked curious, and something like a sparkle ran through the gray eyes, making them seem, momentarily, bluish. He seemed to be considering something. "I'll try to give you a call later. To see how you're holding up."

Like that, he offered me his hand again, and I squeezed it. He wasn't wearing gloves. That probably meant that he hadn't been physically handling the body. For some reason that made me feel better, understanding that had made cultures throughout history declare dead bodies unclean. I didn't want to be near it. I didn't want to touch anything it had touched. And I wanted to drive far away from its smell.

He fished in the pocket of his pants and brought out a business card. "If you think of anything, or anything seems strange, give me a call, okay?" His business card read *Cas Wolfe, Goldport Police Department, Serious Crimes Unit*. "Call my cell phone. If you call the department they're as likely as not to put you through to the other investigator,

Rafiel Trall, and he won't know anything about this. At least not unless it gets really bad and we need to bring in every available person."

I nodded. E waved at him as he turned to say, "Bye, little one. See you later." Even if E didn't trust him enough to talk, the wave was a big honor. E didn't wave at anyone but Ben.

I was conscious of Ben's messages on my cell phone in the purse on the floor of the passenger seat, but I had to get away from the smell before I listened to any messages. I drove carefully out of the parking lot, through the crowd of policemen, who got out of the way. Some looked toward Officer Wolfe, who waved as if to say that I was free to go.

Over the bump and onto the tree-lined downtown street, and then down that and around the corner onto Fairfax Avenue. My house was eight blocks down it and then a sharp right on Quicksilver.

Fairfax was a busy street, the east-west artery of the town. I pulled into the parking lot of a drugstore and got my phone out of my purse. It was not normal for Ben to call me on Saturday morning, certainly not two times in what seemed to be half an hour or less.

Les Howard, Ben's live-in lover, was a French horn player at the symphony downtown, and Friday night was usually concert night, which meant that they stayed up late, of necessity. The earliest I heard from Ben these days on Saturday was midafternoon, when he usually did call, keeping up a habit from our high school days of each finding out how the week had gone with the other. Even while I'd been married to All-ex, we'd kept it up. It was one of All-ex's big all-time complaints, as if he really were in any danger from Ben. And I kept it up now, too, even though, frankly, I could be fonder of his boyfriend—*partner* seemed all too final, and Ben hadn't done anything bad enough to deserve that. I could be fonder of Les Howard, for instance, if it had been his body I'd found back there.

But this thought brought with it an all-too-clear image of the body, and I shook my head. No. I didn't wish that on anyone. And besides, I had nothing really against Les, except the way he looked at me and the suspicion that he wasn't making Ben very happy.

Ben and I had been friends since we were twelve, when he'd rescued me after I'd gotten in over my head in a fight with playground bullies. It would take more than our truly despicable taste in men to break that.

As I thought that, I was dialing my messages, and I got Ben's voice, crisp, clipped, over the phone. "Dyce? Why aren't you answering at either phone? Where are you? Call me."

It didn't sound particularly urgent, but something about it disquieted me. I erased the message and listened to the next. And became

15

far more worried. Ben's voice had lost the patented, almost inhuman calm he seemed to think was necessary when leaving a phone message. "Dyce! Oh, for the love of—" I didn't know for whose love it was, because the next word was slurred. And then, in growing annoyance, "Dyce, answer the damn phone now. Where are you? Would you please answer and tell Les that I—Les, would you *please*?"

The connection ended. I opened my mouth, closed it, and looked at the dashboard, at Officer Cas Wolfe's card. But what was I going to tell him? That I thought Ben had had some sort of domestic scene, what . . . an hour and a half ago? Yes, that would be helpful.

And the thing was that the idea of a domestic disturbance between Ben and Les would strike people as either funny or Ben's fault. Les was all of five-five, maybe five-six, elegantly slim, with the sort of build that seemed made for the tuxes he wore to work, while Ben was six-three and built like an assault tank, and he kept slim only through strenuous and continuous exercise. Any policeman seeing Ben and Les fight would immediately arrest Ben for assault.

And besides, Ben didn't fight with people as such. Even when we met—I'd been involved in trying to punish two bullies at once and had momentarily forgotten that they were eighth graders and a year older than I and probably singly outweighed me by double—he'd walked up and punched the bullies out, and asked me if I was all right. Then he'd dusted his clothes—which didn't need it—and introduced himself, and walked away with me, leaving the bullies in the dust. All without looking even mildly upset, much less angry.

No, I had no idea what was going on with Les, but the idea that they were fighting was absurd.

I dialed Ben's house, just in case, but the phone rang and rang, and no one answered. I closed my phone and was about to put it back in my purse, when it rang.

I opened it. Ben's cell phone number. "Ben!" I said.

"Dyce." He sounded like himself again, and wasn't yelling. "Where are you?" Correction, he sounded terribly tired. He probably had woken up too early.

"Shorty Drugs."

"Where?" Which was justified because Shorty was the local chain and it was all over town.

"On Fairfax."

"Are you coming home?"

"I was about to."

"Good. I'll wait."

I was going to tell him to let himself in—he and my parents were the only people with keys—something he never did without permission. But he'd already hung up.

Two Ciphers

A S I PULLED INTO my driveway—beside the once-opulent blue Edwardian mansion of which I rented the bottom floor—alongside Ben's BMW, E said, "Uh-oh," from the backseat.

I didn't know—exactly—what called for that sound. E shouldn't know anything was wrong. From where he sat, he couldn't see what I could. That the trunk lid of Ben's car was dented, and that his back windshield window had a crack straight across.

Ben sat in the driver's seat. He'd rolled down the window, and he was scribbling on a pad in a leather portfolio that looked like something from work. And Ben's appearance was as wrong as the dent on his normally impeccable car, as wrong as his being here at this time of the morning on a Saturday, of all days.

It's hard to explain how Ben relates to clothes. It's not that he's exacting about them—he is—and it's not that he cares how he looks—he does—it's something well beyond that. Ben is attached to clothes as if they were his armor of righteousness, without which he would dissolve. If he were a superhero, he would be Captain Suit and Tie, and if he had a trademark, it would be to leave behind an impeccably tied tie or at least a drawing of one.

Now, though I suspected it had taken him his college years to get over this, he wasn't so fanatic about it that he wore a suit and tie on weekends. But even then he did usually look as though he'd put himself together to exact measure from some picture in a magazine captioned *The man who has it all relaxes*.

He was still wearing nice clothes—a pale cream shirt with two buttons unbuttoned at the chest. But the shirt was misbuttoned on the uppermost button, one up from where it should be.

As he got out of the car, I became even more alarmed. His khaki pants looked . . . rumpled. And up on the left side of his forehead was a very thin, jagged . . . scratch, I decided; I wouldn't call it a cut. From it a drop of blood had run in an irregular pattern down Ben's square, closely shaven face. And I was sure he hadn't noticed. Or he'd never have come out looking like that.

I couldn't even look. Something was wrong. Very wrong. I thought of the corpse in the Dumpster. Everything was wrong. I'd taken a wrong turn. Reality was askew.

"What's wrong?" I said, as I got out of my car and opened the back door to unbuckle E. He was squirming and screaming, "Bah!" which was the closest he'd ever come to talking near another human being that wasn't me. I had no idea what about Ben prompted the exclamation, and probably neither did Ben, who looked unusually dazed.

E escaped my grasp and ran gleefully out of the car to hug Ben's legs. "Bah."

"Uh," Ben said, somewhere between amused and puzzled. "Same to you, buddy." He looked back up at me, and I became suddenly conscious that I was still wearing my denim coveralls, probably stained all over with stuff from the Dumpster. "Ugh. What have you been doing?"

"Dumpster diving," I said, but unzipped and removed my coveralls and folded them, clean side out, which is normally what I did when I was trying to keep the car clean—what I should have done before I drove here. I put them under my arm to take inside. "For furniture. End of term at the college." I wasn't going to tell him anything else. At least not yet. I didn't have words to tell him anything else. Yet.

Ben visibly hesitated. "Look, your parents—"

"Stuff it. No."

I didn't really want to discuss for the umteenth time why it was profoundly unadvisable for me to live with my parents, and because E was firmly attached to Ben's legs saying, "Bah," up at him in wild adoration, I was free to go to the back of the car and pick up the little table.

Being just a tea table, it could—barely—be lifted with one hand and left me the other free to offer to E. "Come on, E. Let's go in."

But Ben reached down and grabbed E around the waist, lifting him up and sort of sitting him on his right arm. "Come on, monkey," he said.

I'd never fully understood Ben and E's relationship. They were the two people in the world closest to me—the ones who mattered most.

I'd known one of them for seventeen years and the other since before he was born.

It should have been easy to figure out how they related. But their relationship was more complex than some third-world diplomatic negotiations and had all the protocol of a Mandarin ceremony. Somewhere between the fact that Ben lived in dread of what E's spit-covered hands would do to his clothes, and the fact that E acted around Ben like cats act around people who hate them, they had a very strange friendship of sorts. The thing was that Ben didn't hate E. Not even close to it. I was sure of it. You could tell it in times like this, when he carried E even though he could have avoided it. Or the times when he actually babysat, twisting his life all of out of shape to look after E so I could deal with divorce hearings and such. Not to mention the utter panic Ben had gone into the night that E had the ear infection and his fever wouldn't stop going up. He'd all but physically threatened the ER doctors. But most of the time Ben avoided E and called him *monkey* and accused me of having kidnapped him out of the local zoo. And E thrived on this, as he didn't on fawning and petting and cajoling.

I opened my front door and we went into the apartment that had been home to me for the last year and a half. Howsoever dumpy, it was still . . . well, dumpy. It was the sort of apartment that was rented to students, though the landlord had given me a break on the rent because I'd been willing to sign a two-year lease and because—presumably—he guessed my cleaning skills were better than the average bear's. Or college student's. But I repeat myself.

It wasn't so much an apartment as the bottom half of an Edwardian house, relatively sprawling as these places went. I was lady of a domain that comprised a living room carpeted in spilled-ketchup red and wallpapered in prim little yellow roses. This spacious room I'd furnished with an old blue couch and a table that I could never sell for any decent price, mostly because I hadn't yet determined whether the table was wood or cardboard, but I was fairly sure it was glued together with spit and its legs tried to sprawl wide at the slightest touch.

Through the door at the back on the far right was the bedroom. Or rather the bedrooms, which sort of flowed into each other, with a narrow door in between. The bedroom I used had my childhood bed—single, rickety, white-painted—and a makeshift shelf of bricks and boards, which held the books I actually read; no *literature* because it brought out my PTSD from college. It was carpeted in neon-glaring blue and the walls had a wallpaper that looked like a snapshot of spiders involved in an orgy spanning all of spiderdom. All of this over a red background. Through the narrow door was E's bedroom, which someone filled with foresight had refused to carpet and covered instead in poo-brown vinyl. What it was covered in, though, most of the time, was stuffed animals. For reasons unknown to me—though I was sure there were reasons, perhaps involving secret memos and a strategy for driving me insane—everyone I knew, even the most casual of acquaintances, gave E stuffed animals. He had every creature that had ever stumbled into old Noah's ark. Only not two by two. Oh, no. As Noahs went, E was clearly broad-minded, and his beasties marched by three, by four, by multitudinous crowd.

E was a normal little boy. Except for the occasional cuteness mode—which I always suspected was more for my benefit than his—he used his stuffed animals as projectiles, which he lobbed with unerring aim at the head of the unsuspecting. Usually me. From this sea of variously colored fake fur emerged E's crib—which he still used, as I was still looking for a little bed at a good price. In the corner sat a set of plastic drawers and cubes, which contained his clothes and toys-that-weren't-fuzzy. The only one he'd shown any interest in so far was the toy piano Ben had given him for Christmas, which I had regretfully put in a safe place, while putting Ben on my *What was he thinking?* list. My only regret was that Ben was unlikely to ever have kids. Otherwise, the kids would already, pre-existence, be on my *Give a drum set to* list.

Out of E's bedroom, the other way from my room, was a large and ugly bathroom. The sink—stained, squarish, and graced with a mostly rusted faucet—sat on little metallic stilts as if porcelain supports were definitely too expensive for the likes of us. The bathtub, also large and squarish, had had rust stains on the bottom, which I'd covered with porcelain paint. It was an imperfect effort, but it had left the bottom of the tub nicely ridged and definitely a nonslip surface. When I'd moved in, Ben had spent about an hour in that bathroom with cleaning products and a series of brushes—which was very funny, because he paid to have his house cleaned—because he was sure I would catch tetanus, or perhaps rabies, from the tub. It had taken him that long to convince himself the dirt was probably a structural part of what held the bathtub together. And when I'd told him you couldn't get rabies from bathtubs because they didn't bite people, he had removed the industrial-looking rubber gloves, glared at me, and said, "That one might."

The other door out of the living room led directly to the kitchen, which was the only room in the house that Ben approved of. Just as well, because that was where we spent most of the time when he visited. For some reason—and I still couldn't believe it was the benevolent impulses of the rental company, so it must have been to hide something, possibly a body under the floor—the kitchen had been tiled, both floor and counter. The floor was a serviceable clay tile; the counters were large white tiles. There was a plant window over the sink where I kept the only plants—probably weeds—that I couldn't kill, and I loved the effect of the morning light on the counter tiles. I'd furnished the room in Grandma's old pine table, oiled to a mellow shine, and, having tried to balance on the rickety bar stools I'd found at the thrift store and failing, Ben had given me a pair of pine chairs that perfectly matched the table—though they had to be of much younger vintage—and that had probably cost him more than anything in this place was worth. Next to the table stood E's highchair, a baby gift from my in-laws when I was still married, and the finest plastic and vinyl money could buy. Not that I was complaining. It cleaned up easily.

Through the kitchen door at the back, and all of maybe ten steps distant, was what had undoubtedly been designed as a storage unit. I'd made it into my workshop, where I kept refinishing fluids, furniture under processing, paints, oil, and other things that would be an invitation to disaster in E's curious hands. I worked while E napped (rarely, but it happened) or while I could con someone—usually Ben, though Mom had done it once or twice—into babysitting. Or, of course, while E was with All-ex.

I let Ben in ahead of me and closed the door behind us, dropping the little table in the middle of the living room. I was dying to see what it was, and where it had come from, but, realistically, it could wait till All-ex picked up E. And meanwhile there was Ben and whatever was up with him. Oh, he acted like nothing was wrong as he carried E into the kitchen to an ecstatic chorus of "Bah!" but this just wasn't normal. Not Ben here, at this hour in the morning on a Saturday. What the hell had happened to him? Car accident?

I concentrated on Ben to banish from my mind any thought of the body. Look, Goldport is a safe city. An old mining town turned college town, it might have enough crimes for a Serious Crimes Unit, but I thought the annual murders hovered around ten, most of those either crimes of passion or drug related. Neither of which mixed well with a melted corpse in a college Dumpster.

If I turned, right after setting the table down, to triple-lock the door behind me, it wasn't because of fear of burglars, but because E's current hobby was stripping naked and running screaming out the front door, up into Fairfax Avenue traffic. Although I'd not been a bad runner in high school, my glory days were well behind me, and besides, running was a hair-raising sport as E forced it on me.

With the door secured in a way that—so far, at least—E had not defeated, I walked into the kitchen. Ben had strapped E into his highchair and was standing in front of my open fridge. As I came in, he turned around, the almost-empty bottle of milk in his hand. "Dyce!"

"He's going to his dad's today. There wasn't any point buying any more till he comes back on Tuesday," I said.

Ben frowned. "And you intend to eat—?"

"Whatever," I said. "I won't starve."

He mumbled something under his breath, and I said, "You can't be too thin or too rich."

"You can if you starve enough to make yourself ill, Dyce." He looked over at me, his brown eyes closed enough that they were overshadowed by his blondish-red eyelashes, a perfect match for the never-out-of-place reddish-blond hair that had made every woman in high school want to kill him, because of the natural flip in front. He narrowed his lips, but didn't say anything.

And I'd be damned if I was going to be lectured by a man my age who had his shirt buttoned wrong and didn't seem aware of the fact that he had bled—something people normally noticed. "Well," I said, with more heat than logic. "At least I don't have blood on my face."

He was reaching into the cabinet for one of the plastic sippy cups that E used and turned around at my brilliant comeback. "What?"

"You have blood on your face," I said. "And your top button is wrong."

For just a second he frowned at me, as if I were speaking a foreign language, then filled the sippy cup with just about the rest of the milk, capped it, and set it in front of E with, "Here you go, monkey." Then he turned without a word.

In a wild, momentary rush, I wondered if he was going out of the house. Throwing a fit was not exactly Ben's thing. Correction. Ben's fits were cold things, in which he seemed to mentally remove himself from the presence of whoever had pissed him off. He had never stomped out of the house.

But then I heard him cross the bedrooms on the way to the inner sanctum of the bathroom, and I heard water running. Even though one needed to cross three doorways to get to the bathroom, it did share a wall with the kitchen—the one behind the stove.

I filled the teakettle in turn, because, frankly, after the events of the morning, I needed tea. Coffee has never been my beverage of choice, and as for the coffee the police gave me, I was grateful, but I think some of my paint thinner was less potent.

When Ben came back—his face clean, his shirt properly buttoned, but looking somehow less healthy than he had before—I had retrieved my favorite cup, a vast red mug, from the cabinet and was in the process of tying the strings of two bags of Earl Grey to the handle. Ben must have been off balance, because there was no comment about Earl Grey being all perfume and no tea.

He kept his own tea here, mostly because he didn't trust me to buy his tea. Which was just fine, as I didn't trust him to buy mine. Yes, yes, I could stand the whole expensive-looseleaf thing—except that I tended to lose my tea ball and spill the tea all over while I was using it—and I actually enjoyed the Victorian High Tea at Green's Hotel, where Mom took me twice every year, whether I needed it or not. I enjoyed the whole bit of picking an outré type of tea and having it served just so.

It's just that that stuff, tasty though it was, wasn't *tea*. Not the tea of my childhood, not the comforting stuff that made you stop crying or helped you get better when you had a headache.

Grandma—Dad's mom—lived just up the street from us, and until I was six I'd spent more time at her house than my parents'. And Grandma's house meant a cup of inky black tea—Earl Grey by preference—usually stewed by her forgetting to remove the bags and so sweetened that the spoon left a trail in the liquid when you stirred. I couldn't afford that much sugar, but otherwise, that was how I drank my tea.

Ben was getting out his own small teapot and the cup that matched it and doing whatever it was with the tea ball and the container of ridiculously expensive tea he got at the tea store down the road, and I left him to it. For a moment, a truce reigned. The sort of truce that descends on towns just before they're bombed to kingdom come.

I felt my back tense in expectation as I took the tea bags out of my cup, tossed them, added a judicious teaspoon of sugar to the golden mixture, and sat down. And it came, just as I expected it to. "Dyce, your shoes are wearing through at the tip, your car sounds like a UFO landing, and you have no food other than flour and half a sippy cup of milk. Have you considered going back to stay with your parents? I mean, you could go back to college and perhaps . . ."

Ben was my dearest friend in the whole world. He was very much the sibling I'd never had. In many ways he was the adult "relative" closest to me, since Grandma had died. Or at least the only relative who acted like he was older than I. He'd known me for more than half my life, and ostensibly he knew my parents. And yet, I'd never been able to convey to him the layers of wrongness in my little dysfunctional nuclear family. Mostly because Mom and Dad were all smiles and best behavior around him. They had the framed picture of us together at prom over the fireplace. And when I told them I lacked an essential piece of equipment to be Ben's type, they told me I had an awful sense of humor. I'd once tried to explain to Ben the essential issue contained in the phrase *adult children*, which preceded the names of so many therapeutic groups. Adult children of alcoholics. Adult children of abuse. Adult children of drug users. Not that I could claim anything so well defined or politically correct. I was just the *adult child*. I had been the adult in the house from about age ten. I was not going back to that. Besides, it would give Fluffy a heart attack, and she was a geriatric cat.

So instead, I struck back. "What happened to you? What happened to your car?"

He carried his cup to the table and sat down, and for a second, for just a second, there was something in his eyes.

Look, Ben is six foot three and built like the proverbial brick outhouse. He disguises it. He's an investment planner and does his best to project an image of someone who lives by the mind. But somewhere in his genetic background was some ancestor, probably in Ireland, who could plow his fields better *without* his oxen, and who could do the work of ten men in half the time they'd take. And yet the one thing I could honestly say, in our seventeen years of acquaintance, was that I'd never seen Ben furious. I'd seen him upset. I'd seen him withdraw inside himself. But the closest I'd seem him to lashing out was when he'd told the ER doctor that triage be damned, he'd see E *now*. And the doctor had been smart enough to shut up and do it.

But at my question, he looked up and for a moment—for just the space of a breath—there was something very much like burning anger in his eyes, quickly replaced by bewilderment, hurt, and then tiredness. "Les and I argued. I don't want to talk about it."

I opened my mouth to say, *Hell of an argument. It dented you car?* But the thing was, though he was looking at his tea and seemed perfectly all right, I wasn't sure—at all—that he wouldn't give me that angry look again. And even though I was almost absolutely sure the look hadn't been directed at me, as such, I didn't want to see it. And besides, Ben had kept quiet—mostly—through the rather fast breakup of my marriage. Save for his insistence that I should live with my parents. So I bit my tongue and instead said, "Are you all right?"

"Yes," he said. "It was just a stupid scratch." He shrugged.

But he looked so withdrawn—the way he did when he really didn't want to discuss something—that I took a sip of my tea, floundered around wildly looking for something to say, and said the first thing that came to mind. "I found a body in a Dumpster today."

Ben didn't drop his cup, but he came close. It trembled in his fingers for a moment, a massive loss of control as far as Ben's reactions went.

He recovered, not so much by controlling himself but because he was overcome with complete bafflement. He looked up at me, his expression perfectly blank. "What?" he said.

Which is when we realized that E had used his mad Houdini skills to escape his highchair and was somewhere in the living room. I did not have time to worry that he might have left the house, because he was yelling, "Bah, bah, bah," in the demanding tone of an emperor calling his vassals.

And a Scribble

W E WENT. WHAT ELSE could we do? Both of us were in such a hurry that we carried the cups right with us into the living room. Where we found E lying flat on the floor, with his head under the little table. As we entered the room, he said, "Bah!" and then, chubby hand extended to the underside of the table, "B, B, B, B, B."

Out the corner of my eye, I caught Ben's grin. "Dyce. Where's your toolbox? I think your little monkey is spluttering."

I set my empty teacup down, carefully, on the coffee table, and went to remove the little table from atop E, which caused a sound of protest. "Come on, kiddo," I said. "Why are you lying under there?"

But he just pointed at the table and said, "A *B*, a *B*," before trying to get back under it.

"C," Ben said, with every appearance of being helpful.

I ignored him. However, this was new behavior for E, who frankly had never made so many speechlike sounds near anyone else, not even Ben.

"What is it, baby?" I said.

"No, no, no," he said, earnestly. "A *B*, a *B*. An' *N*."

"You know," Ben said. "I know you've been saying for weeks that he could talk, but this is not—"

"Shush," I told him, as I reached over, removed the little table from atop E, and set it upside down on the carpet. There, on the underside of the table, big as life, was a long scribble, which started with something that looked like a *B* and contained at least an *N*.

ELISE HYATT

"You know, you could have a circus act here," Ben said. "If you teach him to stomp his foot twice for yes and once for no. What was that thing with Clever Hans, the horse that could . . ."

He stopped, probably realizing that I was frowning at the bottom of the table and looking totally unamused. I was looking totally unamused because I remembered where I'd gotten the damn table. And if it had some message underneath . . .

"What is it?" Ben asked.

"The table was in the Dumpster. Where I found the body."

For a moment, he didn't move. He exhaled air in a long, long breath. He said something that sounded suspiciously like, "Oh, holy fuck," under his breath, and then aloud he said, "Dyce, are you joking? About finding a body?"

I shook my head, and he put his cup down slowly next to mine. "Dyce!" he said, his voice half reproach and half tight with something that sounded terribly like worry.

Of course I had to look up at him, nothing for it. The expression on his face was all worry, the kind of worry one would expect if he'd just seen E sample a poisonous spider. "I found a body in a Dumpster. I told you," I said.

He cleared his throat. "What . . . what did you do to it, Dyce?"

It crossed my mind to tell him that I had saved the choice cuts for a stew, but the joke caught in my throat in a knot of nausea. "Nothing!" I said.

Ben sat down. He didn't do it, but looked like he would very much like to clutch his head in his hands. He visibly bit his tongue. "Dyce, you have to call the police."

"I did," I answered, and it occurred to me, even as I said it, that my voice came out peevish, like E's when I asked him if he'd washed his hands.

E at this point decided to add to the discussion by walking up to Ben, patting his knee, and saying feelingly, "Phew."

Ben smiled at him. "Just about. With Mommy, you never know. But one *is* rather *phew relieved* she did the right thing."

"I think he meant the smell," I said.

He looked up at me with the kind of look he got when we were seniors in high school and he had come in early one morning to find me treed like an idiot cat atop the giant cowboy statue in front of the school. It wasn't my fault.

You see, my French teacher kept spare panties in her desk. At the time neither Ben nor I could have guessed why, though looking back, she had held long conferences with the principal and . . . who knows? These panties, which I'd found quite by accident when she kept me after school to write the verbs and then left the room to see the principal, were the size of your average washtub, pink and made of the sort of improbable synthetic fabric that, with the roaches and the rats, will be the only thing surviving after nuclear attack.

Now, if you know that the mascot of the high school was a cowboy—with his hat in his hand—and that I loathed the French teacher, you'll understand it was more than human flesh and blood could endure *not* to climb the statue and put Madame Virginie's underpants on the cowboy's head. But the look on Ben's face that morning, before he had to help me climb down from that stone shoulder twelve feet in the air, I'd never forget.

His expression now was exactly like that, half wonder and half shock. "Dyce . . . the table was in with the body?"

I shook my head. "Not exactly. I mean same Dumpster, but there were some bags in between and all. I mean, it wasn't touching it or anything. I'm sure it wasn't related."

"How can you be sure it wasn't related?"

"Because it . . . it was far away from the corpse. The corpse was . . ." I swallowed hard, having become unaccountably nauseous. "It was melted and I . . ."

"I'm sorry."

I shook my head. "Well, it wasn't me," I said. "Or anyone I know."

"But the table . . . should you have kept the table? I thought the police would take everything in the general vicinity."

"They would," I said.

"Except . . . ," he said, looking suspicious.

"I didn't tell them. I mean, it was just in the Dumpster. It wasn't touching."

He just looked at me. He opened his mouth, closed it, then said, "What *am* I going to do with you?"

"Nothing, I'm not your type. Horrible deformity. Important missing part."

It didn't even get me a smile. In fact, he frowned. "Seriously. You have to call the police now. Tell them you forgot about the table. They'll believe you. Shock and all." And the crazy man was fishing in his pants pocket for his cell phone and extending it to me on the palm of his hand. "Call them. Now."

I ask you. He had known me for seventeen years, and he thought that would work. I'd been feeling low and down and about ready to do the girly thing and burst into tears. Until he took that tone. At which point

I crossed my arms on my chest and looked up and up and up to glare at him and said, "No."

"What do you mean, no?"

Poor man, so young and with such sad hearing loss. "Benedict Colm, you know perfectly well what I mean. No. I am not calling the police and telling them I have a table from that Dumpster. They would take it away."

"Of course they would," he said. "It's evidence," he said. He frowned. "That's why you must give it back."

Sometimes I think with men in general there's a sort of skip in the brain—a flat spot. They don't seem to understand that *should* is not the same as *must*. Of course I *should* give it back. Theoretically. Very theoretically. I knew that. I knew it was possible Officer Hotstuff would think it was evidence of a sort or another. But come hell or high water, it was far more likely that the table was completely unrelated to the corpse and had just been thrown away. And if that was the case, then by giving it to the police, I'd be doing myself out of . . .

I frowned at the table. Delicate legs; a drawer that was subtly, not perfectly rectangular; a top that looked like a piecrust edge, but really could be any other kind of carving under a thick slathering of various kinds of paint . . . well . . .

If it was anything even nineteenth-century or earlier, it would probably sell at the consignment store in Denver for maybe even as much as five thousand. Which meant I could pay the rent and afford real food for me and E for more than a few weeks, all of which I had no clue how to do otherwise.

Alternately . . . alternately, it could be a piece of trash, assembled perhaps from bits by an amateur last year, and then inexpertly covered in paint.

I bit the tip of my tongue, trying to clear my head.

"Dyce. Dyce! You must call."

"Shush. Look . . ." I frowned at the table, then looked at Ben. "Do you have to go back and . . . make up or whatever you do?"

He let a breath escape again, with the effect of a balloon losing air. "Whatever I do?" he asked confused.

"After arguments. Make up. Shake hands or . . ." I realized where I was going by implication, shook my head, and shut up.

Ben of course knew what I was thinking, but he had no more wish to traipse there than I. There were things one simply didn't need to know about one's friends. Hell, things one would pay not to know. Real money.

He pressed his lips together. "We've never had an argument before. Don't go there, Dyce. I'm not ready to go back. It wouldn't be a good thing for either Les or me if I did."

"Oh, good," I said.

"Good?"

"Yes, good, because that means you can stay with E while I go out back and look at this thing."

"But—"

"I'll look at that inscription," I said. "And see if it's anything that could even be vaguely related to the murder. I mean, if it says *Mr. Lincoln was shot by John Wilkes Booth*, you'll admit it has nothing to do with the body in the Dumpster, right?"

"*Mr. Lincoln* doesn't start with a *B*."

I made a dismissive gesture, meant to convey to him that he was being nitpicky. "*Booth* does."

He sighed. "It could be this murdered guy is also Mr. Lincoln. Or Mr. Booth."

"Oh, it could," I said, "except the corpse was a woman. And don't ask how I knew, it's the hairstyle. So, will you watch E for an hour? Please? If this is just a modern trash piece, I promise to call the police." I looked up and saw mutiny in his brown eyes. "Ben, please. It could be a month or more of living expenses riding on this, and there's a good chance it's nothing to do with the body."

He looked like he was grinding his teeth, but when he spoke his voice was perfectly calm. "You know how you were voted most likely to change the world?"

"Yeah?" I said, puzzled, wondering why in heck our high school senior yearbook was being brought up.

"They were correct. Hurricanes often change everything in their path. Go. I'll keep an eye on the monkey."

I looked at E, who seemed to be asleep on the carpet, and felt a little better about leaving Ben with the brat. "Okay," I said, but hesitated before I grabbed the table, because now that Ben wasn't yelling at me, I no longer felt like I should resist him with all my might.

"Go," he said. "Before I change my mind."

I grabbed the table and I went. All the way to the back.

The Chamber of Horrors

THE SHED IN THE back was the real reason I'd settled for this student apartment, instead of the hundred different ones downtown, some of which were cheaper, many of which had bathrooms that would have disgusted Ben slightly less.

Not that Ben was particularly fond of the shed in the back. When he was forced to come out here—usually to call me—he was very careful not to touch anything, and he called the place my "chamber of horrors." As far as that went, he was absolutely right. He shouldn't touch anything in here, and someone like Ben, unusually attached to his clothes, could only view this area with absolute and utter horror.

To me—but I have a more romantic imagination—it looked like an old-time alchemist's shop. Oh, I had some of the modern stuff, including some of the nontoxic—or not too toxic—paint remover, of the kind that you can't touch with metal. You buy it at refinishing stores and it costs an arm and a leg. Other things I had were pretty expensive, too, and had been bought while I was still married and the furniture refinishing had been an interesting hobby. Like the heat gun of the sort that puts out eight hundred concentrated degrees and can be used to peel several layers of paint at once.

I also owned some good scrapers, including one that I was told is called a five-point painter's tool but that I called "the vicious tool" because with its flat front, kind of like a sharpened spatula, and the curlicues and bits on the side that could be used to enter the narrowest

32

crevice and scrape the tightest carving, it had always struck me as the tool I wanted at hand if anyone ever broke in while I was re-finishing. Then there was the incredibly expensive but near-miraculously useful set of fine-sanders that Ben had bought me for my birthday last month. Which had been doubly appreciated because I knew how Ben felt about what I did for a living—part discomfort that I was working at a manual profession and part disappointment that I didn't try for something better.

But on the shelves against the far wall, I kept what I mostly used. Alcohol spirits and turpentine, and various waxes and oils that could be bought dirt cheap, as opposed to the really expensive prepackaged stuff. Oh, if I'd had money, I'd have bought the more expensive, name-brand stuff. There were some things I did allow myself, simply because they saved so much time. But when you're living on a narrow margin, anything that saves money helps.

The other feature of the workshop that made it just about perfect was the two narrow windows. They were too far up for anyone to look in on me and see what I was doing, or even to allow much dust in—the screen notwithstanding—to land on any of the furniture I was refinishing. On the other hand, they allowed for lovely cross-ventilation, which one must have while working with solvents. In my first attempts at refinishing, back at All-ex's home, I'd worked in a completely closed garage. Which meant I'd once run into the house screaming when the desk I'd been working on had started dancing and singing show tunes. It had taken my ex's best efforts and several hours of deep breaths before I was willing to admit that perhaps I'd been high as a kite.

However, I never repeated that mistake. For one thing, E depended on me, thank you very much. Besides, I thought, considering Ben's shock at the idea that I wouldn't call the police immediately, if Ben didn't have me around to shake him up now and then, he'd probably turn into granite. And then somehow, sooner or later, a high school student would put pink lacy panties on his head. Bound to happen.

I set the little table down on my worktable. The worktable was nothing fancy. Two sets of kitchen cabinets someone had been throwing away made up the base, surmounted by a thick broad piece of plywood. I put little projects on top of it to allow me to work more easily. The other furniture, like the dresser that sat—in pieces—in a corner, I worked with on the floor. That dresser had been put out on the curb for trash pickup, because it was literally in its constituent parts. However, from the style and the veneer, I thought I was dealing with an empire piece, and I was almost sure it had all the bits there. Or close to it. It was just going to be a bitch and a half to assemble and would have to wait for my three days without E, so I could do it a little at a time.

Against the other wall, next to the disassembled dresser, were the pieces that were ready. Not many, but the kind that were too good to sell in Goldport—at least if I wanted real money for them. There was a little walnut bookcase with a glass door. When I'd gotten it, the glass door and all had been covered in white paint. A couple of nice solid end tables. One of those reading desks where you stood up to read. I had to get them all to Denver, somehow.

Before I did anything at all, I put on my coveralls, which were hanging from a hook at the entrance. They were thick, and the fabric was supposedly chemical resistant. Of course, if you knelt on a patch of solvent, it was still going to stain your jeans. On the other hand, the overalls never let enough pass through for me to feel it on my skin, for which I was grateful. The few times I'd gotten some solvent on my skin, I'd had to wash immediately. With the liquids I worked with, there was no such thing as dropping some on your skin and not knowing.

Then I put on my goggles and mask. Again, it was not worth it to skimp on this stuff. Yeah, the goggles would end up fogging when it was hot, particularly if I was working with the heat gun. And yes, the mask was a pain and I never felt like I was breathing enough. But inhaling particulate from sanding or getting anything in your eye would be far more uncomfortable than that. Seriously uncomfortable. As in, you could end up blind or dead.

I pulled on the chemical-resistant gloves. With all this, I was fairly aware I looked like an alien. If you added the noise-canceling headphones that I used while sanding, I really looked like I'd just landed from outer space. A couple of months ago, a delivery man had knocked at this door after trying the house, and when I opened it in this attire, he'd backed away really quickly.

He'd never delivered whatever it was, and never told me what he wanted. For all I knew he was probably in Wyoming by now, still running and screaming that the aliens had landed.

Properly attired for work, I frowned at the table. Right. What I needed to know was what time period it was likely to be, which in turn would tell me if I was dealing with a fine piece made by relatively primitive methods, or with a shoddy modern piece.

First, I thought I'd take a look at the inscription. From the drawer in the cabinet at the end, I fished out my notebook and one of the flat pencils that you can buy at the refinishing store. A handyman had once told me that they were flat so you could get them in narrow spaces to mark things. I had never had a need for that kind of precision, but frankly the narrow pencil was easier to put behind my ear, which meant I was less likely to put it down somewhere and forget it.

So I grabbed it and the notebook, and copied the note from the bottom of the table. I didn't intend to hurt it at all, but you never knew.

The beginning was in fact a *B* and the word seemed to be *Botched*. Well, either that or *Before* or *Because*, or probably *Ben coughed*, although I found that highly unlikely. Ben's acquaintances in general always struck me as several quarts short of an oil change, but even they weren't crazy enough to write notes about him on the bottom of a table then throw it away. And besides, he was likely to know if they had. Of course, perhaps it was like Mr. Lincoln. I was fairly sure there were several other Bens around town. Still, what were the odds?

Squinting at the letter, I thought it might say *Rocky*. Which was plain nuts, because the table wasn't. After the first three words, though, it was easier to read. It did not pertain to the Lincoln assassination—more was the pity, as I was sure that if it had, it would add a lot of value to the piece. Instead it seemed to be refinishing notes. Or identifying notes. As such they struck me as a little crazy. The first sentence was doubtful, the second improbable, and the third plain crazy.

It said: *Dark cherry. Hand carved. Colonial.*

I looked at the little table and frowned. Could it be dark cherry? Hell, for all I knew it could be anything. What I could see of the bottom, the only part free of paint, was a dark wood, and it had marks, like it had been sawn and someone hadn't bothered to sand under here. Which wasn't rare in old pieces or shoddy ones. Why waste labor on a part that would never be seen, after all?

But that rough surface had clearly collected dust and grime, and if someone could see that it was cherry through all this, they were better than I. Heck, they were better than any normal human being and should try to stay away from Kryptonite just in case.

I turned the table over again and ran my hand over the very edge, which was what had convinced me it was, if nothing else, real wood. In the Dumpster, it had seemed to me like a piecrust edging. Here, in the cold light of day spilling through the little windows, it was a little sort of irregularity on the borders. Could be carving. Or it could be . . . oh, I don't know. A previous owner had had a dog with a habit of chewing and a methodical type of disposition?

I frowned at it. Then I pulled out the little drawer in the front. It fit funny and I immediately realized why. Whoever had painted this, at least one of the times it had been painted, had painted around the drawer and let the paint drip on the sides to form an uneven, ridgy surface. I was fairly sure the topmost white coat was not the only one. It never was. It seemed to me that all decades, but especially the sixties, had been populated with people who—faced with any piece of furniture—could think of nothing better than to paint it, inexpertly and with half-dried paint and brushes missing most of their bristles.

I pulled the drawer out carefully. The back of it was bare, and clean enough to let me see the joining, which was all wood. No nails, no rivets. No staples. The fact that the joining was done in such a way that it did not appear to be glued, either, spoke of an old piece. More to the point, there were only three tenons, irregularly sized and clearly hand cut. I set the drawer down slowly on the table. My hands were shaking. Hand cut. The real thing, not a fake. That meant . . . seventeen hundreds. I ran my nail wonderingly around the edge of the top, feeling the indentations.

They might have been left by someone's teething puppy, or perhaps someone's nail file, but it didn't feel like it. Of course, the table being in good condition underneath the thick layer of paint would make it much easier to actually get good money for it.

I grabbed my mineral spirits and wood alcohol and one of the empty cans I kept around for mixing. A small can, because unless I was seriously wrong, this thing was going to prove to have at least ten coats of paint and might end up taking lye to remove. I didn't like to use lye for many, many reasons, one of which was that I lived in fear of falling in it—as stupid as it might be. But then, when I had a dishwasher—a luxury fortunately absent from my rented apartment—I lived in fear of somehow tripping over my own feet and spearing myself on the knives, so I always set the knives in point down. But there were other reasons. Lye is really strong medicine. Something perhaps to use on a piece of dubious provenance covered in way too much paint, but not on something like this little table, which might—just might—be a true colonial piece. Lye raises the grain and stains the wood a dark brown. You need to apply vinegar to stop it from continuing to pulp and eventually digest the wood of the piece itself, and it—on a more basic level—gave me the creeps.

Eventually I would probably end up using the heat gun and the fine point of the vicious tool on this table, taking it slowly and patiently. But right now I just wanted to know what the indentations were—which meant removing enough paint to see the shape underneath. And for that, provided I didn't run into polyurethane, paint remover mixed with wood alcohol and thickened with a little cornstarch so it didn't evaporate quite so quickly would be fine.

Before I started, I opened the windows to the maximum to get cross-ventilation, and I turned on my floor fan, pointed away from the piece. Right now, the worst it would do to the piece was dry out the mixture and make it impossible for me to work with it. Most of the time, though, having the fan turned toward me would blow tiny bits of dust and fuzz onto a drying piece. So the fan was always pointed away from me.

I set some of the mixture on the very edge of the wood and waited. Waiting is always something I have a huge problem with. I like to be fiddling, playing, or pushing at things, not just waiting for chemicals to do their own thing.

Looking toward the box of lye on the shelf with some longing, I decided instead to fiddle. Fiddling consumes a lot of time I call working. I understand that other people do things like organizing the pens and pencils in their offices, polishing the phone, or whatever. In my line of business, pencils and pens and such were not really a big deal, except for my lovely little yellow flat pencil. So I did the equivalent. I rearranged my cans and flasks, set the various products on the shelf in a neat row, then came back and tested the white paint with the edge of the vicious tool. Nothing. I applied a bit more of the magic mixture and went back to—this time—rearrange the various parts of the dresser, identifying the outer shell and the drawers and looking at the points where things attached.

The dresser wasn't half as good a piece as the table—unless I was seriously wrong, which was entirely possible. I figured it for an early nineteenth-century import from France, though where the marks would be was a question, considering the whole thing had fallen apart and also looked—to be bluntly honest—like it had been soaked, then dried, until it seemed much like driftwood, bleached and dried out.

I started fiddling with getting a drawer together and picked with my nail at the cracked, splintered veneer in the front. It looked like some heavily figured wood, but at this point not necessarily something I could identify.

My plan for it was to do the best restoration job I could, but not break my heart over it. It was a relatively good piece, but with the resources I had it was never going to be restored to its former glory, certainly not in the way to satisfy a connoisseur. The best I could do for it was make it showy and somewhat evocative of what it had set out to be. And then it would probably fetch a good enough price.

I'd done that to the desk and small dresser sitting in the corner, ready to go up at Shabby Chic. If I could make it to Denver in my car—which, considering the state of my car, was highly unlikely.

I returned to the table and tested the edge of the paint with the pointy end of the vicious tool. It peeled back the white layer, revealing a bright green layer underneath. Right. As per script. After all, almost every piece had one green layer. Sometimes several. The only question, really, was whether the metallic layer would be over or under it, and whether it would be gold or silver. I'd stripped a little carved bookcase—of at least as early a vintage as that little table, with a carved frieze of fleur de lis—that had thirty-six coats of paint. Thirty-six. One had to wonder what was going through people's minds. At least I did wonder. Didn't anyone ever get curious about what was under all that paint?

What was under it, in that case, was lovely, solid golden oak and a whole lot of hand carving. That had been a good piece, bought for twenty dollars at a garage sale and sold for two thousand at Shabby Chic.

I applied another layer of the stripper and went back to fuss around with the dresser again. After a while I came back and pulled off the green layer. Revealing another green one. Right, then. That was just fine, wasn't it?

I grabbed a notebook, went to the dresser, and made notes. Part of it was a shopping list. I was going to need a sheet or two of veneer, some of which I didn't even think was available, or not at prices I could pay. On closer inspection, the veneer was almost certainly burled walnut, and there was no way I could match that, certainly not on my budget. Unless I found a trash piece I could cannibalize—but I was unlikely to find something large enough, as I'd need to replace entire drawer fronts.

Just in case, and because I believe that wishful thinking sometimes forces things to happen, I wrote down the wish for a trash piece with a relatively sound and large slab of burled walnut veneer. Who knew, pigs might fly and I might get my veneer. Failing that, I'd get walnut and work it with gel stain to match the pattern on the sound pieces. Then there was the hardware. The one pull left on a single drawer front was wooden and circular, of that type that you find at every hardware store. Not only had it almost certainly not come with the dresser originally, but I would bet my firstborn and all the bugs he could swallow in a year that it had been put in as a pull of last resort the last time the dresser had been whole—and judging from its appearance, doing duty as a hardware or handyman storage space in some old barn. The dead giveaway didn't require higher intelligence than your average cat's. There were two holes and only one pull.

I made a note to hit the thrift stores and the construc-tion-thrift-stores —where bits of demolished buildings and their contents ended up— in Denver when I went up on Sunday—assuming a miracle got me there, of course—to check on my consignment pieces and take the new ones up. Unlikely as it was, you often found old pulls doing duty in modern, haphazardly repaired furniture in thrift stores. Or you found a bunch of pulls taken from built-in cabinets rusting away in a corner of the building recycling store.

That was my best shot at getting something the same vintage as the dresser. Failing that, I'd have to look online, but I'd rather not spend that much money on this particular piece. There might also, frankly, be something modern that fit the style. I made a note of a couple of hardware stores to check, then another note to go and look in our very own building recycling store here in Goldport.

It was a place I tended to avoid, because going there with E since he learned to walk was about as safe as walking into a china shop happily leading a baby elephant. There were light fixtures and mirrors and other such building elements to which E was a clear and present danger. They also had a bad tendency to pile up boards with nails through them, pointing up, or to have piles and piles of removed tin ceilings, jagged edges and all.

Let alone the bugs my son could find, even in the cleanest environment, if I took my eyes off him for a second in that place, he'd eat a black widow spider *and* manage to spear himself on some jagged something, so it would be a race on whether he first bled to death, died of a poisonous bite, or got tetanus.

Trying to keep an eye on E while shopping for anything—much less things that might be hidden in a corner, behind a pile of roofing tile—just wasn't feasible.

I could go when he was with All-ex, which was usually three days one week and four the next. The problem with that, though, was that those were days I used for intensive work in the workshop. However, this time, with two pieces on hand and underway, I might make an exception.

I went back to the table, prodded with the pointy bit again, and this time, amen and alleluia, the green paint came off and brought with it some of the paint underneath—metallic, silver. It wasn't much, only about a thumb's width of paint, but enough to reveal the delicate carving underneath: a fleur de lis shape, delicately cut.

Hand carved. I would bet on it. My legs felt wobbly and I wished there were some place I could sit down except on the floor

The temptation, of course, once I saw what was underneath the paint, was to strip the entire thing.

But I couldn't let myself do it. Though Ben wasn't nearly as squeamish about changing E as he liked to pretend, the thing was that I needed to get E fed and cleaned and his stuff packed for his time with his father. And though I didn't have a clock in here and had, yet again, managed to forget to wear a watch, something about the quality of the light—let alone the fact that I'd gone through three layers of paint on the carving—told me that I'd been in here far more than the one hour I'd promised Ben.

Now, normally that wouldn't be a big deal, and if Ben had been upset about it he'd have come out back and at least told me through the door that he had to go somewhere. But whatever was happening with Ben—and I very much wished I knew what it was, even if it was absolutely none of my business—might mean that he wouldn't complain. Ben had this tendency to go somewhere inside himself and mull things over, which was probably very manly and admirable, and made me think lovingly of denting his skull with something, to get some sense into it.

Of course, barring nuclear devices, there was nothing I could dent his skull with. I'd known that skull for far too long.

Reluctantly and with a loving last look at the table, I started pulling off all the various protective stuff, starting with gloves and ending with the overalls. I turned off the fan, closed the windows—to prevent unlikely and unexpected driven rain soaking the furniture—and walked out, locking the door behind me with the padlock I'd had installed for the purpose.

The chances of anyone coming in there and deciding to steal the table were minimal. The chances of college students getting in there and huffing my refinishing chemicals were huge. And I didn't need the lawsuit or the criminal prosecution for keeping an attractive nuisance.

I walked toward the house and opened the back door. And knew immediately that something was very wrong.

Hanging

T HERE IS A FEELING of wrongness sometimes when you enter a room. It's hard to define. A house that should be empty feels occupied. A place that should be warm feels cold. You can't put your finger on it, but you feel it, deep inside, at a level below that at which thought happens. You could never say why, but you know something is . . . off.

That is what I felt when I first came in the back of my apartment. The back door didn't open directly off the kitchen. Instead, there was a short hallway and a powder room off it, before the kitchen proper. Without seeing the kitchen, without anything being visibly wrong—the floor was clean, the walls clean, no mud, no weird smells, everything as I had left it—I was sure something was very wrong.

Please, understand I'm not a brave woman, I'm simply a motivated one. I didn't get in fights at school because I liked to—or even because I enjoyed Mom's comments when I came home with my dress in tatters, my hair a mess, and a big bruise over one of my eyes. But I enjoyed even less having the big pack of eighth-grade bullies beat up on the smaller girls or boys.

That was why I'd made it my mission in life to beat up on the bullies—even if most of them were twice my size and even if on one occasion I'd needed Ben to rescue me. I'd ambush them when they were alone, at the back of the school or on the way home. I'd learned very early on that most bullies were at a loss when they couldn't scare you. And they weren't smart enough to know that behind my snarling mouth and my pounding fists, I was terrified.

Right now I couldn't imagine anything more stupid than the thought that Ben might need me to rescue him. And yet the sense that something was very wrong in the house grew on me. My heart was pounding, my teeth were clenched, and my throat was closed on itself, so that I could hardly breathe.

I could not—I would not—call Ben's name. If someone was in the house, if something was happening, that would give my position away. Instead, slowly, I pushed the powder room door open, looking inside and around to make sure no one was hiding there. I wished I had my vicious tool with me, but I didn't, but the powder room did provide a useful implement—to wit, a broom.

I grabbed it around the middle, much like Robin Hood and his men would have grasped their fighting sticks. Yes, yes, very funny, and I realize that, because I was five foot five and I weighed a hundred and ten pounds soaking wet, with my pockets full of lead.

But I was born with an odd glitch, you see? Some time ago some psychologists did an experiment with toddlers to find out how they reacted to fright—no, I don't know what the mothers were doing while this was going on—and they found that most of the toddlers ran away from what scared them. A significant minority became frozen in place. And then there were those who ran toward whatever scared them. If they did this while screaming and ready to claw, bite, and gouge eyes out, they were my kind of people.

When I was young and got into fights, some bullies laughed when they saw me coming. They didn't laugh for very long.

Holding that broom, I started into the house, slowly. I looked around, making sure nothing hid in the shadows. The kitchen was empty, and I went on into the living room. It was empty, but as I stood there, I noticed that the front door was unlocked except for the bottom lock, the one that used a key and could be locked from either side. I was sure, as I was sure of standing here, that I'd left the door locked, all three locks.

More important, Ben wasn't sitting on the sofa, reading or writing in his portfolio. Granted, maybe he'd gone into E's room to read to E and had fallen asleep. It had happened at least once. I'd been out back and come in to find E asleep in Ben's lap, both of them snuggled amid a cloud of stuffed animals. I had taken a picture, of course. Sometimes it's impossible to resist the temptation. Ben had a copy of it in his wallet.

I went into my room and checked the closet in the best action-movie style, half-expecting someone to jump at me—which was very improbable because this closet was outfitted with close-set shelves crammed with my neatly folded clothes. The only villain who could hide in there would be Folio Man, the incredible self-laminating nemesis.

I entered E's room, and by now at least part of my uneasiness had taken a rational shape. I didn't hear any sounds, not even breathing. And in fact, E's room was completely empty, though I did look under the crib and kick around the stuffed animals, just in case.

Nothing. I took a deep breath. Of course, it was entirely possible that Ben had taken E somewhere. He usually didn't unless there was some very good reason—like he'd been called to work and I couldn't be reached—to saddle himself with E. For one, my adorable son, though nominally potty trained, was quite likely to fill his Pull-Ups at the least convenient time. For another, taking E anywhere was not for the faint of heart. You had to watch him every second.

Oh, Ben had done it in the past, taken E for a walk, or out to grab an ice cream or something. But never—never—without at least coming out back and telling me.

On the other hand, Ben had also never come to visit this early on a Saturday, with his shirt done wrong and a cut on his face.

Understand, I didn't for a moment think that Ben had snapped and kidnapped E or anything equally ridiculous—it would be a very short kidnapping. The first time E squashed a bug all over one of Ben's suits, Ben would return him to sender.

No, what worried me was less rational. Ben was in the midst of some crisis I couldn't even understand—partly because the wall of silence had gone up and I simply was not going to be allowed in. What if Les had called? What if Les had said, *Come and see me now, or else*? What if . . .

I'd retraced my steps back into the living room. The door started opening. Someone came in. I leapt . . .

And stopped just in time, about an inch from bringing the broom handle down on Ben's head. They froze, too: Ben, holding a paper bag with a smiling burger logo and E, next to him, one arm stretched up to hold Ben's hand, the other hand clutching a travel cup of some soft drink.

Ben recovered first. "Holy Mary Mother, Dyce! What are you doing? Ninja samurai housewives?"

E, who couldn't possibly know why this was funny or even if it was, gave a little giggle. "Bah," he said, superciliously. "Bah nam nam."

Ben looked down at him. "Yeah, but you didn't say *Bah* when you got the burger," he said, letting go of E's hand and turning toward me. "I took E to Cy's. For burgers. You took way longer than an hour, Dyce."

I lowered the broom, feeling sheepish. "I was peeling the thing by layers," I said.

"Obviously," he said. "Well, the monkey got hungry and I couldn't find anything in the house to feed him. He did find some tasty bugs on the windowsills, but I thought that wasn't ideal."

"You didn't tell me you were taking him anywhere."

"I left you a note," Ben said, as he locked the door behind him. "On the kitchen table."

"Oh," I said feeling my cheeks heat. "But . . ." I started to say, but I was feeling so embarrassed over the whole samurai housewives thing that I didn't feel like arguing. Instead I turned to go into the kitchen and looked to the table to see if Ben had in fact left me a note. And my mind stopped.

Ben had left me a note. At least, there was a paper on the table—a notebook page, probably taken from his portfolio—but it had been chopped into four bits. I knew it had been chopped, not torn, or cut, or simply left that way, because my cleaver—one of a set of a good knives that my mother had given me for a wedding gift and one of the few things I'd kept when it all fell apart—had cut long, raw gashes into the mellow wood of the table and was still embedded in it, cutting the nearest piece of paper into two pieces.

I heard Ben gasp as he came in behind me. "What the . . . Dyce!"

"I didn't do it," I said as I neared the table, enough to read the note—or the pieces of it intact enough to be read. It was a normal Ben note, from the joking beginning, *Salute Magistra*, which he'd used ever since we'd taken a Latin class together—and I'd failed spectacularly—to the message: *Monkey threatening to chew off my arm. Taking him to Cy's and letting him play till he's slobbered over every inch of play area. Enjoy the peace to work.* And the ending, which was how we always signed letters to each other, originating in a long convoluted joke in which we'd become "best girlfriends" back in tenth grade: *Love and kisses, Ben.*

And someone had chopped it up. With a will. And half-destroyed my favorite table in the process.

The craftswoman in me was nattering at the back of my head, and I let it come out of my mouth without thinking. "It's not as bad as it looks," I said, running my fingers over the cut, just carefully enough to avoid the splinters. "The cuts are narrow enough even if deep, but the top is thick enough that it would take more than that to split the wood." I poked at it. "A bit of wood putty, a lot of sanding, some oil finish, and you'll have to look really closely to figure out that the table was ever cut. Besides, it probably adds character. Makes it look older. All of this old furniture has gone through some sort of upheaval."

Ben made a low, explicit remark about what to do with the table—which was not only strangely graphic for Ben, and Ben around

E at that, but also so anatomically unlikely as to be mind-boggling. "Ben!" I said. "E."

"He's not here," he said. "Will you stop being an idiot, Dyce, and turn around? The last thing I care about is your fff—your table."

I turned around. Ben was pale, his features tense. More tense than when he'd first arrived, which is to say more tense than I'd ever seen him. He was in serious danger of turning into granite. "Dyce, someone got in and attacked your table. Think . . . oh . . . *Fatal Attraction*."

"What? I'm not having an affair with anyone. Where would I have time to have an affair?"

"No. Don't care. What I mean is the sign of a disturbed mind, Dyce. Sane people don't go into other people's houses and put cleavers into their tables."

"Granted," I said. "But—I don't see how anyone could get in. You have a key, I have a key, Mom and Dad have a key. Did you lose yours?

He put his hand in his pocket, as if to verify, though he must have just unlocked the bottom lock to come in, so he had to know it was there. But then his motto could be *Trust, but verify*. "No," he said. "Still here. Your parents?"

"They're at a mystery convention in Denver," I said. Remembered Murder, the mystery bookstore my parents owned, got enough business, though normally from used-book sales, to make them a decent living. But in the end, the real business came down to doing all the local cons they could, particularly those dealing with books and mysteries. "Till Sunday." My mind was working through the problem. "But the thing is, Ben, why would anyone want to steal my key, or come in and chop my table?"

He rubbed the middle of his forehead with his square-tipped fingers, and absurdly I felt a pang of jealousy at his impeccably kept nails. Between Dumpster diving, refinishing, and all—and never mind that I still bit them now and then—my nails looked like they'd been put through a shredder. That I needed to keep my nails better—and longer—was the only thing my mother and All-ex agreed on.

"When my sister Brigid got Grandma Elly's desk, my sister Dana threatened to break it. Mind you, she never did, but . . ."

"I'm an only child, Ben. And so were my parents. If some relative is jealous of Grandma's table, they had to come a long way to find me."

"People do stuff like that," he said, but didn't sound like he believed it. "You know . . . idiot stuff."

I shook my head. He took a deep breath, noisy in the silence, then said, "You know, it could be . . . I mean." Another breath. "The table."

"No, it couldn't." I refused to even consider it.

"I want you to come stay with us. For a bit."

"With you?" I asked. Because Ben had to be crazy. As I said before, I thought any dislike he feigned for E was grossly exaggerated, if not a reversal of his true feelings. But I also knew what Ben's loft looked like. And what E could do to it in three minutes, without trying. It was a *loft* in the self-consciously trendy sense of its being part of a building downtown that had started life in a nonresidential application.

The building in which Ben's loft was located had been an office building. Three years ago The Loft Bunch, a redevelopment firm in town, had changed it completely and made it into several upper-end units that, on the inside, more closely resembled townhouses than units in a divided building. They ranged from two thousand square feet or so to Ben's modest eight hundred square feet divided over two floors. A combination of a sudden slump in the local real estate market and the fact that Ben's Grandma Elly—whose favorite he was—had left him considerably more than a desk had allowed him to buy it, though it would normally have been way out of his range. And mine. And that of anyone else our age.

As it was, it was not only an upper-floor unit—with a panoramic view of the downtown lights at night, and of the highway up above girding the slopes of the Rockies and shining in the dark like a lighted ribbon—but it was done up in all top-of-the-line materials. Granite countertops. Lovingly polished oak floors enhanced by Oriental rugs. Ben had decorated it to his taste, which ran to expansive glass surfaces and vast antique vases, about which he knew more than I could begin to guess. He had worked for months to find just the right piece for the right place. What E could do to such a place didn't bear thinking—at least not if one wasn't a sadist.

To top it off, the place had a completely open floor plan. Even the bathroom and the master bedroom—accessible by a wrought-iron spiral staircase—didn't have any walls. I remembered that when Ben had bought it, I'd asked him—considering that the external walls of the loft were pretty much glass—if he wanted the whole town to see him bathe. He'd told me if they wanted to take a helicopter up to the twentieth floor and use a special lens to look through the polarized glass, they had earned the right.

E aside, I wasn't exactly happy at the idea of bathing where Les could look up and see me. And I was more than sure the feeling would be mutual. I didn't even have the slightest wish to see Ben naked, something we'd avoided through seventeen years of friendship.

"You can stay in the guest room," Ben said, still rubbing his forehead.

And if it weren't for that gesture, which normally meant he had a massive stress headache forming, I would have laughed aloud. His guest room was partitioned from the living room not with a wall—no—but with an antique mahogany bookcase that he'd bought from the store where I consigned pieces in Denver. Its shelves were filled with Ben's favorite books, all of them in pristine condition, because he could read his books and leave them immaculate, something I'd never managed. And with antique pottery glazed in lovely red and brown shades. E loose on those two things . . . I shuddered. "Don't be stupid, Ben. I can't stay with you." I left unsaid, because I was fairly sure we both knew it, that I'd rather walk on blades in a salt desert than stay with Les.

I was sure that Ben knew it, because he'd gradually given up on having Les go with us when we went out to dinner. Not that I ever tried to antagonize the man. Ben loved him, and I didn't have the power to have Ben committed. And I don't think Les was trying to antagonize me. It's more that we were such diametric opposites that we rubbed each other wrong without even trying.

If petite, slim, blond Les had been a girl, he would have been one of those flawless porcelain blondes who, in school, always brought out the worst in me. Not that—as I told the principal—I had anything to do with putting glue in their mascara holders, or even with the famous live bugs incident when all their purses had been stuffed with crickets. And the principal had never been able to prove it. Seems the pet store didn't know who had bought all those crickets, and the person had paid in cash.

I was fairly sure that the fact that Ben and I had jokes going back years and could smile or laugh suddenly, at nothing that anyone else could understand, drove poor Les insane. Which, admittedly, was a short distance and a good road. Of course, our trying to explain the jokes or references only made him snippy.

"But I can't leave you here, alone, with E. Not—"

At that moment, E screamed. I'm not exactly sure how Ben and I managed it, but we became entangled in the door going into my bedroom. He was bigger and finally got through first, bullying his way through the door to E's room. And then he was silent. Very silent.

"Ben, what—"

I came in after him and followed into E's room and the bathroom. And stopped, looking where he was looking. The only sound was E, who had gone through all levels of siren to *high-pitched fire alarm*. He was pointing a shaking finger at the dark bathroom. And there, swinging from the curtain rod, was one of his monkeys. It had been hanged with the belt of my bathrobe, which was in turn hanging on a hook on the wall.

"Right, you're staying with us," Ben said.

THE LAW

"OH, COME ON," I said. "Don't be silly. It's just a stuffed animal. Not a live bunny." I walked into the bathroom, turned on the light, and started untying the noose from around the animal's neck. It had been tied so tightly that it was indented deep into the fur and took all my stubbornness, not to mention further damage to my already destroyed nails, to get it undone. I was ten seconds from cutting through the belt, but it was my robe's belt, and I liked that robe, damn it. E stopped crying and came up to me, extending his hand for the animal, but at least he wasn't making that brain-blotting noise.

"But it's only not a bunny because you don't *have* a live bunny," Ben said. "And I don't even want to think what they might do to E."

"They," I said, trying to picture someone out there, someone who had killed that woman by making her half-melt and now had broken into my house to . . . cut up my table and hang one of my child's stuffed animals? "Whoever they might be, they're completely insane. There's no sense in this." It couldn't be about the table. Not my lovely, valuable table.

"Is that supposed to reassure me?" Ben asked, and then said in that tone he assumed when he thought he could simply get his way by speaking authoritatively and acting like he was in charge, "You are coming to stay with us and that's it."

I'm sure that this worked really well at his investment firm, but he knew better. And he knew I knew him better.

I got the noose untied and gave the animal—a realistic-looking chimp—to E, who cuddled it. "E isn't going to be here till Tuesday, and I'll be just fine."

"But if E isn't going to be here, then there's no reason for you not to come and stay with us. You're not going to break things or . . ."

I looked up at him. "No. I have a really valuable table in the back. I don't want to leave the place alone."

"But—"

"No."

Ben took a deep breath and looked like he was trying to find sanity or at least strength. "Will you at least call the police?"

"Ben, don't be ridiculous," I said. "What am I going to tell the police? That someone came in, knifed my table, and hanged one of E's animals by the neck?"

"Not after you found a dead body, they're not."

"It's not that simple. Look, there's no reason to associate that dead body with me. Do you want them to think there is?"

He frowned. "There must be something. This is clearly a threat. A way to silence you."

"Really? A threat? Hanging a stuffed animal?" The truth was, I wasn't feeling nearly as sanguine as I tried to appear. And the sad part of it was that if Ben hadn't been trying so hard to convince me that there was a serious threat, I might have called the police of my own accord. But with him pushing at me, I could never do it. And besides, what would I tell them? Officer Hotstuff would think I was nuts. It shouldn't matter, but it did. And I'd be damned if I was going to explain that complication to Ben.

As it was, he was looking exasperated, but he did what he did when he was truly annoyed. He followed me in stony silence, except for when he opened his mouth to be absolutely polite at me. His first gambit was, "Your burger is on the kitchen counter, and I'm sure it's cold by now."

Indeed. If he expected me to pick up on that line, he would be seriously disappointed. There was only one way to deal with Ben in this kind of a snit. Not to admit that you knew he was mad at you, and to carry on in as inconsequential a way as you could manage. And if you could surprise him enough to get him to burst out laughing—one of his rare, sudden eruptions of laughter—then you won. I wondered if Les had figured that out yet. If he hadn't, he'd probably come close to murdering Ben several times—what with the silences my friend could fall into, which could easily last for days. Particularly when he knew he was right—which he undoubtedly did now—and when he was concerned for the person who was annoying him. Which I was sure he was.

I wasn't in the mood to manage a zinger that would make him laugh suddenly, though that might come later. Instead, I decided to try for the light, inconsequential chatter, starting with, "That table is probably colonial. Seventeen hundreds. Cherry." I realized I'd just repeated what was written at the bottom. A long shudder ran over me as I rushed to the kitchen and picked up the burger. It was cold, and I didn't feel like eating.

But Cy's was the best burger around—well, at least for fast food with a play area—made of organic meat. So I wouldn't let it go to waste. I ate it grimly.

Ben was standing at the sink and taking an unusual interest in the cramped porch outside the window, which didn't even belong to me but to the college radio station out back. A look around him confirmed that it was completely empty. I restrained a temptation to sigh and instead said, "Just as long as no one puts pink panties on your head."

He turned around, eyes wide. "What?"

"When you turn to granite. Hopefully no one will put pink panties on your head."

His laugh burbled forth, sudden, starting as a low chuckle that couldn't be contained, and ending with his head thrown back and his laughter echoing in the room. He stopped as suddenly as he'd started, though his eyes still laughed with devilment as he looked at me, "Dyce, if you didn't exist someone would have to invent you, you know that?"

"What I meant—" I said painstakingly, trying to explain, as I usually did, even as I rejoiced inside at my success in making him laugh. Ben was so tightly controlled that sometimes I was afraid he would explode just out of sheer internal pressure. I wondered if he was like that with everyone else, too, and if he knew how infuriating it could be.

"Oh, I know exactly what you meant," he said. "You were imagining me as that damn cowboy statue, with Madame Virginie's parachute-like pink panties on my head."

I made a face at him. "Well, it would help if you didn't try for the stoic granite look."

"Oh Lord, not again," he said.

I had no clue what he was talking about, because I hadn't told him that in two weeks at least, but I chose not to pursue it, because I didn't want to get him in a mood again. "Look," I said. "I'll admit to you it's a little weird that the table is . . . well . . . that someone with some sort of expertise in finishing made the notes on the bottom of that table, but—"

"They did? What did the notes say?"

I told him, and I told him how much I thought it might be worth, what a really great find it was, and in the end he shook his head. "I can't persuade you to call the police, can I? Or to give up the damn table?"

"Well, the fact that I didn't tell them about it would now seem . . . suspicious."

"No, it won't," he said, decisively, but his eyes still looked amused. "I'll tell them you were dropped on your head when you were a baby and that you can't help it."

"You didn't know me when I was a baby."

"So what? Your mom tells me stories, Candyce Chocolat."

"Oh, you will *not* repeat that in public," I said.

"Perhaps," he said, crossing his arms on his chest. "Or perhaps I will call the nice policeman and tell him that Ms. Candyce Chocolat Dare would like to talk to him."

I wasn't going to explain that the nice policeman was the sexiest thing God had put on two legs. I couldn't. Besides, with my luck, if I invested my hopes in the man, he'd turn out to be a member of Ben's club who hid it better. So instead I rolled the burger wrapper into a ball and threw it at Ben. It fell short, of course, on the floor, and while he bent to pick it up, I went out the door and to E's room to pack up his stuff for his dad's place.

Packing for E's three days away was always a weird thing. At some very instinctive level I felt as if E wasn't supposed to go anywhere else. But I knew with absolute certainty that I'd only barely escaped having E removed from my custody altogether, given my lack of visible means of support and my unorthodox approach to life. So I made the best of a bad thing.

Of course, sending E to Daddy actually meant sending E to Daddy's new wife, because on Mondays and Tuesdays Daddy was at work. All-ex's wife was . . . a woman I barely knew. It seemed very strange to send E into her care. It seemed even stranger that E had a different set of clothes there, and a different set of toys. I always wondered if he had the same or a similar plethora of stuffed animals. I'd asked him once, and he'd said something about cars, but at his age it was hard to get an exact description.

Sighing, I got the little backpack that E took back and forth between the houses. When I sent him to All-ex I usually sent back—washed and folded—whatever he'd been wearing when he'd come back the previous Tuesday evening; his favorite sleep-with toy of the moment, which right then was a realistic platypus that Ben had bought him from some online store called Real Zoo; and his favorite read-aloud book, currently an illustrated version of William Allingham's *The Fairies*.

What he brought back was usually the outfit he'd been wearing on Saturday, all washed and dried and folded, plus bananas, apples, and whole-wheat muffins, plus the book and sleep-with toy looking as if they'd never been unpacked.

If something out of the ordinary was going on, there would also be a note written in the new Mrs. Mahr's well-rounded finishing-school handwriting, usually saying things like, "Please give Enoch his antibiotic at nine a.m. and six p.m."

Lately there had been notes about E's Pull-Ups and the need to wean him into big-boy pants, to the point that I had given up on opening the notes. Because, look, they were probably right. I mean, E did need to wear real, grown-up cotton pants someday. On the other hand . . .

On the other hand, he was having fewer and fewer accidents every week. And when he did have them, it was easier to deal with the Pull-Ups than with cotton pants, because I didn't own a washer and dryer and going to the Laundromat was a production, not to mention expensive.

I emptied his backpack—there was still a muffin in there, though I'd managed to make E eat the fruit. The banana had to be mashed with graham crackers and orange juice, and the apple had to be baked, but I had managed to make him eat them. I found a note I dimly remembered seeing. It was under the muffin, looking slightly greasy.

I opened it, sighing at the expected screed about Pull-Ups, and instead found a couple of lines: "Dear Candyce, Alexander and I are concerned about Enoch's speech development. We'd like to take him to a psychologist for evaluation, but Alexander seems to think he needs your permission for anything of the kind. Michelle."

Yes, indeed. Evaluation on psychological issues, problems of development, and such all required my explicit permission in writing—mostly because the lawyer I'd engaged for the divorce had wisely secured it.

I rolled the paper into a ball and threw it in the direction of the door, thinking to take it to the bathroom trash on my way there. And hit Ben on the thigh.

"What?" he said. "I didn't say anything this time."

"I didn't even know you were there," I said. "I was just . . . gah."

"You were gah?" he said. He was engaged in some complex game with E that involved giving him a stuffed animal, getting another one in exchange, and repeating ad infinitum while E said, "Bah, bah, bah," and grinned.

"I'm always gah," I said. "It's just more gah than usual. All-ex wants to take E to a psychologist to figure out why he won't talk."

"Well . . . ," Ben said.

"Bah!" E said.

"Don't you start. Do not start, Benedict."

"No, but . . . you know, I know you speak to him and say he speaks back, but . . ."

"Selective mutism," I said, digging the sentence from my back brain. "It's not unusual for highly intelligent children to refuse to speak to anyone but one of the people around them. Officer Hotstuff said that—" I realized too late what I had said, as I watched Ben's lips form the words *Officer Hotstuff?*

I resisted the temptation to tell him to shut up, particularly because I was aware that he hadn't said anything. A wave of blush came up to my cheeks, causing them to blaze with heat. I turned away and removed everything from the backpack, then got the outfit that E had been wearing when he'd returned on Tuesday—a little pair of chinos and a button-down shirt—and put it at the bottom of the backpack. I gathered the other stuff from around the room, half-expecting Ben to say something, or ask something. But he continued his game with E, seemingly not noticing what I'd said.

Good, then. We wouldn't go down that road. I picked up the platypus and stuffed it into the backpack. I wondered if I should stuff the bran muffin back in on top of it all. It wasn't even homemade but one of those you can buy at coffee shops, all wrapped in plastic.

I'd bet it was full of fiber and organic honey sweetener and whatever else. Organic and natural seemed to be my ex's new wife's touchstones. Without me, my poor child would not even get his minimal daily requirement of preservatives and colorants. Not that Ben helped with that, of course, going and getting him organic burgers.

"What?" he said. "What did I do now?"

"Nothing," I admitted, fairly sure I'd given him a dirty look and even more sure that if I explained that it was because he hadn't given E any colorants or preservatives, he would simply proceed to having me committed. Or persuade Mom and Dad to do it.

The fact that he smiled and shook his head, as though he could guess what I hadn't said, made me want to stuff bugs in his purse. Even if I had to buy him a purse for the purpose.

I edged past him, trying to think if there was anything else I needed to send with E that he would need. I purely hated having to drive across town to All-ex's suburban house to take some little thing I'd forgotten.

Ben's cell phone rang, and he fished it out of his pocket. Something must have been wrong on the home front, because he sounded a little too relieved as he said, "Les. Oh, good. What?" He walked out of the room—and my room—to the living room. I could hear him say things like, "No. No. Of course not." Then a pause. And after a sigh, "Les, I can't.

I'll explain when I get—" Another pause. "Must we have drama? Do you realize how ridiculous that sounds?"

Yep, I thought. His saying such things while sounding unearthly calm ... well, if I were in a relationship with him and he talked to me like that he'd have had a shoe or a stuffed animal thrown at him by now. I wondered if he drove Les as insane as he did me. And then, because I hated feeling any kinship at all with Les-finishing-school-Howard, I thought it was a good thing Ben was gay. Men—at least in my view—tended to be a bit more controlled. Any woman worth her salt would have put a hatchet in Ben's head by now.

He was still talking, in his calm, exacting way, and I decided not to go out to the living room until he was done. After all, it must be hard enough for Les to deal with him, without hearing someone move around in the background. And besides, I didn't want to hear. My arrangement with Ben was that we both stood ready to hear the other's confidences, but unless there was something truly seriously wrong, we didn't ask for them, much less listen in on the other's conversations or read his or her letters or anything of the kind.

It was a hard-and-fast rule come to after I had opened the door of the piano practice room just after class—looking for Ben, who often tried to practice before going home, because his mother's piano was shared with six younger siblings—and found Ben making out with the student council president, who, as far as I could see, did not lean that way.

I'd walked away in confusion, of course, but afterward had tried to get Ben to tell me all, only to meet with a granite wall that all my efforts had only managed to make more solid, until my stubborn friend had stopped talking to me for an entire two weeks. It was the longest rift in our friendship. And I had never found out exactly what had happened with the student council president either, except that he was now married and he and his wife were leading lights in the society of Goldport, the set that All-ex and his wife moved in.

Ben had told me then—and I'd not dared ask now—that it simply wasn't his information to give away or his secret to share. When we'd made up—after two miserable weeks—we'd established the rule that we would each determine what we would and could share with the other, and the other wouldn't push.

It had in a way been a sanity saver as my marriage disintegrated. I knew that Ben was there, should I need to talk about what was going on, but I didn't *need* to talk about what was going on, and he'd accept my silence implicitly.

I now accorded him the like courtesy, and between keeping E occupied—and preventing him from bursting into the living room—and making a list of what I needed to do and buy on my trip to Denver, because I'd left the other one in the shed and felt leery of going there although I had no very rational reason, I stayed out of his way a long, long time.

In fact, I hoped that the fact that his conversation was taking so long meant that Ben and Les were making up. No, I did not in fact think that Les was the best thing that had ever happened to Ben, but I suspected part of my issue with this was that Les didn't look anything like the type of guy I'd imagined Ben settling down with. There is this tendency, when you've known everyone forever or just about, to think that you know exactly who'll make him happy. And Les was definitely not what I thought would make Ben happy. I'd always thought Ben would end up with a guy somewhat like himself. Well, not necessarily as tall but . . . well, masculine. Not small, willowy, and seemingly in need of protection.

On the other hand, of course, Ben was—objectively speaking and my dearest friend though he was—no prize. There were the silences and the reserve. Les had managed to stay with him for a year and change. A line that I suspected came from a Jane Austen movie floated through my mind, and I wondered who I thought I was, that I had the right to determine in what manner my friend should be happy.

At which point my phone rang, and it was All-ex, which made sense because he always tried to interrupt me when I was settled down with a blanket and a pint of Rocky Road in front of the TV, ready to watch one of Jane Austen's miniseries.

"Candyce," he said, which was one of his bad habits. Well, *speaking* at all was one of his bad habits, really. But calling me that in particular.

"Alexander," I said, which was a bad move because the priss actually liked his full name.

"I was wondering if we could come by and take Enoch a little early. You see, Michelle's parents would like us to come to dinner, and I thought we'd make Enoch—" He stopped. "I mean, that we would like to take Enoch with us, and you know, he's quite likely to crush a bug on himself or something, just before . . . anyway . . . Michelle says she'll bring him earlier on Tuesday, too. And that way it will all be even, but if you wouldn't mind . . ."

I minded. Of course I minded. I minded having to send E to his house at all. But the thing was that eventually I'd need a favor of the kind or to keep E an extra day, and for me to be trouble over this—or even to take offense at the unstated fact that they wanted to make E decent before taking him out—would only be a problem for me later on.

"Okay," I said. I turned around the way you do when you're trying to turn away from the person on the phone, and you do it physically. "All right. He's ready, just about."

"Oh, good," All-ex said, sounding only mildly surprised. "We're about thirty minutes away and we'll be there—"

All hell broke loose. As I'd turned away, E had broken away from the room and bolted toward the living room, saying, "Bah! Bah! Bah!"

I heard Ben shout, "No, don't—"

I hung up and ran.

For such a series of sounds, the scene was nothing like I expected. E was holding on to Ben's leg, and Ben was standing looking at his cell phone with the expression of someone who expected the small, compact phone to turn into a three-headed frog.

"What happened?" I said.

Ben looked at me. His free hand went up to rub the middle of his forehead. "Nothing. It's just . . . Les . . . is being a—" He stopped and gave the impression he'd bit his tongue, then shrugged. "I have no idea what's going on, but he had . . . he's been under stress at the symphony. Something about the brass section." He shrugged again. "He'll calm down."

"I'm sorry I let E run out," I said. "I was trying to keep him in his room."

He gave me something that approached a smile. "Well, having the monkey run in and shout didn't help, but it was probably headed that way anyway. He'll calm down. He's just . . . stressed."

Right. For someone who said they'd never had a disagreement before, to the point where he had no idea what the making-up procedure might be, Ben was acting like someone in the middle of a huge flare-up. But there was the rule.

I told him that All-ex was coming to pick up E early.

"All right, then I probably should go," he said. He grimaced. "You know how well we get along. But I really don't want you staying here. Can you go stay at your parents', or something? I know they're not there, but—"

I didn't want to go stay at my parents'. Too many reasons to list, but at the end of them all, Fluffy would piss on my bed. She always did, even when I tried to shut her out of the room. And besides, again, she didn't need that sort of stress. "Yeah, sure."

He looked doubtful. As he'd pointed out before, he knew me rather well. But he said, "Okay," and petted the top of E's head. "See you later, monkey. Be good for Daddy and Stepmommy."

"Bah."

"Yes, but you probably shouldn't tell them that."

The doorbell rang.

I detached E from Ben's leg, and Ben took two steps toward the door. So All-ex had gotten here early. Which meant there was no point at all to Ben's leaving to avoid a confrontation.

I walked quickly, peevishly, to the door and flung it open. And found myself staring—no doubt disapprovingly—at the confused face of Officer Hotstuff, aka Cas Wolfe.

"Ms. Dare," he said.

"Officer Wolfe," I said.

He blinked at me and looked over my shoulder toward Ben. "Did you know your car is . . . that someone slashed the tires?"

THE BRIGHT EYES OF THE LAW

"THE VOLVO?" I SAID, starting toward the door.

"The BMW," Officer Hotstuff Wolfe said.

Ben made a sound that might have been an explosion and headed out the door to his car.

"I'm sorry. I didn't mean to upset your husband."

Honestly. Should a grown man look that sheepish? "He's not my husband. Just a friend." And then, realizing that *just a friend* these days could be an entire category of dating, "Not . . . a romantic interest." And then of course I wanted to bite my tongue off, because why in hell should I be telling this to a total stranger? Next I would tell him that Ben was just so incredibly gay . . .

But he didn't seem surprised, and nodded as he asked, "May I come in?"

"Of course," I said, stepping aside, more than a little confused. Part of the confusion was the fact that Ben was now looking at his tires. Part was that Officer Cas Wolfe really was *all that*—broad shoulders and perfect features and all. My mouth wanted to drop open and drool and it was all I could do to keep it decently closed.

He walked into the house, but stood by my side looking out at Ben. I knew where he was looking without turning to glance at him. I could tell from the heat radiating from his body that he was standing very close indeed, and felt tenseness from him.

Ben came back to the house, talking on his cell phone. As he got close to us, he said, "Just a second," then to me, "I called roadside assist. They'll send someone out." He shook his head, frowning, his look at me intent.

I knew what the extraordinarily focused gaze meant, but I didn't want to say anything one way or another. He wanted me to tell Mr. Policeman about someone coming in, knifing the table, and hanging a stuffed toy by the neck. He thought it was related to the slashing of his tires.

Which beggared the mind. For one, it couldn't all have happened at the same time. Clearly, the stuffed chimp had already been swinging, the table knifed when Ben came home. Clearly, too, Ben and E had not been riding around in a car with slashed tires.

So . . . My mind reeled, trying to make sense of all of this. Ultimately, the stuffed animal and the knifed table couldn't have anything to do with the slashed tires. The slashed tires were probably the result of parking a BMW in this neighborhood. After all, when I'd decided to move in, Ben had brought up all sorts of scary statistics, including but not limited to the fact that this neighborhood had more bashed mailboxes than any other in town. It wasn't that far from bashed mailboxes to slashed tires, and I'd be damned if I was going to tell Officer Hotstuff Wolfe that people were out to get me, were targeting me, or—or gave him any other reason to think I was paranoid.

And then, in the way these things happen, the roadside assist people arrived, and Ben went to deal with them. Which meant he was standing at the edge of the driveway as All-ex and Mrs. All-ex pulled up in their car. I didn't know if All-ex had actually steered toward Ben, but Ben stepped out of the way anyway. I was curious enough to watch them load the car onto a trailer while Ben gave them instructions. But he didn't go with them. This seemed at best impolitic, unless he thought he needed to defend me from All-ex, which wouldn't be the first and probably not the last time.

It all happened very quickly. All-ex and Mrs. All-ex got out of the car, and Ben walked toward me, hands in pockets, looking far more casual than if he were actually at ease. For one, he never put his hands in his pockets when he was at actual ease, because it ruined the line of the suit. "Dyce," he said, before All-ex could talk. "If you wouldn't mind giving me a ride home, then Les can give me a ride to the shop to pick up my car."

"Sure," I said, as All-ex came up the steps to the front porch—a little cement enclosure just up from the street—and glared at me as if I had personally offended him by talking to Ben. He glared at Ben, then glared at Officer Wolfe, just as Michelle—blandly pretty and wearing a pink skirt suit with just a bit of a lace collar showing, and a set of matched pearls around her neck—gave Ben and Officer Wolfe a pale, embarrassed smile.

All-ex was dark blond and barely taller than I. I'd always thought part of his problem with Ben was Ben's height. If so, Officer Wolfe wasn't helping, and from the look All-ex gave each of them, you'd think All-ex and I were still married and he'd caught me in flagrante delicto with both men. He straightened his neck and gave the men a ferocious, challenging glare.

I'd seen that glare before. It was the year Grandma kept chickens and she had two roosters. The smaller of the two looked at the world with that same mad, defiant expression. "I need to talk to you," he said to me, before I could even introduce Officer Wolfe. Which is probably just as well, because after his look, I wanted to tell him that yes, I was carrying on with Officer Wolfe and that all his darkest suspicions about Ben were true. The gay thing was just a ruse. A very well-carried-out ruse. It required him to make out with the student council president in high school and to live with Les Howard.

Instead, I tried to discipline myself to say hello. Somewhere behind me, in the living room, I was aware of the sound of little running feet, and wasn't sure if E was coming forward to greet his father or to hide behind me as his father attempted to take him away.

Before I could open my mouth, though, All-ex said, "We have to talk."

"Oh no," I said. "Isn't that the woman's line?"

He looked confused. Poor All-ex had spent a great part of our marriage looking confused. He frowned, bringing his eyebrows low over his eyes. "Did you read the note in Enoch's backpack?"

"There was a note?" I asked, all sweetness and light.

"You know damn well there was a note," he said. "The thing is, Michelle and I were talking in the car, and we really need to take Enoch to a therapist. He's over two and a half now, and he should be saying something. At least *Mom* and *Dad*."

And Ben—Ben, who normally would have sided with All-ex on this—blurted out, "Well, he says *Bah*."

All-ex gave him a withering look, then glared at me. "He says all sorts of things," I said. "Selective mutism is not unusual in gifted children. He will speak more to other people as he becomes older and . . ."

"There is no proof that he speaks to *anyone*," All-ex said. "Just because you keep telling me that—"

"She's right," Officer Wolfe put in, all too helpfully. "Selective mutism is quite common in smart kids. I didn't talk to anyone but my mother for—"

"Enoch is my son, not yours," All-ex said, in the voice of a man holding fast to that one basic truth in the face of his ex-wife's obvious and clear lack of morals, which had enlisted all these men to her cause.

At that moment, E pushed forward, keeping close to my legs and holding on to me, turned his innocent face up to his father's enraged countenance, and said, "Oh, holy fuck."

It rang clear as a bell and, unmistakably, in Ben's intonation.

Run, Baby, Run!

"WELL," I SAID, BECAUSE sometimes, frankly, the quilt frame is already on fire and the cat is going to get burned whether or not she jumps through it, "as you can see, he can talk."

All-ex swallowed. Our married life together had ended the day he slapped me, something I didn't normally tell people about because I didn't think it was that All-ex was necessarily an abuser or would ever slap any other woman. And it wasn't so much that I blamed myself as that I knew, to quote my mother, that I could make a saint turn devil. Since then, All-ex had gone out of his way to not even raise his voice at me. But right then, he clenched his fist by the side of his body, and I could see him physically hold himself back. "What kind of language—" he said.

"Dear, remember your blood pressure," his wife said.

"It was my fault," Ben said, as if it would help anything. "I don't normally swear . . . well . . . not in front of him, but it escaped. You see, Dyce found . . ."

"A problem in a piece of furniture," I said, cutting him short. Not only was his admission of fault not going to buy him any slack, but if he went around talking about me finding a body, let alone having my table slashed and a stuffed animal hanged from the shower curtain bar, All-ex would call in the lawyers. And he would do his best to keep me from seeing E ever again, for the rest of my life. Hell, that was why I never took him to court over missed child support. Because it could be worse.

"And he swore?" All-ex asked.

"I'm like that," Ben said. "Very empathetic. I swear whenever Dyce feels like it."

From my right side, Officer Wolfe cleared his throat. I was afraid he would say something. In fact, the man was almost guaranteed to say something. But before he could, E saved the day. Not that I in any way approve of what he did, of course.

He sprang up from behind me and ran full tilt toward the street. It took me two seconds to realize that he was stark naked, and a quick look to my side to realize he'd taken off his clothes and his Pull-Ups and left them in a bunch on the floor.

By that time, he was running hell-bent for leather up the sidewalk on Quicksilver, toward Fairfax—the largest, busiest artery in Goldport. At rush hour.

I took off after him before I was fully conscious of what I was doing. But I was almost a block behind E and behind Ben and Officer Wolfe, both of whom had reacted with remarkable promptness, and both of whom were now beating a mad pelter after the toddler.

As I ran behind them, my lungs were bursting, my legs felt like they would fall off, except that I must keep running, I must catch up with the crazy kid. And yet, at the same time, some part of my brain—the part that was rarely concerned with motherly things—noted that Officer Hotstuff was steadily gaining on Ben and muttered, *Aha, I knew he was a runner.*

Which was all very well for the cavewoman, but I, of course, was far more concerned with my son.

I saw him turn from Quicksilver onto Fairfax and start to run along Fairfax to the next intersection. The problem was that the next inter-section was Pride Street, which had almost as much traffic on it as Fairfax. I braced as the little figure reached the corner, fully expecting him to step out into the stream of crosswise traffic.

However, against all expectations, he stopped.

To this day I think he stopped because he hadn't actually expected to see traffic moving in front of him. On the other hand, Ben claims he stopped because at the corner of Pride and Fairfax, facing us, was the George. The George was a diner that had recently been refurbished and renamed. Part of the refurbishing was a big neon sign in the shape of a dragon flipping pancakes. Though we were still in full daylight, that side of the street was in shadow, and so the light flickered very brightly and it might have caught E's eye.

For whatever reason, E did stop. And before he could start up again, Officer Wolfe caught him about the waist, saying, "Got you," just in case E didn't notice.

Ben caught up with them then, and stooped, drawing breath. I caught up with them after that, though frankly what I was doing was more like coughing and moaning and it seemed like I'd never breathe again. Ben helpfully tapped me on the back, as though by this means he could start up my breathing mechanism, even as he muttered, "I should run more."

Officer Wolfe looked from one to the other of us, amused, which frankly made me want to tell him I'd like to see him holding a lighted quilt frame, and then we'd see how good he was. But of course, I said nothing of the kind. Instead, I noticed that E was holding on to him and saying delightedly, "Oh, holy fuck."

Ben groaned. "Monkey, perhaps it would be a good idea to not display your linguistic ability quite so much?"

"A very good idea," Officer Wolfe said as, more or less by common accord, we started walking back toward my place with me walking between the guys. "Don't make me take you in for violating the language decency rules."

E looked doubtful. "That means he locks you up," Ben said, then coughed. "Then again, a locked room and all the bugs he can eat . . ."

"Stop it," I said. "Just stop it. Oh, damn. All-ex is going to sue for custody."

"Why? Because his son acted out when he saw his parents argue?" Officer Wolfe said. "I don't think he'd have a case. Remember, I'm an officer of the law."

"Good one, that," Ben said, sounding very much like Officer Wolfe had gotten his job just to give us cover.

At the corner of the street I took E back from Officer Wolfe, who gave him to me without protest, and I walked slightly ahead of them, bracing. As I expected, All-ex hadn't even left the front porch, which made perfect sense if you understood how All-ex's mind worked. It wasn't that he didn't care what happened to our son. It was that, in his mind, E's taking off running down the street naked was completely my fault, and therefore it was my responsibility to get him. Also, in his defense, he was wearing a suit and wingtips.

As I approached I could tell his lips were pursed in complete disapproval, and I walked a little faster, distancing myself from the men behind me, who seemed to be talking to each other anyway. I repressed a strong urge to sigh. Maybe I'd been right—maybe Officer Wolfe did play on the same team as Ben. Well, whatever. I told myself I didn't care at all. At least—though it might be the first time in Ben's life that he'd had anything to do with a person involved in one of the more masculine professions—he'd be an improvement on Les.

Mrs. All-ex had gotten little clothes from the back of the car. Not Pull-Ups, I noted, and what looked like a miniature suit, exactly like the one All-ex was wearing. Wasn't that just too precious? It was all it took to put the cap on what was fast becoming a truly foul mood.

I handed E to All-ex, watched E open his mouth, then glared at him and told him, "Don't you dare."

I don't know what E had been about to say, though I suspected it was his newly acquired vocabulary. Instead, he looked confused and clamped his mouth shut. *Yeah, that's right, Dyce. Make the kid hate you, too, why don't you?*

A part of me, the part that had a tendency to go maudlin and feel sorry for herself, was trying to say that perhaps it was better for everyone if E hated me. After all, I was clearly an unfit mother. But not even I could convince myself of that. I wasn't an unfit mother. On the other hand, it surely looked like it, as I watched All-ex and his Michelle dress my little boy in stiff, all-too-proper clothes.

My eyes blinded by tears that I did not remember feeling forming, I ducked into the house and brought back a backpack, which I handed to Michelle. E waved at me and at Ben and Officer Wolfe and said, "Bah!"

Officer Wolfe looked amused, Ben waved, and All-ex said, giving the impression of speaking between clenched teeth, "I'll bring him back on Tuesday."

I said, "Good," and that was about that.

Except, of course, it wasn't. Officer Wolfe and Ben stood side by side on the front porch. I wanted to tell them to go off and do something, but I didn't know exactly what to say, and besides, even if Ben was in the middle of an argument with Les, surely he couldn't just throw him over like that. I confessed to not being privy to the inner workings of Ben's emotional life, but I was fairly sure he wasn't that shallow.

I watched All-ex drive away, and pointedly ignored Ben and Officer Wolfe, but I couldn't quite shut the door in their faces and before I could retreat into the house, Officer Wolfe was there, clearing his throat. "I was wondering," he said, "if I could invite you to have coffee with me or something, and we could . . . well, I'd like to talk to you about what you saw . . . see if perhaps you could give us any insight."

"Insight?" I asked, completely confused. It wasn't so much that I didn't understand what he was saying. It was more like I'd forgotten my command of the English language. A confusion of thoughts went through my mind, from the shock of the attack on a table and a stuffed animal—but who the heck attacked tables and stuffed animals?—to the fact All-ex was going to try to get custody, to the fact that Ben and Officer Wolfe seemed to have hit it off, and it wasn't fair. It just wasn't.

It might be a cliché to say that all good men were either married or gay, but damn it, that seemed to be the way it played out. Except, of course, that All-ex was married, not gay, and he wasn't very good. But that only made me more confused. I wiped my dripping nose on my sleeve and caught Ben's disapproving glare. "What type of insight?"

"Well," he said. "We've found that the body was ... that is, that either the dead person was killed, or the corpse was immersed after death, in a lye vat."

"A lye ... as in a refinishing vat?" I said.

"Exactly," Officer Wolfe said. "And I remembered you said you refinished furniture.

Oh. Of course, it would all come around to Dyce being suspect number one. Who would ever doubt it? Only, this time I almost had proof—as far as one could prove a negative—that it hadn't been me. After all, an operation the size of mine simply couldn't afford any type of vat, lye or otherwise. "I don't have a lye vat," I said. "That's usually the really big refinishing places. You know, the ones that do architectural components and the like. At best, with all the goodwill in the world, I could have dipped her leg in a lye bucket."

Officer Wolfe's lips twitched, which was weird, because I was sure I hadn't said anything funny. "I didn't think you'd done it," he said. "This is not an official inquiry. I just thought because you refinish furniture, you might know about other places that refinish furniture here in town, and you might be able to tell me where to start looking."

"Uh ... I don't think I know any more than you could find from looking in the phone book," I said, even as I caught Ben giving me such a disbelieving look that I wanted to ask him what was wrong with him. I was fairly sure my nose wasn't painted red, which was the only thing that would justify those eyes open wide in shock and the head shaking slowly in disapproval.

But Officer Wolfe clearly had comprehension problems. He only smiled wider at me and said, "Humor me. May I pick you up for dinner in a couple of hours? I have some errands I need to run, but I would love to take you to dinner afterward."

I opened my mouth to say no, but Ben looked so frantic that all I could do was swallow and say, "If you think it will be any help. But you don't need to take me to dinner."

Ben looked like his eyes would explode out of his head, like the eyes of a cartoon character in an old-fashioned reel. His lips were pursed, and he was clearly trying to tell me something without making a sound. I had no idea what it could be other than, *Help, there's steam climbing up inside my head.*

"I'd like to," Officer Wolfe said, and I wondered if Ben had told him I lived on pancakes and that he should improve my diet. Give him ten minutes with Officer Hotstuff, and they'd probably cut off my supply of pancakes and of colorants and preservatives forever.

"Oh, all right," I said.

"Good." He smiled. "At seven, then." And he left, at a trot, to the car he'd parked at the corner.

He had barely shut the door to his car—a small red car of Asian make—when Ben crossed his arms on his chest and said, "What are you trying to do, woman?"

"What?" I realized that my hair had come loose during my run, and I removed the elastic and started to pull it all back into a ponytail. "You shouldn't have told him to buy me dinner, you know? It's not like I'm a famine victim."

"Told him . . . ? What?" he asked in turn. "I didn't tell him to buy you anything. Clearly the man wants to take you out."

"Why?"

Ben threw his arms out in a gesture of exasperation. "How do I know? Some men like women. Search me if I know why." He shook his head at me. "And clearly some men like you. You've been married. You figure out what he wants."

"Don't be stupid," I said. "You were very cozy with Officer Hotstuff."

"Oh, don't I wish. Well, no. Actually I don't. He's not my type. Nice, but not my type. Yeah, he's Officer *Hotstuff*, but the only reason we were talking is that you were walking ahead of us and to talk to you, we'd have needed to scream. What do you think—" His phone rang, and he fished in his pocket for it.

"Hello," he said. And then went very still. "Oh," he said, after a while. And then, "I'll come as soon as possible."

He hung up, and all humor was gone from his expression. He looked pale and tense and distraught. "Dyce, can you drive me home? There was a . . . fire in my place and the fire department was called. I . . . uh. I need to go assess the damage. Les . . . Les isn't there."

CREATIVE DESTRUCTION

T HERE WERE NO COMMENTS on my sudden speeding up, no comments on my slamming on the brakes at the intersections, not even the ghost of a flinch as I tore across two lanes of traffic at the last minute to pull into the visitors' parking area of his building and slam, more or less willy-nilly, into a parking space.

No, I don't normally drive that badly, but I do drive horribly when I'm perturbed. And frankly, seeing Ben so silent gave me the screaming willies.

He got out of the car as soon as I stopped, and didn't wait for me. There was a fire truck parked in the middle of the parking lot and they were doing something with hoses and ladders, but Ben didn't even give them a second look, nor the police car beside them. Instead, he hurried toward the door to the building. I followed.

When we were little, this building stood in the heart of what was then the downtown shopping district. And it remained the downtown shopping district. Sort of. Gone were the mom-and-pop stores and the strange, sometimes dusty shops of our adolescence. In their place were a lot of chain restaurants, a couple of chain bookstores, and a whole lot of trendy clothing stores, with names like *Virgin Forest*.

The building that had become Ben's place had been one of those massive, stone structures, nine or ten floors tall. The bottom floor held a used record store, the floor above a funky and somewhat scary used office furniture store, and the levels above that the sort of small offices that evoked images of Dickens.

A few years ago, local developers had bought it, stripped it down to the bones, and then rebuilt it much taller as a steel-and-glass structure.

I still resented the idea that it had taken the place of the familiar build-ing of my childhood, but I couldn't deny that it was far more pleasant. The bottom floor now held a combination bookstore and coffee shop. The entrance for the people who lived above it was through the back, straight out of the parking lot. Ben had let himself in with one of those key cards reminiscent of the badges used in office buildings.

I followed him into the elevator. He punched the button for the nine-teenth floor, then leaned back against a faux-marble elevator wall, in silence. I hate elevators, and having to go that far up in one to go home would have dissuaded me from living where Ben did. But Ben didn't seem to mind. At least I presumed the hard-set face and narrowed eyes were not fear that the elevator would take him very fast between floors, then drop him. When he saw me staring at him, he looked away. The nineteenth floor was as far as the elevator went—one floor from the top but the lofts up here were two floors. Ben was fumbling in his pocket for his key, but he needn't have bothered.

There were three doors leading out of the marble hallway onto which the elevator opened. One to the left, one to the right, and one right in front.

The left and right ones led to the bigger lofts on this floor, both big enough for large families—not that I thought large families lived in this building. The one in front of us led to Ben's loft. And it was open, because someone had axed the handle—and lock—clear off the door. I say *axed* because there were marks around it, of the sort someone leaves when swinging an ax wildly.

Ben made a sound. It wasn't a sigh and it wasn't a whimper, but it might have been something in between.

He pushed the door open the rest of the way and went in. I walked in behind him. My feet squelched on the entrance rug—a Persian or a good imitation in tones of red. I looked down. The rug was soaked. And the polished wood floor around it was covered in a fine, shimmering veil of water.

"What—" I said.

"The sprinkler system," Ben said, as he walked very slowly into his place, as though he were afraid either of waking someone or that someone would jump out at him. "It's a multistory building with more than three stories. Sprinklers are mandatory. I already told the building manager to call the disaster recovery people."

"A fire?" I said.

He didn't answer. Instead, he prowled into the big open room that constituted most of this downstairs floor. The leather sofas were soaked, the massive mahogany coffee table awash in water. The bookcase with all his babied books was soaked, too. But there was more to it than the sprinklers or an accidental fire. Someone had taken the oxblood vases, lovingly picked one by one, that used to occupy niches in the bookcase, and smashed them and then—it looked like—jumped up and down on the fragments till they were tiny pieces and dust. We walked on pieces of priceless antique porcelain as we rounded the bookcase and looked at the soaked guest bed, then back again to the kitchenette on the other side.

Ben didn't make a sound, but his hands were on either side of his head, his fingers touching his temples, as if he were afraid his head would explode. I half-expected the very thorough destruction out in the living room to continue in the kitchenette, but it didn't. The glass-fronted cabinets were intact, the dishes and glasses in them untouched by the destruction, and the granite countertops shimmered, covered in water but otherwise undisturbed. The only thing out of place was on the cooktop, which was set into the counter between the kitchenette and living room. There, there was a pile of what looked like papers, wood, metal, and ash on the now turned-off, soaked, and cold gas burner. The exhaust fan over the stove was still going full tilt.

Ben looked at it with a blind-seeming, flat gaze and said something that sounded like, "He didn't mean it."

I wasn't about to ask him who didn't mean what, particularly because it had just hit me—because of bits of glass and Plexiglas in the mess—that the pile on the burner was the remnants of framed photographs. The framed photographs that used to decorate the room were mostly of Ben and Les at various occasions. Okay. A woman would have been more merciful, I thought. She would have put *Ben* on the burner. And I was at a loss—if this was the work of Les Howard, how he could not mean it?

Did one just accidentally drop every vase on the floor and stomp it to pieces? And then it hit me. Ben thought Les hadn't meant to set off the fire alarm. The dumb bunny had started the fan over the stove, even as he cooked the personal mementoes of their life together.

I bit my tongue. Hard. What in heck good did Ben think that did, exactly? Oh, sure, he'd broken thousands of dollars' worth of porcelain, but he hadn't meant to soak the apartment and destroy everything else, so goody. They could kiss and make up. But even I wasn't about to tell Ben that right then. He looked like a man looking for a reason to blow up.

I'd never seen Ben blow up. Not really. I didn't want to. Which is why I jumped half out of my skin as he made a sound like he had blown up—or at least expelled a vast quantity of air from his lungs in a long hiss. I never knew what would come next, because someone knocked at the open door. "Mr. Colm?"

Like that, Ben looked perfectly normal. Still pale, but perfectly normal. You'd think that he looked at the ruins of his home every day. "Yes?" he said.

A man came in. He was middle-aged, short, and dark-haired, and apparently rejoiced in the name of Mr. Aretruse. Behind him was a taller, bulkier man, in a police uniform.

The policeman wanted to know if Ben wished to make a complaint of arson, but Ben just said he was sure it had been an accident. The man looked at me for sanity, but I was fresh out. In the end, he had to leave and be satisfied with the idea it was all a big accident. Or at least that Ben believed so and that it was unlikely he could get Ben committed.

Mr. Aretruse, the building manager, had come to tell Ben that the disaster recovery people had arrived, as well as the locksmith to put a new lock on the door. Not that I had any idea what anyone might steal from here now. Water, perhaps. This was Colorado, after all. Water was almost as precious as gold.

The conversation between them was a miracle of tentativeness and attempts not to offend, with Mr. Aretruse mumbling something about Ben's roommate leaving a few minutes before the alarm went off and Ben, even as he disposed of burned pictures and picture frames, making polite noises about an accident. Yep, it had been an accident all right. If Les had thought about it, he'd have put the pictures in the oven. And possibly set the timer.

Men came in carrying very large fans. Ben fished his phone from his pocket, called a number, and said, "Les, it's all right. Seriously. Call me, we can talk."

So he wasn't about to blow up. He was about to implode. I resisted a strong impulse to take both of his ears and tie them behind his head. Maybe I'd been as stupid when I was married, but I didn't think so. I'd left All-ex after he slapped me the first time. This didn't *feel* like a first temper tantrum. And it sure as hell didn't feel like a slap either. More like a roundhouse punch.

I gave my very tall, broad-shouldered friend a jaundiced look, then bit my tongue before I said that abused wives came in all sizes. But something must have shown in my eyes, because he said, "Yes, Dyce?"

"You can talk?" I said. "After this, you can talk to him?"

He pushed his lips together until they just about disappeared, and I thought he was going to invoke our "stay out of my business when it comes to love affairs" rule. But one of the men working with mops and squeegees, hanging up bedspreads, and upending the sofas came over. "We think we can save the leather sofas. There wasn't that much water." He shrugged. "And we have ways to dry things. It should take about three days, but we think we can save most things, and ..." He went on to quote a price for the drying, for conditioning leather and reoiling wood, for removing the smell of smoke from walls and drapes.

The price almost made me swallow my tongue. It was a lot of pancakes. It could keep us in pancakes until E was in high school. But Ben just nodded and got his wallet out. "You take Mastercard?"

Apparently they did, and a happy arrangement was struck, after which the gentleman made it known that Ben really shouldn't hang around the place while it dried. Which was just as well, because you'd think Ben would have gotten this from the fact that not only was everything either dripping or covered in water, but three turbine fans big enough to propel a medium-sized plane were parked in the living room, and two others in the loft-bedroom.

Sleeping there would have been kind of like sleeping in a World War Two hangar. So Ben went up the stairs to his bedroom, which was—in addition to wet and squelchy—thrown about as though someone had packed in a great hurry and not bothered making the bed. He held his breath and threw open his closet doors.

And then came my confirmation that Les Howard was, indeed, as blond as he looked. Because sure, he'd hurt Ben by breaking the vases and burning the pictures, but how could someone who had lived with Ben this long and who was this mad at him not have realized what the real go-for-the-jugular move would be?

The closet was miraculously untouched. It was possible, of course, that Les had forgotten it, because it was obvious that he didn't keep his clothes there—every space was still taken up with Ben's clothes. Immaculate hanging shirts and suits; a collection of ties on a special motorized turning rack; his lovingly folded cashmere sweaters on shelves up the center. "It's all dry," I said.

Ben made a face as he reached to the uppermost shelf for a couple of suitcases. "Yeah," he said. "It's probably a violation of fire codes not to have sprinklers in the closet, but I don't care just now."

He set the suitcases on folding luggage racks the likes of which I hadn't seen since Grandma's house. Only hers had been mahogany and Ben's were chrome. He packed quickly and efficiently, and I refused to say anything about the fact that he was packing up most of his clothes for a three-day absence. Unless he intended to change five, maybe ten times a day, it was gross overkill. Knowing Ben, this was probably the equivalent of packing a security blanket. Particularly because it looked like he'd be leaving a key with the disaster recovery people. So he was probably protecting his favorite stuff.

I had no idea what other valuables Ben had in the house. I suspected most of the other stuff was decent, serviceable, perhaps nice household accoutrements, but nothing like the broken porcelain. I did, however, know—as no doubt he did—that no employee of a bonded, insured company was going to make off with a stereo system or a sofa. But they might take one of Ben's ties, and I suspected that right then such a thing would finish breaking Ben's heart.

Of course, when he disappeared into the bathroom and came back after a while with two—count them—two travel cases, one of them the size of a gym bag, with what he no doubt considered absolutely essential toiletries, my tongue got bitten so hard it was going to make it hard to eat pancakes for a while. Yeah, okay, I was aware that Ben used the sort of shampoo you had to order over the Net and more creams for this and that than an aged dowager. And I wasn't going to argue over it, either. After all, I had no room to argue. It's not like he didn't try to make me see the error of my ways, or hadn't on several occasions given me a full line of facial products. I treated cosmetics as I treated just about everything else that wasn't immediate, important, or interesting to me. I set it on a shelf and hoped it would somehow improve my skin by its mere proximity. A fleeting thought that Officer Hotstuff might like me better if I thought of essentials as something beyond my toothbrush and comb crossed my mind. Men. Who knew what they might like better or not? And what did I care what Officer Hotstuff thought?

Ben had zipped his suitcases and looked at me. I took this as, *Are we going, then?* Oh, sure, we were going. I might as well lead the way, and so I did, treading carefully around the small army of recovery people, past a gentleman who was on his knees collecting fragments of porcelain and another who stood nearby separating books into what appeared to be a "salvageable" pile and a "nonsalvageable" one. Then past the fans, which gave me the impression of being on a movie set designed to make it look like I was walking in a windstorm, and past the locksmith kneeling by the door to fix it, and out into the elevator again.

I considered raising the subject of Les, but decided that Ben had suffered enough. Let him get some sleep, and then tomorrow morning I'd sit him down and do my abused-wife intervention. Of course, as with lion taming and Dumpster climbing I knew there was a way to do this, and of course, as with the other work, I knew I had no clue how. I was also perfectly aware that at the first word out of my mouth that sounded like *Les*, Ben would clamp his mouth shut tighter than an oyster protecting a pearl. Too bad. I still intended to sit him down and read him the riot act. And if at the end of it he was granite and fit only for someone to decorate with pink panties on his head, that was entirely his problem. One thing was shutting up when I had doubts about Les's ability to make him happy. Another thing, and totally different for me, was to keep my mouth shut now that Les had proven himself stupid and dangerous.

Ben put his suitcases in the trunk of my car and opened the passenger door. By the time I got in, he was fully buckled in place and looking like a lord of the manor waiting for the chauffeur to start up the car. I put on my seat belt, started the car, and turned around. "Where to?"

He looked surprised. "What?"

"Where are you staying? Where should I take you?"

"Oh." He opened his mouth as if to argue. What? He'd packed and everything, and it had never occurred to him that he'd need to stay somewhere?

But when he spoke again, the words came out hesitantly, more as if he were trying something on and not sure how to get it across. "Uh . . . I thought I'd stay with you."

"With me?"

"If you don't mind," he said, humbly.

"I don't mind," I said, even as I tried to figure out what was going on. Ben had never asked to stay with me, not even while he had work being done at his place. "There's only the sofa, you know?" I said, as I steered carefully out of the parking lot. "That is, I don't think you'll fit into E's crib."

"I'm sure I won't fit into E's crib," he said, with a little smile that made him look almost human. "And the sofa will be fine."

I opened my mouth to point out that my ratty tenth-hand sofa, covered in a slipcover I'd made myself and which was therefore crooked and had lumps of seams in all the wrong places, was quite a drop in his standards, when I remembered the Mastercard being passed over to the disaster recovery team leader. Right. Of course he'd be tight on money.

I opened my mouth again to ask if he was sure he didn't want to go home to his parents', but then realized not only that it would be churlish when he'd asked for my hospitality, but also that he was as likely to like the idea of crawling home to Mom and Dad in the middle of a disaster as I would enjoy crawling back to my mother and father's place in a crisis.

Ben's family was not like mine. In fact, in many ways it was the opposite of mine. I'd often thought that he kept urging me to go home to Mom and Dad because no one can really understand other families.

No matter how much we're exposed to them, in our minds we see them through the lens of the only family we knew really well and early enough.

I was the only daughter of aged parents who not only had married late but had never expected to have children. In fact, if I understood the gist of the conversation between my parents when talking of my birth, they'd gone to some trouble to avoid children. You see, they'd met at a mystery convention where Dad was selling books and Mom was trying to find a buyer for her manuscripts. I wasn't absolutely sure how they'd courted, much less married, because Mom was a romantic soul and Dad was as dry and impervious as his collectible books. But court and marry they had. I'd come along ten years after that, and my advent had caused such a quake in their otherwise ordered lives that Mom had left Dad for a while—if either of them was to be believed over what they were going to call me. They'd reconciled in the candy store just as Mom went into labor, which both of them seemed to think justified my name.

After that flurry of activity concerning me, they'd ignored me and returned to—mostly—babying the bookstore while leaving me to be raised—mostly—by Grandma. Not that I resented this, mind you. It was very much a case of their not doing what they were not equipped to do.

Ben, on the other hand, was the first of seven kids and his mother and father—even if his dad was a high school teacher—made it a point that their main job was to raise the kids. To wander into their house, as I first had at twelve, was to walk into a veritable hail of questions over how you were doing, what you were doing, if you were having any trouble with your homework, and could you grab a mop and do something about what the dog had just done on the floor by the piano?

Ben's mom didn't work, except for giving piano lessons at home while the kids were at school. Ben's next two sisters were in the grades after us and had counted on him to help them with the homework. His sister after that was the beauty of the family as well as a talented singer, and I don't think I'd ever visited when she hadn't been practicing scales somewhere in her bedroom.

His three brothers were much younger and just a year apart from each other. When we'd been twelve, the youngest one had still been in diapers, and he was now a senior in high school.

The Colm household was referred to by my high school counselor as a three-ring circus, and that it was—even now when only the three younger boys still lived at home—but with all that, I couldn't go to his family's house to drop off something, pick up something, or attend a party without becoming the object of his parents' protective attention.

During the long years of our friendship, I think they had completely forgotten I wasn't one of theirs. Unlike my parents, they had never had the slightest illusion that Ben and I might be an item. Instead, they treated me as though I were an additional daughter, squished somehow between Ben and Dana, who was a year and a half younger. I'd never been able to figure out how they thought that, particularly because their brood ran to tall, well built, and varying shades of strawberry blond, but I was small, dark, and Mediterranean-looking.

However, after I'd started coming home and doing homework with Ben for six months or so, they began setting a place for me at the table, and his mom was as likely to tell me to go wash my hands or fix my hair as she was one of his sisters. And I swear his mom was far more vigilant and interested in the boys who took me out in high school than my mom ever was. For that matter, she'd never really approved of All-ex, and I should have listened to her.

Of course I had no clue how she felt about Les. I was fairly sure they knew that Ben was gay. The simple fact that his mom had never pushed girls at him was evidence enough. I didn't know if Ben had told them—it wasn't any of my business—but he hadn't exactly hidden Les. Even if it would be easy to do. All he had to do was stuff him in that oversized toiletries case.

"Dyce!" Ben said, sharply, and for a moment I thought he was rebuking me for my inner thoughts. Turned out he was reminding me that the light in front of me had just turned red. I stomped hard on the brakes, and he made a sound that wasn't quite a protest as I returned to my thoughts. No. Ben couldn't go home to his parents. What the heck was he supposed to tell his mom when she asked what had happened to his place? I got a feeling he'd rather eat his own tongue sautéed in parsley than discuss Les's temper tantrum with them.

"Fine," I said. "I'll give you sheets and a blanket."

He looked amused. "Oh, good. I was afraid you were going to make me sleep on the coffee stains."

It didn't deserve to be dignified with an answer. "Tea stains," I said, as I pulled into my driveway.

GENTLEMAN CALLER

WOULDN'T YOU KNOW IT that Ben wouldn't let me just go out to dinner with Officer Hotstuff without fussing over me? It started as soon as we got into my living room. He put his suitcases on the floor by the sofa and said, "Go get dressed."

I looked down at my jeans-and-T-shirt-clad body, then back at him. "I'm naked?"

He rolled his eyes. "You're not dressed to go on a date."

"I'm going on a date?"

"You know, Dyce, just repeating back what I say can get very tedious. Didn't Officer Wolfe say he was taking you out to dinner?"

"It's not a date," I said, realizing that an edge of desperation had crept into my voice. I'd seen Ben in this mode, usually trying to persuade his sisters to dress up for the one suitor he considered worthy.

Of course, I had no idea why he considered Officer Hotstuff worthy. Or perhaps he didn't. Perhaps he expected me to use my feminine wiles on the law and . . . and what? Make him search high and low for whoever had hung a stuffed animal?

I looked at Ben out of narrowed eyes and met with a clear stare and features firmly set.

So I went to my closet and put clothes on, and of course they weren't *right*. My slacks were too "business." My blouse was too "blousy"—which gets a prize for redundancy. My good skirt looked like I was trying to sell real estate.

He nixed my little black dress before I put it on, which was a good thing because frankly I wasn't even sure it fit me anymore and I thought there was a good chance the moths had gotten to it. He said we didn't want it to look like I expected the man to take me to an expensive restaurant. I didn't want it to look like I expected the man to take me to any restaurant, even if he had invited me.

In the end, he marched me into the bedroom, stood staring at my closet, then grabbed a wrinkly cotton skirt that had an elastic waist and a dizzying array of colors. "That," he said, "should do it. Do you have a bright blue T-shirt?"

I didn't, but I had a bright red one, which he approved of. "Hanging earrings," he said. "And let your hair loose, just kind of run your fingers through it. Yeah."

"Didn't your sisters let you play with their Barbies?"

"What?"

"Never mind." I'd never seen Ben like this when it came to me going out, and it occurred to me, as I made that remark, that it was probably as much displacement activity from his own troubles as anything else.

"No makeup, I think," he said. Which was very good, because I didn't think I had any. Oh, I'm sure there was a ziplock bag with some stuff in it in the depths of the linen cabinet. But I'd bet money the lipstick was dry and the mascara reduced to black powder.

The doorbell rang and he went to open the door, leaving me to throw my clothes on. Yeah, yeah, I know, technically it should be okay to get dressed in front of Ben, and of course I'd known him forever. But it didn't feel right.

When I emerged from the bedroom, Ben and Officer Hotstuff were talking together in the middle of the room. For two people who had no interest in each other, they sure talked a lot. However, the minute I emerged, Officer Wolfe turned to me in a most gratifying way. And grinned in an even more gratifying way, while his eyes opened just a slight bit, that hint of *oh wow* every woman lives for.

If I hadn't caught a smug *I told you so* look from Ben, I'd even have felt grateful for his dressing advice. But the smug look annoyed me, so I looked at the policeman and said, "I hope you don't need to take up my entire evening, Officer, because I need to get up early and drive to Denver to take some furniture up."

He should have looked wounded at least, because he was clearly appraising me as more than someone to interview. Instead, he looked amused. That was it. I was going to ask him to go to the burger joint around the corner, answer his questions in five minutes, then leave.

Possessed of determination and righteous indignation I stalked ahead of him up the driveway, then said, "Perhaps I should follow you in my car?" It had occurred to me, after all, that as weird as things had been lately, it might not be the brightest thing in the world to get into a car with a strange male, even one who was a cop.

But Officer Wolfe was not a *gentleman*, something he proceeded to prove by smiling lazily at me, gray eyes sparking blue, and opening the passenger door of his car to allow me in. There was, in that smile and the sparkling eyes, a sort of challenge. If I refused the invitation now, it would be the same as admitting I was afraid of being alone with him. And I had no intention of letting him—or any man—know I was scared of him. I got in the car, sat down, and strapped on the seat belt.

Let him do his worst. It wasn't like no one knew I was with him. And Ben might be running mad these days, but it was a madness that applied to Les only, and had nothing to do with how he viewed the rest of the world. I very much doubted he was about to pretend that I didn't exist or not to look for me if I didn't come home.

I suspect my expression must have been as weird as my thoughts. Officer Wolfe, having closed the door, rounded the car and came in on the other side. He gave me a look with raised eyebrows and I half-opened my mouth, ready to tell him I'd go to Cy's—even though two burgers in a day might be too rich for me. But he just said, "I have reservations. It's not very far."

Reservations. That meant we were going somewhere with tables and chairs, probably not made of plastic. There was even a chance that there wouldn't be a play area anywhere in sight. Well, if he thought he was going to soften me up by treating me as an adult, he had another think coming!

But I confess as we drew up outside a tall square building that I vaguely remembered as a bank and that now bore a sign saying *Stock and Cattle*, I gave him an odd look. Perhaps it was his idea of fun to go eat at a savings and loan, chow down on contracts, or eat piles of notes. Who knew? I had no idea how the other half lived. Particularly if the other half was police officers.

"It's a new place," he said, and managed to sound much younger and suddenly defensive. "Steak mostly." And then, in a sudden rush, "You're not vegetarian, right? Your friend said you were pancakarian, but I think he was joking."

The rat fink had discussed my eating habits with a strange man. "I eat anything," I said, and then, in belated recollection of my fears, "except bank notes and contracts."

His eyes widened for a moment, an effect I tended to have on people, but then he nodded, as though I'd made the most reasonable of comments. "Oh, good. You wouldn't want to eat those. Too dry by half."

He got out, opened the door for me, and led me into the restaurant. It *had* been a bank. Once we went in the door, I recognized the subdued parlor with its rosewood paneling, the polished marble floor, and the greenish glass globes on the wall casting an … expensive light over the proceedings.

In front of the entrance that had led once to the sanctum sanctorum of bank counters and desks where people stood ready to discuss your investments, there stood a lectern that seemed made of the same rosewood as the paneling. Behind the lectern, a slim blond woman in a little black dress to end all black dresses raised eyes to us, as though seriously doubting that two such uncouth beings could have access to her establishment.

She would have been perfectly justified in this, had Officer Wolfe not changed out of his T-shirt and jeans. But because he was wearing a dark suit, which somehow—and I failed to understand how—made him look both dangerous and refined, the blonde was out of luck. Officer Wolfe knew it, too. You could tell by the way he looked at her and said, "Wolfe. I have reservations."

She checked a list, condescended to smile, and motioned for her identical twin to come and lead us into the vast resonating hall of the . . . now restaurant.

It shouldn't have worked. I mean, the whole point of a bank is to be too large and have architecture that is too crushing and imposing, so that one feels appropriately small in the midst of monetary transactions. And the point of a restaurant is to create a sense of intimacy.

To convert a bank to a restaurant, they should have needed to lower the ceiling by ten feet and partitioned the floor with booths everywhere.

Instead, some intuitive genius had kept the lights low—really low—on the wall, the sort of lights they show in movies when an airplane loses power. And then, at each of the small tables covered in white tablecloths, they'd put subdued white globes that looked just a bit too strong to be one candle, but were not too much more. The light barely extended beyond the tablecloth.

The result was to make each table a little island of light amid a sea of encroaching darkness. In this darkness floated blond waitresses and waiters in black. I started to wonder if perhaps, just perhaps, the restaurant cloned one waitress and one waiter. I mean, surely they couldn't just hire blonds with the same body build. It had to be against some law.

Such was my confusion, as I followed the blonde through a dark pathway among the islands of light, that it took me a moment to realize I was hearing some sort of old-fashioned music. Looking in the direction of it, toward where the bank vaults had been, I saw that there was a ... big band ensemble and a dancing area in what had once held the holy of holies.

This whole thing was starting to sound very much like Ben's hand had been in it. He was the one who knew where every band played in Goldport, and also one of the few people who knew I could dance, because we'd taken a class together in our last year of high school. Granted, he'd taken it because he'd had a crush on the guy who taught it, but I'd taken it because I enjoyed dancing.

This impression was increased as I sat down and I saw Officer Wolfe's gaze on me, with that hint of confusion a man wears when he's not sure his efforts will meet with success.

"Officer Wolfe, do you normally talk to suspects in expensive restaurants?" I asked, in a conversational tone.

For just a moment he was confused. "Susp—" Then he stopped and smiled again, the long, lazy smile he had given me as he opened his car door. "Well, no," he said. "I much prefer to take them to bars and get them drunk. But your friend Ben said that when you get drunk you just cry and don't say anything material, so I realized my best bet was to feed you."

My friend Ben had told him entirely too much and was capable of a multitude of sins, but he hadn't told Officer Hotstuff *that*. Among other reasons, because it wasn't true. When I got drunk, I got very quiet. "Actually," I said. "Ben says that when I get drunk I get hyper-rational."

The smile became more comfortable. He unfolded his napkin onto his lap. "Oh, I'm glad I didn't get you drunk, then, because the last thing I need is to question someone who is rational."

"You prefer your witnesses irrational, then?"

"Are you a witness, Ms. Dare? Did you actually see anything?"

"Ah, I see how they train you in the police academy."

"Indeed."

The current blond handed us menus. Mine didn't have any prices. I wasn't so stupid as to ask for a non-defective menu, but I did wish to know whether I'd be bankrupting the man with what I picked.

"I highly recommend," he said, "the sage seared beef tenderloin and the watercress salad." And he sparkled his gray-blue eyes at me above the menu, as if to dare me to ask if he had brought many people here. "And save room for the white chocolate jalapeño mousse. It's worth it."

Right. Saving room was all I had done for the last several months, so I doubted I could pass up such a thing as chocolate mousse, even if it came with such an unexpected accompaniment as jalapeño. I considered explaining to him that if he thought some hot pepper was going to keep me away from chocolate, he was sorely mistaken. I'd eaten bitter-sweet chocolate, I'd eaten chocolate with coffee beans in it, and I'd even eaten Mom's unsweetened baking chocolate, though I confess I had attempted to melt it with sugar and butter once. However, that hadn't ended well—even if most of the upper cabinets were salvageable once refinished—and after that I'd just eaten it straight.

I ordered his recommendations, put my own napkin on my lap, and looked up. "You wanted to ask me about refinishing outfits in Gold-port?" I said.

"Yes," he said. "Are there many?"

One of the waiters came and served a red wine I wasn't even con-scious of his having ordered. Perhaps he came here so often that they knew what wine he wanted. I looked across the table at his classical profile, and the thought that he came here every week, each time with a different woman, made me bite my lip. Right. He probably did. And what business was it of mine?

I tasted the wine, and it was lovely, smooth, and almost sweet. The bottle said something of Toscana, but the days were so long gone since I'd drunk wine regularly that even if I could read the whole label, I would have no idea what it was *supposed* to be.

The waiter set a basket of rolls in front of us, and Officer Wolfe took one and tore it apart before setting the halves on his plate and starting to slather them in butter. The bread crackled as it broke, and his fingers were large and square-tipped, with very clean fingernails. I imagined those fingers cupping my chin, felt a wave of heat up my face, and grabbed a roll very fast. "I don't know," I said. "I didn't have time to look in the phone book. I can tell you the companies I've had some interaction with."

He raised his eyebrows at me, "And they are?" he asked, before taking a bite of his bread. His teeth were large and square, too, and very, very white. *What big teeth* . . . I had to bite my own bread to keep myself from imagining kissing him, those teeth grazing my tongue. What in heav-en's name was wrong with me? I wasn't old enough to become—what was the current slang—a cougar, was I? Maybe it started like this. Another ten years and I'd be dragging the UPS man inside to have my wicked way with him. Well, at least if UPS got rid of the current guy who delivered at my house. He had a squint and the worst case of acne scars I'd ever seen.

"Well, they're both far bigger than I. One, I don't know for certain if he uses lye vats. That's Oak Friends down on Madison. They're a little . . ." I tried think of a delicate way to say that the owner of Oak Friends was loonier than a moon-phase clock. He dressed like a refugee from a Tolkien book, for one. "Poetic," I said.

"Poetic?"

"Well, the owner . . ." There were no two ways about it. "He's very creative about . . . okay, fine. He dresses like an elf. He says that the furniture must be freed from the oppressive layers of finish."

Officer Hotstuff was giving me a jaundiced look. "You're making this up, right?"

I looked back at him. "Do I look that imaginative? No. I'm not making it up. He calls himself Inobart Oakfriend. He will only oil furniture, never varnish it or paint it. And now that I think of it, he would never ever use a lye vat."

The policeman looked at me with a look of frozen horror. "Right . . . and he is . . . as yet . . . staying out of a mental ward, I assume."

"Most of the time, at least, because he puts furniture up for consignment in the same stores I use in Denver."

He asked me for their addresses, and I assured him I'd make sure he got them. "There's also Rocky Mountain Refinishing. I'm pretty sure they do have a vat. They're very big. I'm not sure how many they employ. They do the really expensive antiques. You know, when someone dies their estate goes up on the block, and they buy the whole lot—good pieces, bad pieces, everything. Sometimes they throw bad pieces out." I stopped talking for a moment as the server paused to top off our wine. "Or at least," I said, as the server moved away, "pieces that are too much work."

He was looking at me in an attentive way—the sort of way one expects can see beyond the front to what's inside the person. I let out air with an explosive sound, "Yes, all right, I go by the back of their workshop on trash days. Thursdays."

He grinned at me. "You're forgiven. Anything good back there?"

I shrugged. "Sometimes. There was this golden oak bookcase with a fleur de lis carved edge. It had . . . sixteen coats of paint, two of them metallic. You couldn't see the carving at all, so I think they thought it was just a plain bookcase. Or perhaps they thought it was too much work. I don't know."

"But I'd think with a lye vat it would be no work at all, would it?" he said. "I mean, it would eat through everything, wouldn't it?"

I looked up at him and thought of the corpse, turned gelatinous by the lye. I had to gulp, and I knew that if I looked at the plate and the bread I would be sick.

"No," he said softly, as though figuring out what was on my mind. "Not like that. Don't think about that. But, I mean, it would take all the layers and layers of paint, wouldn't it? I'm amazed that not every refinisher uses one, at least for the pieces that are covered in a lot of paint."

I continued to look up at him. "A lot of people disapprove of lye," I said. "I don't use it for the good stuff, for instance."

The waiters floated in out of the darkness and set salad in front of us. Salad was good. There was nothing about salad to make me think of flesh or lye. I collected a forkful of greens. It might be called a watercress salad, but it contained far more than watercress—sweet, bitter flavors mingled in an explosion enhanced, not occluded by the vinaigrette dressing. I realized that it had been years since I'd eaten food like this—stuff that was designed to taste good, not merely to stop one from being hungry. Cy's had become the pinnacle of my culinary enjoyment these days, because there was nothing bad there to detract from what I liked. But this . . . this was like music to the ear, like a good book. Things you enjoyed because they were enjoyable, not just necessary.

And I realized I had eaten almost the entire salad, like a starving orphan on a deserted island. I glanced up. Officer Wolfe looked very amused.

"Why not use a lye vat for good pieces?" he said. "And I thought you didn't use one at all. That you could only have a bucket of lye or so."

I nodded, then shook my head, then shrugged. "Well, you see . . . well, yes, sometimes there are small pieces, but the only one small enough to use a lye bucket in terms of immersing it would be a jewelry box. And the jewelry box . . . there would be a very narrow space between the time when the paint would be softened enough to pull out, and the point at which the wood would dissolve. So you see . . ."

He nodded. "So you don't immerse anything, but you do use lye."

"Sometimes," I said. "On sturdy, not very good pieces. I think the last time I used it was this Oriental chest that had clearly been painted to begin with, and then painted again and again. It was probably not more than five years old. But the inside showed it was solid pine, and I thought it could be made to look antique. Not that I would sell it as antique, understand, but . . . people pay for what things look like."

"Yes," he said. "They always do." He sounded tired. I wondered if he paid for anything, but again bit my lip. Right. This man would not need to pay for sex. And if he did, it was none of my business, and besides, why was I thinking of this stuff? "But why do you talk about lye as if it should be something disapproved of? And say you wouldn't use it for the good pieces?"

"Lye has to be neutralized," I said. I took a sip of my wine and finished the salad at a more sedate pace. "You have to rinse the piece as soon as the paint is softened; otherwise it starts pulping the wood." I took a deep breath, again not wanting to think of pulping. I would definitely *not* think of pulping. "I apply it with a brush, then wait, then rinse. And after you're done rinsing, you have to apply vinegar; otherwise the residual lye will keep working. It sounds easy, but it's a mess, unless, you know . . . you have a big workshop and lots of people working on the piece at once and can time things exactly."

"Ah," he said. "So your objection is the danger of ruining the piece?"

"Not just that," I said. "Even when it all works fine, lye is very caustic and it burns the piece. If you're working with maple or oak, it can darken the wood quite a lot." I finished my salad, and the plate was collected by hands moving out of the pervading darkness. "Of course, sometimes you want that, like when you're working with a relatively new piece but want it to look older, but if you use it on cherry or mahogany, it can completely obscure the figure."

"Figure?" he said, as two plates with steak and tastefully arranged—what looked like sculpted deep-fried or baked vegetable sticks—were slid onto our table.

"The . . . you know how wood is all one color, but it has veins? Even when the veins aren't very big or very visible?"

"Of course," he said.

"Well, if you use lye, it doesn't remove the figure, but it can obscure it. You get . . . opacity, the sense that you can only see one layer of wood anymore, not that feeling a really good finished piece gives you, that you're looking into layers and layers, into the core of the wood itself."

He nodded. "I think I get it," he said.

I had taken a bite of my beef tenderloin and was experiencing culinary nirvana, so I didn't answer, and that gave him a chance to say. "So, how did you get into furniture refinishing? It seems like . . ."

"An odd job for a girl?" I said. "Yeah, my mom tells me that all the time. So does Ben . . ."

"Ben is very protective of you," he said, his eyes half-closed, with a note of something—was it suspicion or just curiosity? I got a feeling he was trying to verify that Ben and I truly weren't an item. Well, I didn't expect Ben would have told him about his own private life. However, he was very good at giving hints, so Wolfe might be unusually suspicious.

"Oh yes. You see, he's like an older brother in many ways, even though we're only six months apart. But he's the oldest in his family and I think his manner stuck like that. He's always picking up . . . birds with broken wings. Even though most of them are human, if you know what I mean." And I found myself telling him all about my friendship with Ben and how I'd come to learn refinishing, though—thank heavens—I wasn't so far gone as to tell him everything about the weird attacks today. I was still convinced they were some sort of college prank, probably from the students who lived upstairs from me. Perhaps their key fitted my door. I knew that the rental company could be very careless like that. Okay, so slashing Ben's tires was over the top, but then Ben could be the original cranky old man and had probably already done the equivalent of shaking his fist at them and telling them to get off his lawn. Suddenly I worried about him alone in my place at night. He had been known to object to the noise from upstairs.

I realized I'd fallen silent and that Officer Wolfe was looking at me speculatively. He had finished his steak without my realizing it. He was resting his elbows on the table, and his hands were crossed well above his plate as he looked at me with a speculative expression. I wondered if he was auditioning me for the part of first murderer.

"So . . . your ex-husband has part custody of your son?" he asked.

Oh. The last few words I'd said were about All-ex, and now he probably thought I was one of those embittered divorced women who thought all men were scum. I shrugged. "Sure," I said. "We have different styles . . . different approaches to parenting, but he's still E's father, and I think E will benefit from knowing his parents at least agree that he's important enough for us to bury our differences." Those eyes were still fixed on me, attentive, inquiring, and I added, "It's not that he's a bad person, you know? I wouldn't have married him if he were. He's . . . we are very different people, and he drove me nuts. I think I drove him nuts, too." Nuts enough to resort to physical violence, which I didn't think had been in All-ex's repertoire before or since.

"And that's it," Officer Wolfe asked. "For refinishers in Goldport?"

"Sort of," I said. "There's someone else who does occasional refinishing, but usually only to order. You know, someone buys a piece and calls him and asks him to work on it. Most of the time he does antique reproductions. Very detailed, commissioned antique reproductions. He once said that two or three pieces a year support him."

"Oh? Would he have a lye vat?"

"I don't think so," I said. "Not normally."

He raised his eyebrows at me, even as someone removed our plates and set little glass bowls filled with white chocolate jalapeño mousse in front of us, accompanied by little cookies shaped like dessert spoons. "I sense," he said as he spooned up the mousse and licked at the spoon in a way that should have been worthy of arrest for lewd and lascivious right there on the spot, "that you don't want to talk about this man. Is he a friend?"

I giggled before I could stop myself. "A friendly acquaintance," I said. "We met back when I was taking things to flea markets, and he was just starting out and put some stuff there, too. You know, small stuff like shelves. He has since developed a very select clientele and lives *quite* above my pancake level." I tasted a spoon of mousse and had to bite my tongue to keep from moaning. Oh, this was . . . oh, where had this been all my life? There was only the edge of a bite, the tip of a sting in sheer delicious chocolateness. It was like a slow kiss with the teeth scraped lightly across the tongue.

"So why the giggle?" he asked, with just a hint of a smile.

"Oh, because . . ." I took a deep breath. "You see, you were so confused about Inobart Oakfriend, I'm afraid you'll think I'm crazy and making stuff up."

He put the cookie spoon down and looked straight across at me. "Not another elf lord?"

"Oh, no," I said. "Nothing as simple as that. You see, Charlie Manson—"

"Excuse me?"

"Well, he prefers to go by Michael Manson, because Michael is his middle name."

"I should hope so," Officer Wolfe said. "I should *hope* he prefers to go by it."

"Yes, he does. Because of the . . ." Laughter was threatening to erupt behind my composure, and I was having all I could to keep it down. "Because of the associations."

"I'd say." He resumed eating his mousse. "So, the poor man has an unfortunate name . . ."

"Yeah. Well, two . . ."

"Two?"

"His other name, that he goes by when he's . . . er . . . wearing different clothes is Miss Charity Jewel."

The cookie spoon went down again. "I beg your pardon?"

"See, I told you you'd think I'd gone crazy," I said.

"Uh . . . not really, I'm considering whether I might be asleep and dreaming. Only my dreams aren't usually this . . . interesting. Are you telling me this . . . gentleman is a transvestite and . . . calls himself *Charity Jewel?*"

"Yes. He wears miniskirts and six-inch stilettos, which would be more appropriate if they weren't size thirteen, and if he weren't about six-five to begin with." Officer Wolfe's mouth had fallen open, and I was sure he was considering one of several quiet establishments with padded rooms where I could rest quietly till I came to my senses, but his expression goaded me on, and I couldn't stop. "He's an ex-Marine and has the craggiest face I've ever seen." I had to pick up my napkin and press it against my mouth to stop what promised to be a shout of laughter from erupting between my lips. "But he thinks . . . he thinks with false eyelashes, rouge, and lipstick, everyone believes he's a woman." My laughter could not wait. All I could do was prevent it from being loud enough to have everyone look at us.

"Good Lord!" Officer Wolfe said, at last. "I suppose he's a friend of Ben Colm's?"

I raised an eyebrow at him. "You mean, all gay men know all transvestites?"

He looked surprised, then shrugged. "Well, no. But . . . my cousin is gay, so I'm fairly well informed. There are two bars in town: the Branding Iron, which Ben doesn't look the type for, and the Pool Queue, which is where my cousin hangs out. Been there a couple of times. They do good steak."

I pressed the napkin on my lips to prevent myself from laughing aloud again.

"You have a dirty mind," Officer Wolfe said—not like someone who disapproves, either. "So, I take it this Manson doesn't run in Ben's set?"

"Oh no," I said, speaking in a strangled voice through the napkin. "No, no, no, Michael Manson is strictly hetero. And let me tell you, it's creepy beyond belief when he hits on you while wearing a miniskirt and speaking in what he thinks is a feminine voice."

"Good Lord," he said again.

"See," I said, lowering my napkin. "I told you you'd think I was making it up."

"You were wrong," he said dryly, though a shadow of a smile still twisted his lips. "I don't think even you could make up a tale half that funny, I mean starting with his names."

Even I. Uh. The man had known me for half a day and he thought he knew what I could make up.

"Good Lord," he said again, apparently expecting divine intervention right then and there, and impatient of getting it. "I didn't know the furniture refinishing world was this . . . exciting."

"Well, think about it," I said, setting my napkin back on my lap. "By and large we're loners who want to do something we can live from independently. And if we actually procure our own refinishing pieces, it involves some creativity and initiative. It's no wonder we get all sorts of misfits."

"And in what way are you a misfit, Ms. Dyce Chocolat Dare?"
I squeaked. I'm sure I did. "He told you."

"Who?"

"Ben told you my middle name."

"No, it's the name your car is registered under," he said.

"You looked up my car registration!" I said, shocked.

"Not really, we were seeing whether you also had a truck registered to you, that's all."

"Why?"

"There were tire prints at the scene of the . . . near the Dumpster. Huge tires, the sort for a truck . . ."

"Oh. No, all I have is the Volvo." And a car registration I'd need to change somehow.

He was quiet a moment, as though finishing the mousse took all his concentration, and then he asked, "So, do you want to dance?"

I should have said no. If I were sane, I would say no. After all, what was the point of this man buying me an expensive dinner and dancing with me? What did he want? I was fairly sure it wasn't my home-cut curls, or my all-too-short body that commanded this attention. And yet he must want something.

But like with the steak and the mousse, it had been too long since I'd engaged in the civilized business of dancing.

So I danced with Officer Hotstuff, who insisted I really must call him Cas.

When he drove me home, I was feeling very mellow and my view of the law had softened considerably. I'd almost forgotten what had brought us together. Perhaps the man—who was an excellent and intuitive dancer, who could lead a woman around the dance floor while making her feel like she was part of a seamless whole—just had trouble finding women who could slow dance with him. Perhaps he suspected I could, and perhaps that was why he'd asked me out.

But then on my doorstep, I realized that he'd paid for a very expensive dinner, and I wondered if he wanted something else. The idea left me tongue-tied and turning red.

"I'd . . . I'd ask you in for coffee," I said. "But . . . Ben is staying with me and . . ."

I looked up to find Cas Wolfe smiling, amused. "We had coffee at the restaurant," he said. "Was it that unmemorable? I thought it was very good."

"Oh, it . . . it was," I said, and looked down at my shoes. They were still shoes, and still there. Flat Mary Janes, with a little strap. They were

Ben's despair because he thought I should have at least a little bit of heel, given my lack of height.

"Good," Cas Wolfe said, and his big, square-tipped fingers came under my chin and tilted it up.

I knew it was going to happen a second before it did. I always wondered if other people had more warning of these things. Surely men at least knew? Or did they just find themselves kissing women without knowing how it came about?

His gray eyes flashed amused-blue and soft, and then his lips were on mine, demanding and very sure of themselves. The tip of his tongue pushed gently in between my lips, and I let it. His mouth tasted of coffee and milk and his touch sent a feeling through me that I wasn't used to and hadn't experienced in a long time. Perhaps never. I realized, rather shamefully, that if Ben weren't staying in my living room, I'd probably ask Cas Wolfe in. I wouldn't be able to stop myself.

Yes, I thought, as Cas leaned back and I was left with a befuddled mind and confused thoughts. In a few years, I was going to be a serious danger to the UPS man, acne scars and all.

Cas's hand pulled my curls back and he said, "Thank you, Dyce Chocolat. For a very enjoyable evening. Now, please open your door; I want to make sure you get in without any problems."

I unlocked my door and opened it, almost slamming into Ben, who seemed to be getting hastily up from his knees. I stepped in quickly and turned around, hoping Officer Wolfe hadn't seen that very undignified scramble. "Thank you, Officer Wolfe. I liked dinner very much. And . . . and the dance."

He smiled and touched my cheek, just the barest of touches with the tips of his fingers. "The pleasure was mine."

THE TRIALS OF FRIENDSHIP

"HONESTLY," I TOLD BEN as I came in. "What were you doing? Looking through the keyhole?"

"Don't be ridiculous." He looked dignified and offended. "The letter flap. The keyhole is one of the modern ones, you can't see anything through it."

"Benedict Colm!"

He shrugged. "Oh, come on. Did you really expect me not to look or listen in? Besides, if you'd decided to invite him in, I'd have liked some warning, so I could make up an important meeting somewhere right now."

"Well, you didn't get out of the way when he said I should open the door!" I said.

"That's because," he said, his voice filled with a tone of long-suffering patience, "you didn't give me enough warning. The next time, try to say something like, 'You really want me to open the door, right now?' to give me time to get up and out of the way. Or else, consider kissing him again. That ought to be good for a delay."

"The next time? There won't be a next time," I said.

His eyebrows went up. "So, okay, you don't put out on the first date, but I understand hetero guys find that nice, you know? He probably thinks you're an old-fashioned girl and is even now considering how best to slip the engagement ring onto your finger."

Out of nowhere something like a black tide of rage came over my mind, obscuring all. "Don't be stupid," I said. "He took me out because he wanted to ask me about refinishing places in town, and he hoped I could dance."

"Yes, of course," Ben said. He mumbled something I couldn't make out, which was just as well, because I felt suddenly very tired.

"I'll go to bed now, okay?" I said.

He didn't say anything, and I went to bed. Which didn't exactly help. I did very little sleeping, as my mind kept kicking up all sorts of images of bodies gone gelatinous in Dumpsters, or, more pleasantly, Cas Wolfe's lips on mine.

By the time I woke up, with the gray light of morning coming through my window and the subdued noise of Sunday traffic picking up outside, my blankets were all tangled in a mess around me, and I felt as if I'd been riding a storm all night and woken up exhausted by the lightning and the wind. And in a foul mood. Which did not improve when I found my bathroom door locked.

I knocked. A mumble answered me. "I need to use the bathroom," I said.

"Use the powder room?" he suggested, speaking as though he were talking between his teeth. Okay then. I made it to the powder room and peed, and washed my face and hands, glaring at myself in the mirror. Then I went back to the kitchen. Seeing my table like that erased all thought of coffee or breakfast—even if I'd had the slightest notion what to make or get for breakfast, which I didn't. Instead I put on my slippers and went out back into my shed.

It was just as I'd left it yesterday, of course. I grabbed wood putty, one of the smaller spatulas, and some fine sandpaper. Back in the kitchen, I realized the slashes on the table were clean. Meaning someone had inserted the cleaver, then pulled it up from the pine, without really wiggling much. Also, they were deeper than I'd thought, but they didn't go through.

I sanded around them carefully, wiped up the dust with a paper towel, then dabbed on the putty. It was the sort that's made from wood dust, so that it would pretty much match the table once dried, sanded, and waxed.

That done, I started the coffee. And then I realized Ben was still in the bathroom. Because I hadn't heard the shower, and still didn't—any water running through the pipes anywhere in the house could be heard all over the house—I wondered what was going on in there. Um . . . I walked back to the bathroom and knocked on the door.

"Yes?"

"Ben, did you get lost in there, or something?"

He opened the door. I screamed. He glared. All over his face, from forehead to chin, was a green-blue substance. "What on Earth?" I said.

"Did I make you go on the warpath for some reason? Are you going to take my cattle and burn my house?"

He glared. Moving his lips minimally—which accounted for the constrained voice—he said, "It's a mask. Maybe you should try it sometime."

I waved it away. "Have. It's sticky and unpleasant. Must you do that now? In my bathroom?"

He only sighed, and I realized that was an unproductive line of questioning. If Ben had decided this was the time for warding off the demons of old age, this was the time for warding off the demons of old age. As someone who didn't attend that church, I had no right to criticize the rituals.

"There's coffee when you're ready for it," I said, and noted as I said it that he was dressed in a robe of a color that very nearly matched his mask. So he hadn't showered yet. That would be fun, because there was only one shower in the entire apartment.

He mumbled something and closed the door.

I went back to the kitchen and had a cup of coffee. I knew I really should go to Denver today, as I had some finished pieces I needed to deliver, but as far as I knew I hadn't sold anything from the consignment already at Shabby Chic. The owners would have called and told me if that were the case. And my car was running funky, and the only way I could figure to get money for gas would be to go to the convention and borrow from Mom and Dad. But the convention was in Denver, so I'd have to get there in order to borrow the money to get there. It seemed like one of those puzzles they give you in math class, where you have three goats and a lion and you're supposed to transport them across a river in two trips.

I chewed on my lip, thinking. Last month had been an unproductive month; my money to buy good but abused pieces had been almost zero because E had had a growth spurt and had needed new clothes. And the discarded things I'd found hadn't been all that good. Which was what had prompted yesterday's trip to the Dumpster. I shuddered at the thought.

But if I went to Denver and took the few pieces I had finished, at least it would increase the variety of my work at the store, and the chance I would sell more. It would also allow me to look for veneer, where I had a better chance to get it. And though the dresser in bits wasn't a good piece, it was sort of showy, the kind of piece that would attract people to my area of the consignment store. So getting it done as soon as possible was of the essence. If only I could figure out how to get the lion not to eat the goats. I'd never understood why, in that puzzle, one couldn't just muzzle the lion.

Ben stumbled into the kitchen as I was deep in my thoughts and poured himself a cup of coffee. Like me, he drinks tea during the day but coffee in the morning, and, thank heavens, he didn't care if his morning coffee was a particular brand or brewed in a particular way.

"Do you mind if I shower first?" I asked.

"No," he said. "Go."

I went.

Maneuvering around the bathroom was harder than normal, because every possible surface was covered in Ben stuff. The man had brought his own bath sheet—though I supposed I shouldn't chide him for it, because it was oversized and he bought those on purpose. Also, I supposed in the end, it was a concession to my housekeeping because he knew how hard it was for me to do laundry. Unfortunately he'd also brought a myriad of beauty products at which I could only stare in half-shocked wonder. The green-blue thing in a plastic tub atop my toilet tank was, apparently, essence of blue-green algae, and it promised to remove ten years from your skin if used every day. Right. Ben could look nineteen. Sure thing. If he ungrew about four inches and lost all his beard and half of his body muscle.

"You can use any of that if you want to, Dyce."

"Right." And I could also dance the polka in my underwear. I'd just never seen any good reason to. I went back to my room and got jeans and a T-shirt and underwear and socks. I'd gotten out of the habit of walking out of the bathroom naked and dressing in the bedroom when E had become ambulatory and started noticing things. The day he'd asked me what had happened to my penis—logical, because he had one and therefore it must be standard equipment—had been the last day I'd been casual about nudity around him.

I took the clothes with me back into the bathroom, showered quickly, dried, brushed out my curls, and got dressed. And opened the bathroom door to the sizzle of bacon and the smell of cooked eggs mingling with the coffee.

I was fairly sure it was too early in the morning to be hallucinating. Perhaps I hadn't woken up and had just dreamed I had woken? It would at least explain that horrible green-blue thing on Ben's face.

But as I walked into the kitchen, I found that Ben was responsible for the smell. He was at the stove, frying bacon and eggs in my largest frying pan—a big aluminum thing I had bought at a restaurant supplier during one of the more delusional times in my marriage.

"Well, good morning, Mrs. Cleaver," I said. "I see you're making the house a home."

He gave me a smile. "I thought you might be hungry. If you're not, I'll feed it to the dog."

"I don't have a dog."

"Don't care. My mom always said that and we don't have a dog either. If I go out back, wave the pan and call 'Dog,' I'm sure one will show up."

"You'll get Doug," I said. "The college student next door."

"Well, maybe he'll appreciate me more."

"Unlikely. He usually has a different girl over every weekend."

"Yeah, yeah, it's always like that," he said, seeming completely undaunted by this as he dished the food into two equal portions on the plates. "All the good ones are straight or taken."

I grinned at him, amused. He set the pan in water in the sink, put the plates on the unblemished portions of the table, and said, "I see you've been working already."

"Just on the table. And it's not as bad as it looks. I see you went shopping. Yesterday?"

"Yeah, while you were on your date."

"It wasn't a date."

He opened his mouth, but must have seen my expression and shrugged. "Fine, Dyce, have it your way. You know, you should stop kissing random guys on your front porch."

"I know. The UPS man will be so surprised."

He gave me a look as if I'd taken leave of my senses. "Dyce, I've seen your UPS guy. If you kiss him—I repeat *if* you kiss him—I will have you committed. Unless you can prove you have a damn good reason to think he will turn into a prince, or something."

"No, it's just . . ."

"Yes?"

"I'm afraid as I get older," I said, sitting down to note that Ben had set the table with napkins and silverware, "I'll start attacking guys on the street and . . ."

"And?"

"Having my wicked way with them."

Ben choked on a piece of bacon, and I had to pound his back before he could breathe again. But he picked up the napkin and pressed it against his face while his shoulders shook.

"What is so funny?" I said.

"You," he said, setting the napkin down. "I will not ask what gave rise to this undeniably charming illusion that you're in danger of becoming a nympho. Instead, tell me what you intend to do today."

"I don't know. Depends on muzzling the lion."

His eyes went big. "You have a lion?"

I shook my head. "Remember Mr. Ziggler and those problems he used to give? You have a boat and three goats and a lion. You need to get them across the river. You can only take two animals at once and you don't want the lion to eat the goats. How do you do it in two trips?"

Ben frowned. "First, I haven't had enough coffee. Second, why do you need to solve that now, and third, I think you have the problem wrong."

I sighed. "Well, probably. I never understood why anyone was keeping a pet lion with their goats either, or why they needed to take it across a river, or why the lion didn't have a muzzle." I looked up to meet with a glance of utter incomprehension. "No, I'm not trying to solve the problem right now. I mean, it's just an example."

"An example of muddling . . . er . . . muzzling the lion?" he asked, and that slip of the tongue was totally intentional.

I sighed again. "Look, most of the money these days seems to come from my consignments at Shabby Chic. But last month I could only leave a very few pieces with them, not enough to take up my space. Because the store is arranged by craftsperson—mostly—the fewer pieces you have, the less chance someone will wander to your area and buy something. I now have a few—unfortunately not many—pieces finished, and I should go to Denver and put them out. But I can't, because I doubt my car will make it that far and I don't have money for gas. But if I don't do it, chances are I won't have money next month, either. I could ask my parents for a loan, but they're in Denver, so I would have to get there first."

He looked at me a long time, then sighed. "I could loan you money," he said. "But I'm not sure your car would make it that far." He drew a figure in bacon grease with the tip of his fork. "Dyce, isn't Mahr supposed to be giving you child support?"

I shrugged. "Some. Not a lot, because it's shared custody."

"And he had better lawyers. So, does he? I never hear you—"

"Well, not in the last six months."

"Uh . . . why not? I assume the child support is court—"

"Because he has better lawyers. If I take him to court, he'll end up with full custody. Anyone looking at my life . . ."

Ben sighed again. "I have friends who are lawyers. And I could lend—"

I thought of that total for fixing his home. "No, Ben, please. I'll manage. Now, if I could just figure out—"

"How to muddle the lion? Easy. We take my cow . . . I mean my car."

"What? First, your car is in the shop, and second—"

"You can take me to get my car. Your car is good enough to go four miles. They called earlier to say my car was ready. It's what got me up."

"Oh. Weird, I didn't hear."

"They called my cell. Of course you didn't hear."

"Oh."

"Anyway, my car is ready and if you can take me there, we'll pick it up."

"And you want to go with me to Denver because . . ."

He shrugged. "I can't go home. Les isn't answering my calls. I figure I have nothing better to do. We can go to Denver and do . . . whatever it is you do there, and then have dinner and come home."

"Right," I said. Normally I would have asked him if he was all right. Normally I would have been sure he shouldn't come with me. I mean, he had other friends and a life. There were, however, a few things militating against that. The first was that Ben was at loose ends. I thought of how many times he'd called Les, and from that *He's not answering my calls*, I suspected he'd tried again today. And then the other thing was that the Volvo had the worst habit of dying in Denver, in the middle of Colfax Avenue, so even if I had the money for gas it would be unwise. The other thing was that a drive of three hours each way was much better passed in company, even if the company was Ben. Also, if we were taking his car, he would more than likely insist on driving, because no one touched his baby but him.

"Fine," I said. "You can come with me, and we'll go in your car. But you're going to be bored out of your gourd."

"Unlikely," he said. "There are many things you are, my dear, but boring isn't one of them."

We finished our breakfast and he went into the shower while I was doing dishes. And while I was doing dishes, I got to thinking. About a lot of things. Like that note on the bottom of the table.

So much had happened since yesterday that it seemed I hadn't slowed down to think till now. That note written on the bottom of the table still chilled me. I didn't want it to be related to the murder. Positionally, it was unlikely it was related to the murder. I stacked the cups and plates carefully. The thing was, see, that it was clearly written by an expert in antiques—and one who didn't mind working on things that had multiple layers of paint. Which meant someone who had a lye vat and wasn't afraid to use it. Maybe. But it could be. And that would mean the table was related to the murder, and my chances of setting my financial life on a somewhat even keel would be gone.

Which meant that—as far as I was concerned—figuring out who had written on the bottom of the table, and, if possible, proving the writing had nothing to do with the murder was of the most urgent essence. But how did one go about doing that?

The way I saw it, there were two ways. One was to solve the murder—and even I snorted at that thought. The other was to figure out who had written those words on the bottom of the table.

Unfortunately the note didn't say something like *The spirit of the tree wishes to come out.* So that maybe ruled out Oakfriend. The scope of the project or lack thereof, no matter how good the piece, probably ruled out Rocky Mountain. They simply didn't bother with fussy small projects. Not worth their time, I guess. But frankly I saw neither Michael Manson nor Miss Jewel—whichever one he was at any given moment—engaging in careful notation on the bottom of an old piece. At any rate, if he was refinishing anything at all, it would be by private contract, and not something freelance. At least the only things I'd ever heard of him refinishing had been to match furniture he was also making. Usually for hotels or some big McMansion.

No matter how I turned it—or thought about it—the only outfit in town with the knowledge to make the note was Rocky's. Perhaps it had been put out by the curb for some particular someone to pick up? And perhaps that someone had given it to a student, who had decided that it was too painted over to carry with him when he moved on from college. But then I thought that there was no reason the note had to have been made here in town or by Rocky or anyone else, just like there was no reason why the corpse and the table—and the chairs—had to be related at all. But I still had to prove someone in town wasn't involved. If I could. To myself. For my own satisfaction. Someone in town with a big, handy lye vat.

It could be, perhaps, that someone not even connected with furniture refinishing had filled a barrel or a trash can with lye and dipped a corpse in it. Why not? It could happen.

Sure it could. And pigs could fly, given a fortuitous genetic mutation, but I hadn't seen any wing it past my window lately.

I wasn't a genius, like Ben, but even I had retained something from my science classes. The simplest explanation is usually the true one. Occam's razor. And the simplest explanation was that the note on the table had been made by a local refinisher who'd discarded it when he or she realized how much trouble it would be to peel. And if it was related to the murder—though I very much hoped it wasn't—it would have had to come from a place with a lye vat.

The only place I knew where there was a lye vat was Rocky's. And the fact that the lye vat was stationary might provide a reason why the body was discarded before being fully dissolved: if they only had time for so long before someone was due to come into the workroom.

Besides, Rocky bought really good, if often work-intensive pieces to start with. The kind you find at estate sales, brought from all over the country. Stuff you otherwise couldn't find in Colorado.

In the unlikely event the table was related to the murder, then it all had to hinge around Rocky's.

I got the phone book from where I normally kept it, on the little stool by the living room window so that, by standing on tiptoe on it, E could look out at the cars.

Rocky Mountain Refinishing was in the Yellow Pages. It wasn't till the phone started ringing that I thought of such things as *What am I going to ask them?* Or *What will they be able to tell me?* Or even *Why in hell would anyone be at the refinishing workshop over the weekend?* This last occurred to me after two rings, and I was about to hang up when a voice—sounding much like someone had a severe cold—answered, "Rocky Mountain Refinishing. Nick speaking."

Nick? I'd only ever talked to Rocky himself. Yes, his name was actually Rocky. Well, it was Arthur Stone, but he went by Rocky. But I supposed he had several people working for him and this was one of them. "Hi, Nick," I said, as if the name conjured any image at all in my mind. "This is Dyce Dare. I was wondering . . ." And out of the blue, as if someone or something had taken over my mouth—which is true, because I was channeling stupid recklessness straight from the source—I found myself saying, "if you know anything about a small occasional table, or perhaps a tiny writing desk. Dark cherry. Hand carved. Colonial."

There was the sound of heavy breathing from the other side. Slow, deliberate heavy breathing. However, considering how the man's voice sounded, perhaps he was just sick. At long last an answer came. "Uh . . . you mean a piece in this workshop?"

"Or something you've seen recently," I said. "Yes."

"Uh."

There was another long silence filled with heavy breathing. "No."

"Okay," I said. And then a devil took hold of me—a sensation like that of setting fire to that quilt frame and waving it around Mom's book-stuffed living room. It made my heart pound. My mouth continued on without the least input from my mind. "One other thing. Do you have a woman employee there? Blond, with kind of short hair and curls?"

"No." The answer was instant and surprisingly clear. "No one like that here."

He hung up very quickly, leaving me wondering if the haste betrayed anything more than exasperation with my questions. Probably not. And speaking of exasperation, I heard Ben's voice from the living room. "Look, Les, I'm not mad. I understand I can be very difficult to live with. Just give me a call. We'll talk it over."

Right. I marched right out to the living room. The door to my bedroom was open to expose the only full-length mirror in the house. Ben's phone was closed and sitting atop the coffee table. Because I didn't think he had progressed—yet—to talking to himself, I assumed he'd just hung up and set the phone down. He was now doing something I'd seen him do the few times we'd stayed in the same house overnight or we'd gone somewhere together and I'd arrived early. He was untying and tying his tie, his expression one of concentrated, frowning intensity, as he adjusted the length so that it fell just over the top half of his belt.

I knew from experience that it was no use at all expecting him to break from this life-and-death activity to give me any attention. The fact that—on a Sunday when he knew I would drag him over the half of creation that was composed of thrift shops and construction materials—he was wearing khakis, a white shirt that looked good enough for work, and a dark reddish-brown tie that had surely been picked for the fact that it matched his eyes in most light spoke for itself.

After standing behind him with my arms crossed for a while, I gave up on getting him to even so much as ask me what I wanted, turned around, and headed for the back, where I brought the ready furniture to my car—the little bookcase, end tables, and reading desk. I put them in the back of my car. Then the thought hit me that I was leaving the house with a very valuable table in the back.

It was stupid to worry, of course. I knew that. I knew that as well as I knew it was, if not impossible, highly improbable to find a decomposing body in a college Dumpster. As well as I knew that my house could not be broken into—because there was no reason for it to be broken into, of course. But someone had broken in for the express purpose of hanging a stuffed animal and knifing my kitchen table. Insane.

Which meant . . .

I made it to my workshop, put the drawer back in the table, and carried it all through the house to the car. I might leave it there, or I might put it in the trunk of Ben's car for the trip to Denver. I was very attached to this little table. This little table would make me enough money that I might be able to buy some severely distressed good pieces at thrifts and sell them for a high profit. This little table could be the beginning of my going respectable and not having to worry about keeping E in pancakes.

I looked up from closing the trunk to find Ben watching me with an unfathomable look. As I came into the house, he said, "Why, Dyce?"

I shrugged. "I don't feel secure." And I didn't know if I was reassured about the soundness of my judgment or scared when he didn't dispute it. "The table is worth a lot of money."

"You're going to take it all the way to Denver, aren't you?"

"Probably," I said. "Do you have everything you need? Do you wish to measure your tie or self-flagellate by calling Les again?"

"You know that's out of line."

It probably was. After all, Ben's romantic life was his own, but I felt like he was not giving himself the respect he deserved and found myself annoyed at it. I fumed as I put the finished pieces in the car. I had no idea at all what Ben might have done to bring about this rift with Les. I was perfectly willing—eager at times—to certify that Ben was the most annoying male ever to walk—or drive, or run—the Earth. But in my opinion none of this justified smashing his beloved oxblood vases, much less starting a fire on his stove.

Even if Les had been stupid enough not to think it would set off the fire alarm—and I was fully willing to believe that Les was stupid enough for that, hence his building the fire on the stove—it was inexcusable and reckless. Wasn't breaking the frames and ripping the pictures enough?

I thought of my own departure from All-ex's home—packing my bags and driving away, without so much as smashing the framed wedding picture. It could be done. If I could do it, just about anyone could. Truly.

But I didn't say anything. Instead, we got in the car and drove to the garage where Ben's tires had been replaced. Apparently they had been punctured in such a way that the tear could not possibly be fixed, something the man spent some time explaining to Ben, possibly to justify the expense of something he called radial belted—which led me to wonder if there was triangular belted, and the inevitable paisley belted. Tires to me were whatever came with the used car I bought. If I was lucky, they didn't require changing before I sold the car or ran it into the ground.

Ben, apparently in a show of goodwill designed to mitigate whatever ill will might be caused by keeping his mouth shut tight all the way to the garage, moved the table to his trunk and the other furniture to the backseat himself, without my even having to ask. And if there was a little smile on his lips, I suppose he could be forgiven.

The ride to Denver was uneventful. At this time of year, it was neither parched dry nor too cold. In winter, setting out to Denver was always an adventure. You could leave with the weather in the high eighties, only to see light flurries an hour later and find yourself plowing through a blizzard within an hour and a half or less. I'd driven this road when I could not see any more than a couple of feet in front of the car and had to go very slowly in case another car suddenly appeared in that space.

But in spring, absent the occasional hail shower, it was a pretty if somewhat boring ride—sparsely treed hills, the occasional house or fast-food joint off in the distance off the highway.

Ben and I didn't talk much—not beyond "Is this music all right?" and "Do you want the air conditioning on?"—because to talk would mean that both of us would touch subjects we didn't wish to. At least I assumed it was both of us. I knew I had no intention of talking to Ben about what was bothering me. Not about the vandalism in my house, not about my concern for the little table that had prompted me to put it in the back. Not even anything about my date with Officer Wolfe.

And he, for all his through-the-letter-flap curiosity, also didn't seem intent on prying. And I supposed because of that, I had to honor our gentlemen's agreement and not ask him about whatever in heaven was going on with Les. More than that, I think he was afraid I would ask him what he thought he was doing in that relationship, what he hoped to gain, and whether he should allow himself to be treated the way he was being treated.

Ben was a smart man, and—for all his silences and touchiness—fairly mature. He had seen the same specials I had, and I knew he read more magazines than I did. Surely he knew the signs of spousal abuse as well as I did. If he wanted to be a doormat, I wasn't going to say a thing. Not a thing.

It wasn't until we pulled in front of the consignment furniture store on South Broadway in Denver, and Ben had parked, carefully, in one of the metered spaces, right in front of the store—which itself was wedged between a wig shop and a used bookstore—that he turned to me and allowed his lips to twitch.

"Dyce, are you really imagining me being bullied by Les?"

I glared at him, though it was truly hard to avoid the return smile when he wore this expression. "I fail to see what is so funny."

He grinned. "Comparative size alone. And besides that, when have I ever let myself be bullied?"

"It's different when you're in a relationship. You let yourself be told things and do things to that you'd never allow . . ." I let it trail off. I was not going to enter into candid confessions.

But he didn't seem to realize how close I'd come to breaking the rule on my own behalf. Instead he shook his head. "Trust me," he said, in that tone men use when you truly shouldn't trust them, because they're head down in some sort of weird fix that they couldn't ever find their way out of on their own. "Les is having some . . . issues at work, and he's misinterpreting stuff at home, but this is not that big a deal or that important, truly. He didn't realize he'd set off the fire alarm."

I could believe that last, because Les was blond, but all the same, leaving the house after creating that much of a mess seemed . . . well . . . a little excessive. "What happened to your window?" I asked. It had been replaced at the shop, and the dent in the back had been pulled out, but I remembered them.

He gave me a pained look and seemed about to tell me it was none of my business, but he had opened the discussion. "Les threw a couple of . . . small things from the balcony, as I was driving underneath."

I didn't ask what small things. Not Les's brain, because—though no one might notice he was functioning without one—it would be too small to dent anything at all. Doubtlessly more pictures. Instead I said, "It could have killed you, if it had come through the windshield."

He shrugged. "It was nothing that big. He wasn't thinking."

"Okay, then," I said. "I need to bring new pieces in." And see what the owner had heard from the refinishing world, which would hopefully prove the table wasn't related to the murder. Like that roving bands of refinishers were leaving notes on the bottom of antique tables, or something. The emphasis being on the *or something* and fishing for info, though I hoped I wasn't going to make it that obvious, and I certainly wasn't going to tell Ben about it. Because if I did, then I'd have to explain why I felt like investigating, and I could just see him rolling his eyes and telling me I was too big to play Nancy Drew.

But he didn't ask anything—no doubt relieved we weren't discussing his less-than-sane partner anymore. Instead, he got out, as did I, after monitoring for a few minutes for a break in traffic that would allow me to open the door.

Broadway had been a fashionable shopping area in the early part of the century, till about the fifties. It was now one of those *interesting* shopping places that artistic types shop in—as well as people with an eye for antiques who wish to get a bargain. Which the pieces in this shop were.

I wasn't stupid and was very aware that the stuff I sold here—even the things that weren't exactly antiques—would sell for a lot more in the antiques places around Cherry Creek Mall. But those places weren't consignment, and I'd have to sell them to the owner at con-siderably less than I got from Shabby Chic, even after the owners took their cut for keeping things there on consignment.

Inside the shop, it was an Aladdin's cave of interesting furniture, no two pieces alike, most of it glistening with varnish or polish, all of it artfully arranged under carefully placed lighting—one of the reasons this shop did better than most of its kind. It smelled faintly of polish and old furniture, like the parlor of some obsessively clean grand-mother.

There were a few things that weren't furniture, too. One of the peo-ple who placed work on consignment here regularly was a stick-thin woman whose name I could never remember, who must have had the fastest hands west of the Pecos River, because every time I went in she had another set of intricate crocheted curtains. They hung sus-pended on rods from the ceiling and were worked from some antique book—the figures on them ranged from what could only be classed as colonial houses, to fantasy castles and horse riders, to—at the mo-ment front and center—a bald eagle swooping down toward a moun-tainscape in snowy cotton. There were also abstract designs reminis-cent of Art Deco or twenties lace curtains. I'd once looked at the price on one of those and almost had a heart attack. Too bad Grandma—the last woman in the family to be gifted with the knowledge—hadn't seen fit to teach me crochet.

There were also, arranged against the far wall on a permanent table, a set of meticulously beaded lampshades. Ben always shuddered when he looked at them, but I could imagine that they would work very well if your objective was to be completely period in your decoration.

Here and there, amid the furniture, were other objects also for sale. Mostly things that the furniture seller or refinisher had acquired at an estate sale or a garage sale. Sometimes there were quite good re-productions of statues—I remembered one of Rodin's *The Kiss*—but more often there were vases and things, most of dubious provenance. However, these were enough to keep Ben amused, and he went flitting away from me to look at something or other sparkling in the crowded depths of the store.

Me, I made my way to my little corner—with the big, hand-let-tered sign on the wall proclaiming the furniture under its aegis *Daring*

Finds—the corner being all I could afford. You paid more of your sales to put pieces on consignment near the front.

And I let out a big relieved breath. I'd called yesterday and been told I hadn't sold anything, so I must have had a very good morning today, because only a couple of pieces were left in the corner—a tea cart and a gateleg table. In my mind I went over what had been there. A quite good twenties vintage bedroom set of burled walnut. Not exactly a known manufacturer and not exactly antique, but very nice. Bought at a garage sale for fifty dollars. Bed, bedside table, and dresser, all covered in ten layers of sickly-sweet pink paint. An oak rolltop desk that was not even remotely vintage, but was real wood and had come to me covered in layers and layers of paint, only to leave with just a light waxing, as pure and virginal as if it had come from the Oak Friends workshop. And a kidney-shaped vanity table, which I'd French-polished to a mirror shine after liberating it from coats and coats of—for some reason—purple paint.

Well, it looked like I would have a decent paycheck coming to me, which was good, even if Ben had gotten me enough food probably to last a month. I was sure of it if he'd gone shopping. The man didn't know moderation. If he shopped, he shopped in quantities. But this money would cover the rent and food until the pieces now in the car sold. Perhaps I could get my car fixed, buy E a new pair of sneakers, and stay away from the dreaded pancakes for a while.

I looked around for the shop owners and focused on movement rounding the corner of a massive wardrobe. But it was neither Janet, the white-haired grandmalike lady who ran this place, nor her husband, Mike. No. The person who rounded the corner of the wardrobe—resplendent in a cowled green robe that, other than the color and the fact that it was obviously polyester, could have come from any medieval monastery—was none other than Inobart Oakfriend.

Inobart had a peculiar trick of always looking at you without looking at you. He'd swivel his head around so that he was facing now the ceiling, now the floor, now the side wall, now the shop window. The wardrobe next to him seemed to hold his attention, then the coffee table on the other side, and finally the tip of his scruffy shoe. And all the time—all the time—he was looking at you from the side of his less-than-focused, not-quite-all-there pale blue eyes.

It was vaguely unnerving until you got to know him. But then most of the stuff about Inobart was vaguely disturbing, whether you knew him or not. Ben had once said that Inobart had gone on an acid trip sometime in the seventies and hadn't come down from it yet. Much as I hated to say it, Ben was probably right.

As Inobart inched toward me, looking at me out of the corner of his eye, even as he stared—ostensibly—at the wardrobe next to him, I found Ben materializing behind me. It had the feel of his coming to act as my bodyguard, which was ridiculous because—as far as I knew—Inobart had never hurt a living soul. Well, at least not a human living soul. I'd never been near enough to his house to know whether he killed bugs. On the other hand, given his respect for long-dead trees, he probably let the rats and cockroaches run free through his abode.

"Hello, Candyce," he said, speaking to the tip of his shoe and watching me out the corner of his eye. "Hello, Mr. Colm."

Ben had once, long ago, introduced me as Candyce Dare and himself as Mr. Colm. Inobart was the sort of person who filed this stuff away—in the roach-filled depths of his mind—only to extract it at need. The standoffish hauteur that Ben had attempted to introduce had been quite lost on Inobart. Names were just handles. Ben might as well have told him we were Maryhadalittlelamb and Thebigbadwolf, and we'd have been that for the rest of Inobart's life.

"Hi, Inobart," I said, being a little more friendly than I would be to anyone else, because Inobart did give me the creeps and to compensate I went out of my way to make sure I didn't offend him.

My warmth must have startled him because for just a second he looked directly at me. Then he looked at my corner and gestured with his chin. "I guess you sold a lot of things. Janet was telling me someone bought your stuff just an hour ago . . ."

"Yeah, I guess so; have you seen Janet?"

"Oh sure," he said confidently. "She's in the back there." He pointed a long, trembling finger vaguely in the direction where I knew from previous visits there was a sort of breakroom with a coffeemaker and such. I saw Ben turn to look in that direction and had a sudden idea that Janet was dead somewhere back there. Which was silly, as I saw her come through the door right then.

She waved at us and started walking in our direction, which would take a while because she had to walk the aisles between the furniture displays.

"She gave me a check, too," Inobart confided to the tip of his left shoe.

"Oh, she did? Good," I said. And then because Janet was still not next to us, and because I wanted, after all, to find out more about who might have murdered someone—particularly if the situation was going to force me to carry occasional tables around on the back of whatever car I was in—I said, "Do you have a lye vat?"

Inobart gave an inarticulate cry. He stepped back so hastily, he almost tripped. He looked at me—fully at me—his eyes full of terror. A bit of spittle formed on the side of his mouth. His hands came up and did something odd that took me a moment to recognize as an attempt to form a five-pointed star—I guess the same way that people would lift a cross toward a vampire.

I was too speechless to say anything, but Ben asked from behind me, "What is wrong?"

What was wrong, clearly, was that Inobart had inhaled a bit too much refinishing fumes. Then again, perhaps he knew about the body in the lye vat . . .

I looked back at him. "Well, do you?" I asked his terrified expression, even as he breathed rapidly like someone on the verge of a panic attack.

"No," he said, though there is no way to reproduce the sound he actually made, which was sort of a long, drawn-out exhalation crossed with a high-pitched whine. "Noooooooo," he repeated. "I'd never. The lye is bad. The lye burns the wood." Spittle flew as he spoke, and his eyes rolled in his head, as if he were in some sort of frenzy. After stepping back away from me, he now stepped very close, to give me the benefit of life-sucking halitosis and a shower of spittle that made me wish I had brought an umbrella. "The spirits of the wood cry out," he said. "It burns the nymphs captive in the grain. Lye is worse than the paint it removes. It gets in the fibers and darkens them forever."

"I see," I said, fighting an urge to interpose my open hand between his mouth and my face.

"Rocky uses lye," he said. "Rocky is evil. I told his wife, Nell, that it was evil, and she said it was true. That she knew it burned the soul of the tree. And then they got divorced. You see," he said, confidentially, bringing his face closer, "Nell is an enlightened being. I'm very sure she's close to making the transition. I could help her." His eyes now burned with intent and something approaching fanaticism. His white hair clung to either side of his face, looking like it hadn't been washed since the acid trip had begun.

"The transition?" I said.

He waved his hands around, sort of like someone who thinks he's gotten hold of the secret to unaided flight. "To a light being," he said. "One of the shining ones. I could help her. That way . . ."

Janet's hand came to rest on Inobart's shoulder. "There, Inobart, you're delaying Dyce and I need to talk to her about accounts."

Like that, the sudden smarmy intensity was turned off and Inobart was looking at the ceiling while spying Janet out of the corner of his eye and saying confidentially to the ceiling beam, "Yes, yes, I'm sorry. I shouldn't keep her. I have a long drive back to Goldport anyway."

He shrugged, and looked almost like a normal person. Well, a normal person wearing a lime-green polyester monk's robe with a gold and black upholstery cord at the waist. Okay, right, not a normal person at all, but at least better than what I'd seen in the last few minutes. He started to shuffle away, but then turned around and flashed me the weird sign with all his fingers bent and trying to form a star. "Don't use lye," he said. "Remember that. Lye hurts the living soul of the wood. People who use lye are hurting the spirit of the wood."

And he turned again and walked off. Janet, looking at his back, said softly, "I wish he'd take his meds. It really worries me when he drives in that state. But," she said, in a rallying tone, "I just paid him for a large oak entertainment center that sold, so he should be able to afford his meds again, for a little while."

"Meds?" I said.

"Oh, a slew of them. He's bipolar and I think schizophrenic. He told me once, in one of his better times, you know, but I don't remember."

"Ah," Ben said from behind me, and wandered off to look at stuff again. Janet smiled at his back. "There is one of those vases you collect, Mr. Colm. It's over there on that large dresser."

Ben headed that way—Janet was not his main source for his pottery, but she was one of the cheaper sources. And now, I thought, he had a lot of them to replace.

Janet was walking toward the counter where the register was and where she kept the account books, as she said, "I thought you knew better than to talk to him about lye."

"I'm sorry," I said. "I didn't realize he had such an objection to it."

She hesitated, then shrugged. "Well," she said. "You see . . . the lye really isn't good for real antiques. I wish that Rocky would stop using it. Oh, we'll still take their things on consignment." She gestured toward one of the larger areas, crammed with a dining room set, a couple of bedroom sets, and some very showy armoires. "I mean, it's money, and you know, their stuff looks good. But it seems almost a crime to use a caustic method of refinishing on the real good furniture. And it's not like they need it. I mean, he has what? Two, three people working for him and all those machines? They could afford to do the work slower."

"He needs to pay the people who work for him," I said, and Janet nodded and shrugged as she got behind the counter and got out her little black book, where she kept the accounts for all of us. I'd once asked her why she didn't use a computer, and she'd told me that she'd used it every day of her working life, her last ten years in the office. This was her retirement job—something to do for fun in her golden years—and she had neither the time nor the patience to fuss with technology.

She showed me the page, and I had to smile, because everything had sold for the asking price. Which meant I had almost two thousand dollars coming to me. "All to one client?" I said.

"Yes, young couple furnishing their first home. And your stuff is always reasonably priced. They left just an hour ago or so. Do you want check or cash?"

"Cash," I said. I did have a bank account and most of it would probably be deposited, but right now was the weekend, and I didn't feel like depositing the check and waiting for it to clear. Also, I had nowhere near that amount in my account and if I deposited a check they'd probably put a hold on it until they received the physical money from Shabby Chic's account in Denver. Meanwhile, I needed to buy veneer and who knew, there might be something else in the thrift shops or construction recycling stores up here that might be useful or needed. Besides, I thought, with a pang of guilt, thinking of Ben's bill for fixing up his place, I probably should buy Ben dinner to compensate for the gas I'd made him use to bring me here.

At any rate, with the records Janet kept—and the ones I kept, of necessity—there was no question of evading taxes or any such thing.

She counted out the notes and handed them to me, then handed me a receipt to sign and gave me the carbon copy of it. I went out to the car, got the new pieces, and brought them in, and we priced them.

At which point Ben showed up carrying a vase and a marble bust. Oh, goody. The vase, which he set on the counter, was a red one and looked almost exactly like one of those he'd lost. The marble bust looked like a young man—or a somewhat butch young woman—with curls and head thrown back, laughing. It also looked very much like a classical statue.

"Ah, I'd forgotten we had that, otherwise I would have pointed it out to you," Janet said.

Ben signed a check for just over five hundred dollars—Janet didn't take cards—but he didn't look at all upset about it. I took the opportunity, as Ben and Janet were telling each other what a nice piece it was, to say, "Inobart said something about Rocky's wife . . ."

"Ah, Nell," Janet said absently, as she wrote down Ben's cell phone number on the check, under his address. "Rocky's ex-wife. She divorced him about six months ago."

"On her way to becoming a light being, we understand?" Ben said, managing to sound both amused and puzzled.

Janet rolled her eyes. "Inobart had a thing for her . . . you know, became convinced that she'd left Rocky because she agreed with him that Rocky is evil or something."

"That's not why she left him, I assume?"

Janet sighed. "Oh, no. The usual, complicated by the fact that they both worked in the same place. You know—she complained about how he didn't give her enough power and treated her like a child, which he probably did, Rocky being Rocky."

"Yeah," I said.

"But Inobart had a crush on her, and you know, he's really inoffensive, but he's like a child, and he makes up these things in his head. About how she was really in love with him, and that's why she divorced Rocky. When Nell was up last week, she told me that she was going to have a restraining order filed against Inobart because she was sure he was looking in her windows at night."

I thought of that straying eye looking one way and then another, all the while slyly prying through the window, and shuddered.

The creepiness stayed with me all the way through my visit to the construction store and to a couple of thrift shops.

All in all, the trip was good. In one of the thrift stores I bought another tall reading desk, this one probably of twenties vintage. It was, of course, covered in paint, but a look inside the drawer, and at the frame once I'd removed the drawer, gave me hopes that it was real mahogany. The other piece was a desk with inlaid leather, and the inlaid leather might have to be replaced, but then maybe not.

Both of them were a pain to fit in the backseat of Ben's car, but fortunately my friend—possibly knowing he might get stuck driving with me and furniture—always carried a couple of blankets in his car, which he used to protect the upholstery from the dusty wood.

In the construction recycling store, I found a lot of veneer that had been pulled off someone's paneling or wall or something. I truly didn't care, except that I got the lot for less than twenty dollars.

And yet, through it all, and even if Ben hadn't complained about the very dirty veneer in his car, I felt creepy and out of sorts. I kept thinking of Inobart looking in some woman's window, in the dark. What if he was far more dangerous than we thought? How often did he go without his meds? Janet said he was inoffensive, but was he?

Night Drive

"You're very quiet," Ben said when we were almost to Goldport. We'd stopped to eat at this little place that served—of all things—squid steaks in the heart of the Rockies. Ben knew the owner and insisted we go there, and I hadn't complained because Ben also insisted on paying.

His bad mood seemed to have lifted since he'd bought the bust and the vase—both now safely nestled in cloth in the trunk with my unfinished table. He'd even poked around the construction recycling place and expressed regret that his home didn't lend itself to the application of an entire tin ceiling that must once have covered a room the size of Shabby Chic.

On the way back, he tried to start several conversations, most of which went nowhere, partly because I still felt as if I could see Inobart looking in my windows in the night, and partly because I tend to fall asleep in cars if I'm not driving—all the more so if it's dark out.

I kept hearing Ben asking something, and I'd try to answer, but my eyes would close and my head would nod.

Close to Goldport, as I saw the lights of the city in the distance, I started to perk up, and I actually answered Ben, "It's Inobart. I was wondering how dangerous he is without his meds. You know, how out of touch with reality he might be."

Ben gave me a curious look out of the corner of his eye, even as he watched the dark road ahead. "Dyce, he dresses like and seems to think he is some sort of elf lord; what do you expect?"

"I don't think so," I said. "I think he dresses like or thinks he is a pagan priest."

Ben rolled his shoulders in an elaborate shrug. "The point is, sane pagan priests don't wear robes. Of course he's out of touch with reality. But you've known him how long? And he hasn't hurt anyone, right?"

"Right," I said. That we knew of. Of course, lye eats through everything, doesn't it? I mean, leave something in it long enough and it would all be gone to hell, wouldn't it? I didn't know what it actually would do—I'd never tried to submerge any pieces, and I certainly couldn't submerge them in the sort of volume a commercial lye vat would have. But I'd heard stories of entire Spanish Colonial tables turned into a little bit of sludge at the bottom of the caustic liquid.

And then it occurred to me—if a person submerged someone in lye, either after killing her, or because she was dead—why not leave her in the lye till she, too, was just a bit of sludge at the bottom of the vat? It would seem the logical thing to do. That it hadn't been done would mean the person who'd done it wasn't logical. Which meant . . .

Inobart would be my main suspect. "What if we just haven't found out?"

Ben seemed to think that was funny. He gave a little chuckle, deep in his throat. "Oh, come on," he said. And then, stealing a glance at me, "You are creeped out. I should have known, because you haven't teased me about the bust."

"Teased you?" I said confused. "It's a very nice bust, though I'd think classical antique—"

"Not the original," he said as we hit the main lighted strip into town. "The original is in a museum in Europe. The Prado in Madrid, I think. Mind you, this is a nice reproduction and probably Italian and bought by someone who traveled to Italy, where they sell all this stuff."

"Ah," I said.

He took this for encouragement. "Antinous. The lover of Emperor Hadrian."

"Ah," I said.

"All right," he said, after a silence. "You are creeped. No jokes about buying statues of ancient gay guys? Nothing about building a historical gallery and am I going to find a bust of Marlowe next?"

"It's a nice bust," I said, absently.

He sighed. "You should tell Officer Wolfe about Inobart," he said.

"I did."

"What—that he might have a restraining order against him for spying on naked ladies? How? Are you telepathically linked to Wolfe now?"

"Oh, no," I said. "Just about Inobart in general."

"Well, you probably should tell Wolfe about what we found out in Denver," he said. "And look at it this way, it gives you a chance to call the big-not-so-bad Wolfe, right?"

"Right," I said, and heard clear as day in my mind my mother telling me not to call strange men.

We passed the George at Fairfax, and then we turned down Quicksilver and drove the two blocks to my house.

And I realized I didn't need an excuse to call Officer Wolfe. In fact, I would have to call him anyway, no matter how reluctant I was to do it.

Someone had taken a bloodred spray can and written the word *Bitch* in five-foot-tall letters next to my door—which stood wide open.

Ben pulled up and cursed. He took his phone out of his pocket and dialed, before I could. To my surprise, what he dialed didn't seem to be the police department. Or if it was, it was a direct number and Officer Wolfe worked Sunday evenings, because Ben said, into the phone, "Wolfe? Colm." A pause. "We're at Dyce's place. Outside. In my car. Yeah. Someone has broken in." Pause. "Because the door is wide open." Pause. "Yes, I'm sure I locked it." Pause. "Okay." And he hung up.

"What?" he asked me, and I realized I had been looking at him openmouthed.

"He gave you his number."

"What?" he said, then made a very weird sound that might have been a laugh. "Not like that," he said. "He wanted me to . . ." He paused. "Uh. He thought because you'd found the body, you know, and then someone slashed my tires in your driveway, that you might be in danger. He gave me his number in case something else happened."

"Ah," I said. I felt suddenly very numb. "And that's why you're staying here, isn't it?"

He looked at me. "Well, I couldn't exactly sleep at my place," he said. "Between the fans and the—"

"No, but here, instead of at a hotel. You'd much rather stay at a hotel, wouldn't you?"

He opened his mouth, then closed it, then shrugged. "Considering how much I'm paying for the disaster recovery service," he said, "I think I can use the savings, don't you?"

"You bought the vase and the statue," I said. "Without blinking."

"Well, yes," he said. "And I'm not going to tell you I'm going to be stone-cold broke after I pay for the disaster recovery, but you know . . . it's going to take time to get back to where I was before, and staying with you helps."

"But you're staying here in case you need to protect me."

He opened his mouth again, then closed it, and finally opened it again. "Yes," he said.

"I don't need your protection," I said. I knew it wasn't true. Or probably it wasn't true. I had needed Ben's protection in the past—or we wouldn't have met over his rescuing me from playground bullies—and I might very well need it in the future. And if truth be told, I was scared. Very scared. But the fact that I was scared, looking at those huge letters, terrified of what might have been done inside the house, only made me want to act tougher. "If I needed someone's protection, I'd have stayed married, or gotten married again." I reached for the door handle.

"Where are you going?" he asked.

"To look inside my house," I said opening the door.

Ben reached over and grabbed my wrist. I tried to shake it loose, but Ben—for all that he makes his living as a financial planner—has a hand like a paw, a hand that doubtless did justice to his manual-laborer ancestors who'd probably come across the ocean at the time of the potato famine. He grabbed my wrist in a vise grip. "Dyce, no," he said.

"Why not?" I asked. "You think I'm such a fragile flower that I'll break down crying at the sight of another big *Bitch* spray-painted inside? You think—"

"No," he said. He spoke very quietly and evenly. "I'm afraid that the person who painted that is still in there. I'm afraid he's lurking in the dark with a knife. I'm afraid by the time I get in there, you'll have been sliced, diced, and filleted." He took advantage of the fact that I was speechless at the image to add, "Do you mind? I like Dyce Dare very much and I'd prefer she stay alive."

I swallowed. I was too far gone for the cajoling to make me laugh, but it jolted me out of my panic fear and into something resembling mere terror. I swallowed again and took a deep breath that hissed in and out of my lungs. "Do you think it was Inobart?" I asked. "Off his meds?"

"Could be," he said.

He was spared saying anything else because at that moment Officer Wolfe pulled up behind me, and moments later a police car—lights blazing—arrived.

Broken, Searched, Sprayed

"**D**O YOU HAVE ANY boyfriends you broke up with?" Officer Wolfe asked, looking intently at me. *What big eyes you have!* "Someone who might think you betrayed him?"

We were sitting at my kitchen table. The wood filling had dried very nicely, but I took no joy in it. Ben had made coffee and was serving it to Officer Wolfe. He'd given me my tea with a week's worth of sugar. All the while he fussed with his special tea. I knew he didn't drink coffee during the day because he was—as he put it—working on a stress ulcer.

For the first time I wondered what the stress was all about. I'd always assumed it was work, but the thing was that I'd never heard Ben refer to his job with anything but unalloyed interest and enjoyment. He'd come out of the College of William and Mary—where he'd gotten an MBA on a scholarship or a grant or something—and gotten a job with an old, established firm in Goldport. A better job than he had hoped to get, making more than he expected. And from the little bits he let drop—not a lot, of course, because a lot of his work was, after all, confidential—he really seemed to enjoy himself. And according to what he'd told me when he'd had his first-year review, his bosses were quite happy with him.

I'd thought it was just Ben being Ben and getting fussed over the work and trying to be perfect at it, like he tried to tie his ties perfectly. But now I wondered if it was Les. The scene in the loft stuck in my head, and I wondered how many such scenes I'd missed. Yeah, okay, so Ben said they'd never fought before. But then again, Ben also said that Les hadn't really meant to do anything bad by setting fire to pictures and frames on the stove. It was entirely possible that Ben's ideas of *slightly disturbed, eccentric,* and *crazy as a loon* were a bit off.

It occurred to me that, being my friend, he was probably used to a high degree of insanity, and I hid my face in my hands. Only to feel Ben's hand on my shoulder as he slipped another cup of tea in front of me. "Come on, Dyce, you're going to have Officer Wolfe thinking that you're the object of disputes between many of the single males in Goldport."

At which point, of course, my tongue answered before my mind caught up. "Not all of them," I said. "I think there are one or two who have other girlfriends."

Ben gave me a serious look, and I realized I was being an idiot. "I'm sorry," I told Officer Wolfe. "No, I haven't been dating. In fact, I haven't dated since my divorce. I was afraid of the . . . disruptive effect of dating and bringing new and possibly temporary people in contact with my son, particularly after the divorce. Why?"

"Because this has all the feel of a *crime passionnel*," he said, and gestured around the apartment. "The whole thing, from your underwear drawer being turned out over most of the bedroom, to your closet being ransacked, to . . ."

The *to* . . . was the word *Bitch* written twice more, in the same excessive size and same red color, once over the sofa and once over my bed. The intruder had also tried to write the word *Fuck* in the shower, but had run out of spray halfway through and therefore had written what looked like *Fuch*, which I thought was a brand of electronics.

At least, I thought, E's stuffed animals had been left alone this time.

"So," Officer Wolfe said. "It seems like an intimate assault. Particularly the underwear drawer and the one box they tore apart in the closet."

That box was my collection of mementos. Mostly silly stuff from middle school all the way through my wedding. I'd even kept the mementos of my wedding, as memories of how I'd once felt about All-ex and why I'd married him. I figured I might need it as fortification in the days ahead. In which case I would have to do some really good work of collecting all the pictures that I'd saved in two envelopes—the marriage had been too short for me to put them into albums—because they'd been strewn all over the room, and a few of them had been crumpled. The prom picture of me and Ben—the same one my parents had in a huge enlargement over the fireplace at their home—had also been crumpled. The blue garter from my wedding had been torn through. My dried bouquet had been pulled apart.

Yeah, I could see how Officer Wolfe thought it was the work of a man scorned who—though he might not be as great a fury as a woman scorned—was surely no piece of cake. But the thing was that I was telling him the absolute truth. "I really didn't give anyone the idea that we were involved. I mean, me and someone, some person, some guy," I clarified, afraid Officer Wolfe would think I was claiming to be involved with him.

"What about someone who might have gotten the idea without your giving it?" he asked. "Someone who is prone to fantasy or something?"

"I don't know anyone like that either," I said. "The type of life I've been living, I might as well be a nun. The only people I know, just about, are other people who refinish furniture or who work in thrift . . ." My voice slowed down. I'd remembered Inobart. I told him the story of my encounter with the man. Ben chimed in to point out that he'd always found Inobart strange and worrisome.

"And he'd have come back to town midway through the afternoon, so he'd have had plenty of time to do this."

"Yeah," Officer Wolfe said. "We'll look into him. You know, his real name is Melchiazar."

"What?"

"Melchiazar Jones. I checked him out this morning when I was looking at refinishers, you know, the names you'd given me. Perhaps he went a little crazy because of that name. I mean, it's possible."

"Or perhaps it's hereditary insanity," Ben said. "And I thought Dyce's parents were bad."

"Yeah, but . . . I didn't see a restraining order against him. Of course, if it's very recent it may not be filed yet. In fact, the paperwork may not be completed. But I'd agree that he sounds like a good candidate for this." He took some notes, then drank his coffee. "You know, we'll know more once we go through the results of the scene workup."

He looked at us. "You should know, though, that the door was not forced."

"But I did lock it," Ben said. He'd made his tea and was now holding the cup and frowning at Officer Wolfe. "I remember."

" I didn't mean to imply the door was open, just that it was not forced. You're absolutely certain that you locked it?"

"Someone came in before," I said. "When I was sure the door was locked." Officer Wolfe gave me a look, and I told him about the knifed table and the hanged stuffed animal. His eyebrows rose during the narration.

He sighed. "And you didn't think this was something I needed to know?"

"Ben wanted to tell you," I said. "But I thought it was students playing a prank."

"I told her it could be important," he said. "Right after, you know . . . she found a corpse."

Officer Wolfe didn't seem to be listening anymore. He was drumming his fingers on the table. "And you're sure the door was locked that time?" he said.

"The front door?" I said. "Well . . . Ben is compulsive about it." I heroically abstained from saying that Ben was compulsive about everything. "And he said he had locked it. Only, you know, I thought . . . but . . . once he might have missed it. Twice . . ."

Officer Wolfe drummed his fingers some more. "It sounds," he said, "like somehow someone got hold of a key to your house. Is that possible?"

"I think so," I said. I rubbed at my nose, not so much because it itched, but because I felt like I would burst into tears at any minute and I didn't want to. "I mean, it's never happened, but then . . ." I cleared my throat, trying to keep tears at bay. "See, that's why I thought it was a student prank. I got the apartment . . . I mean, the landlord is Pads and Flats, which rents mostly to students at the college, and you know what they can be like. I think they don't change the locks in between renters, you know . . ."

"Um," he said, which was not nearly as reassuring a sound as perhaps he might have thought it was.

"She gave me a key and one to her parents," Ben said, helpfully.

"Where do your parents keep it?"

"I don't know," I said.

"Could they have lost it?"

"Nothing more likely," Ben put in helpfully. "They lose everything. Frankly, it's a miracle they haven't lost the bookstore yet." This about the people who considered him a son. "Dyce, have they come in with it at all? Recently?"

"Not that I remember," I said. "Wait, maybe the week I moved in. Mom came in to pick up some stuff for E because they were keeping him." No use telling him Mom had been looking for a baby emetic after catching E eating spiders in a corner of the bookstore. She hadn't found it, anyway.

"So someone may have gotten their key," Officer Wolfe said, making another notation. He frowned down at his notebook for a while. He sighed. "I don't want to alarm either of you, but I'm going to call a friend who's a locksmith to change that front door lock. I have to tell you I'd feel better if the two of you didn't stay here tonight. The house hasn't been broken into as such, but if someone who didn't have a key wanted to, it wouldn't be at all hard."

"We could go to a hotel," Ben said.

"I don't have the money for a hotel," I said. Yeah, I still had almost two thousand dollars in my purse, but there was rent coming up and the car to fix, not to mention various supplies for the workshop. And then there was E. He was about to need shoes, and it wasn't like All-ex would ever buy him sneakers. Left to his own devices, he'd probably get him mini wingtips.

"I'll pay," Ben said.

But I thought of that bill to the recovery service. The thing is that I knew pretty well, within a close approximation, what Ben made. Not that he'd ever told me, but I could guess from the monthly expenses he incurred and from what he thought was too much money.

He'd never have been able to afford his lovely loft if he hadn't bought it with the inheritance from his Grandma. And he would never be able to afford the payments on it if he hadn't put down such a substantial down payment that the mortgage was less than half the original and if the inheritance hadn't paid for his car outright, too. This left him enough for what I considered a dream life. He bought decorative stuff for the loft. He bought nice furniture. He ate well. He and Les went out to eat two or three times a week. And he had enough money left over for nice clothes—very nice clothes—and to give E and me gifts well above our reach.

But he and Les didn't take foreign vacations or do any of the things All-ex did. Weekends in New York City, summer in Italy. That sort of thing. So I knew Ben was comfortable but not wealthy—oh, he was rich beyond the dreams of avarice compared to me, but that wasn't difficult.

And the bill for that cleanup and recovery had truly been staggering. Okay, he'd put it on Mastercard and he'd pay it off by bits, but... he still had to live while he did it. As far as I could determine—and of course I'd never asked—Les didn't contribute anything to the household. It was Ben's place, and it was Ben's expense to maintain it.

"I don't want you to pay," I said. "I don't. Please don't argue."

He looked like he was going to argue anyway, so I said, hastily, "I'll go stay at my parents' place."

Officer Wolfe looked at Ben, who expelled air with an explosive sound, but then sighed. "Do you think they'll put me up, too?"

I looked up at him and was about to ask if he'd taken leave of his mind. Did he really want Mom to start thinking that her dreams were finally coming true?

Officer Wolfe spoke first. "I'd feel better knowing Mr. Colm is with you," he said. "You see, I would like to assign an officer to look after you, but I don't think I can. We're a small department, and assigning someone to guard you full time would mean getting approval to make one of the part-timers full time for a week or so, or moving someone from another case. And until then . . ." He shrugged. "Well, you know, you say your parents may have lost the key."

"I didn't," I said. "Ben did."

"Right. Is it possible that they lost the key?"

"Oh, yes."

"Well, then, if they lost the key, they may have lost keys to their house as well, and I understand they're elderly."

I sniffed. Yeah, okay. I had been born when both Mom and Dad were on the wrong side of forty, and because I was now nearing thirty, they were in their seventies. But if Mr. Policeman Wolfe thought that my parents were defenseless, or even at risk because of absentmindedness, he quite mistook the matter. They approached the world as if reality and everything in it were a distraction from the all-important business of reading. That was Mom and Dad's armor of righteousness, their unpierceable shield.

It had allowed them to sail through all the less-than-well-thought-out adventures of my childhood without ever wondering if I would turn out all right, or even if I would kill someone by the time I was ten. They had taken my broken marriage in stride, and they were able to hold on to their confident notion that I'd eventually marry Ben—whom they regarded as a second child, the son they always wanted—because they hadn't taken their noses out of a book long enough to realize that Ben was in fact gayer than a dance reel.

If a murderer or vandal broke into their house, Dad's sheer impervious lack of noticing him would send the man screaming into the night—that is, if he didn't get co-opted into finding the book Dad was currently reading—*It was right here, I swear. Rats. I must have set it facedown somewhere. It has a blue cover. Or it might be green. On the other hand, perhaps brown? It's called* Murder *something. Or maybe* Death. *Might be* Crime *of something or other.* Or Mom might assume the intruder was there to help her find a particular book in her prodigious collection of favorite books with such sheer force of belief that the poor creature—and yes, I would feel pity even for a murderer in such circumstances—would be trapped forever in the basement, with its makeshift bookcases and Mom's less-than-stellar instructions—*It's a Van Gulick. I'm sure of it. Oh, dear. I can never remember if I shelved it under V or G. Or perhaps K because, you know, that final sound is so forceful. Or C because the mysteries are set in China.* So I was not really worried about Mom and Dad. Not really.

On the other hand, having Ben around—even if it would encourage Mom's delusions—would make going home somewhat easier. I could leave him to find Dad's book or Mom's favorite novel and sleep late. Ben was very nice to them. This was one of the reasons why I was an only child, but still not my parents' favorite.

It was only for a night. I somehow suspect that Ulysses told himself that, too, when setting off to return home from Troy. *It's only one night. How bad can it get?*

We waited till the nice locksmith had changed the lock and given us the new keys, and then Ben and I drove separately to my parents', furniture and bust still in the back of his car.

THE FLEDGLING RETURNS

I T WAS CLOSE TO midnight as we drove up Mom and Dad's street. The neighborhood was composed of brownstones built side by side, connected like townhouses, though they were far too big to be townhouses. I'd always wondered what the rationale had been for building them—maybe someone was really homesick for the East.

In the beginning of the twentieth century, they'd been inhabited by the upper middle class, but by the middle of it they were all—except ours—run-down apartments. However, in the last twenty years the place had become pricey again and was full of young couples, most of whom ran commercial establishments on the bottom floor. All of those cafés, art galleries, organic delis, and bicycle shops were now closed and dark. All except Mom and Dad's house, which blazed with lights. Even the bottom floor, which was the store.

Mom and Dad's house was three stories tall—four if you counted the very short attic where my bedroom was. It had been the home of Dad's grandmother and left to him in her will. I expect she'd thought Dad would sell it and perhaps use the money to finance a college education. The house was, after all, big enough to turn into a small hotel, and she probably thought no sane person could have wanted to keep it, not in the fifties when the fashion was all for one-story homes and streamlined furniture and when—from what I understood of the history of this area—this street had been going downhill, with all the grand brownstones subdivided into apartments inhabited by entirely the wrong sort of people.

Great-Grandmother had made only one mistake in her calculations. She'd failed to consider that Dad might not be sane. It should have been glaringly obvious to just about everyone. I'd seen pictures of him in his teens and twenties, when his grandmother must have decided on the inheritance.

He was a gawky young man, with curly dark hair and the sort of glasses that, though not bulletproof, would probably have stopped a shot because of their thickness. From behind those lenses, his eyes shone with the glare of the fanatic.

In previous centuries Dad would probably have gone into the church and ended up as an hermit or an anchorite somewhere. One of those holy men who never washed and sat in a corner thinking increasingly complex thoughts about dancing angels.

Born in the thirties into a white, Anglo-Saxon family, bearers of a decent sort of Episcopal faith—the kind that believed in God but thought it was bad manners to speak about it in public—he had lacked the religious background to become a holy man. Instead, he'd turned the basement of his parents' house into an ever more complex maze of book piles.

He'd graduated from high school—to believe my Grandma, at least—because his parents went down and found him every morning, stuck him under a shower after wrestling the current book out of his hands, forced him into clean clothes, and dropped him off at school. Where he had to get through the day before he was allowed into his basement again.

Eventually his labyrinth of books got too complex for him to be easily found. Fortunately, this was after he graduated.

And shortly thereafter his deluded grandmother, who probably thought he only needed an opportunity, had left him her house, which was right next door.

So it was easy for him to move there with his books and line every wall with bookcases. I was still not absolutely sure he'd decided to open a store so much as one day someone stumbled through the door, decided that this must be a bookstore, and offered him money for one of the books he was least attached to.

Over time, he'd caught on to how the store worked, at least to the point of moving the books he didn't want to sell to the basement or the upper floors, buying a register, and giving the store a name and a sign.

How the store survived and made money was a bit of a puzzle. Well, from what I understood, from reading mystery books and from talking to the mystery authors who came by for signings, it is always a bit of a puzzle how independent mystery bookstores survive. My favorite theory was that of the best-selling author who told me that she always figured that the stores were fronts for numbers games.

But I knew Dad didn't run numbers. And heaven knew he made even less effort to sell books than the average mystery bookseller.

I truly had no idea at all how he'd survived till Mom married him. After that, Mom—for all her dreams of being an author—had taken the matter of their livelihood in hand, made sure the sign was big enough to be seen from the street, persuaded Dad to sell some of the better books, and made it clear to him that when they went to mystery conventions he was to spend less buying books than they made selling books. She had also persuaded him to carry a limited number of newly printed books—multiple copies of each, even. These he was not nearly as attached to as his used, vintage, and collectible books.

Selling those books was still a nerve-racking endeavor for my father, and right now, after he'd returned from the mystery convention, I knew what he was doing. He was in the store, alone, reshelving the books that had escaped what he viewed as the horrible fate of selling, and reassuring the other ones, left on the shelves, that they had a good three months before the next convention and that he would do whatever was needed to avoid parting with them.

I drove into the nearest alley to the back of the row of houses, and Ben followed me to the circular driveway that surrounded the backyard and ended in a large three-car garage. On the far side of the garage, a driveway, now walled off, used to lead to the house my dad grew up in, which had been sold to strangers a few years ago. I pulled up in front of the short brick wall and got out to tell Ben to pull into the one open space in the garage. He didn't argue, which was good, because I would have had to tell him I was doing this because his car was so much better than mine. The truth, though, was that I was afraid someone would figure out where we had gone, and get into the trunk and hurt the little table. I just hated to lie to Ben.

The driveway encircled the backyard, where, except for one area given entirely to crabgrass—the reminder of my incident with the gasoline bottle—there were big maple trees everywhere, with a few tall pines to break the monotony. In summer it had been a wonderful place to play at being lost in a magic forest. In winter it had created a winter wonderland to play at being at the North Pole and breaking into Santa Claus's ultra secret workshop, which was usually the shed under the largest pine tree.

Right now, on a spring night, it was a backyard to get through as quickly as possible. My luggage consisted of my toothbrush, shoved hastily into my purse. I still had jeans and T-shirts in my closet here, and thank heavens, my size hadn't changed much.

Ben, on the other hand, was lugging his two shoulder bags. I occurred to me to wonder, after going through everything in my closet, tearing through my souvenir box, and upending my underwear drawer, why the intruder had left Ben's things completely untouched. Which could mean that either Officer Wolfe was wrong and the mayhem wasn't caused by some man who had a crush on me, or the man knew me and Ben well enough to know Ben was no threat. Or was afraid of Ben.

Or perhaps, of course, the intruder simply understood that a man who traveled with his weight in cosmetics was not having an affair with any woman under the sun. But it still seemed very odd.

We walked as fast as we could, avoiding being tripped by oak tree roots, all the way to the stairs that led to my parents' kitchen door on the second floor. The staircase had always scared me a little. I didn't know when it had been built or by whom, though I suspected—both from the workmanship and the look of it—that it had been built by Dad under Mom's direction and at her insistence after she married him and explained that he couldn't be cooking and sleeping in what was, technically, a store and that the door into the house from the store had to be permanently closed.

It was sort of what a wrought-iron staircase would be if it had been built by a man who had neither iron nor the slightest idea how to build a staircase. Supports of irregular lengths and widths, nailed with the sort of nails one expects to hold down railroad ties, held a spiral of sorts, only one whose basis was the square rather than the circle. The construction had been somewhat complicated by the fact that though Dad can calculate and measure like nobody's business, he can't cut anything straight or to the proper length. So each step was slightly different from the previous one: wider, thinner, longer, shorter. Also, the distance between them was slightly different, so that you had to concentrate on going up the stairs and couldn't get into a rhythm.

Frankly, if a psychiatrist saw that staircase, he'd probably have Dad committed, and Mom, too, for not realizing Dad was less than sane. But of course, Mom and Dad's friends included booksellers, book buyers, book writers, and cover artists but virtually no psychiatrists. And the staircase, for its appearance of having been built by monkeys from found materials, had stood firm for all of my childhood, and still didn't shudder as we walked up it.

At the top of the stairs was a little platform—it would be much too much of an honor to call it a porch—where I paused to dig through my jeans pocket for my keys. Before I could get them out, Mom's psychic powers struck.

I'd never understood this, unless of course she had some sort of sensor set up under the floorboards on that stair, but Mom always knew when someone was at the back door. She was particularly good at knowing when Ben was at the back door, as she proved right now by opening the inner door, pushing the screen door open, and beaming up at Ben. "Hello, Ben." And then smiling at me. "Hi, Candy." She backed into the house, keeping the door open with her body as she did so.

Mom looks more or less as I know I'll look as I get older—small, skinny, with the sort of face that people call interesting, because it was never pretty. She had two things going for her, which I had quite failed to inherit: her golden hair, which had now turned a fluffy, sparkling white, and china-doll-blue eyes. Her eyes were, right then, full of gratified expectation. "I was just about to go to bed," she said. "I'm glad I stayed up, though, so I could be here when you came in."

Oh, boy. She had the look of a mom who expects an announcement. And I doubted the announcement she expected was that I'd found a body and now someone had vandalized my house and therefore I must sleep somewhere else. But then I realized I could never tell her that. It would be wiser to say that Ben and I were getting married and driving to Vegas in the morning. At least then she'd let us go. If we told her I'd been anywhere near a murder, let alone a murder and break-in, I'd be a permanent guest. They might lock me up in the attic until I gave them the crucial clue to who had committed the crimes.

No, to even let Mom suspect the whole story would be suicidal. So I was ready as Ben started to say, "We're only here because—"

"Ben's place is getting renovated," I said. "And my house has . . . a gas leak. That's it. A gas leak."

Ben looked at me. The man had a very odd addiction to the truth. But he must have caught something in my eyes, because he said, "That's it," and cleared his throat. "A gas leak."

"Oh." To say Mom's face fell would be going too far, but the pleasant expectancy left her eyes. Instead, she stepped back near the sink. As she did so, Fluffy rose from her basket near the stove. At twenty-some years of age, she was more fur and bones than cat. In fact, most of the time all you saw of her was patchy fur sticking out at all angles. And most of the time, people seeing her in her basket thought she was just a bit of abandoned fur. More than one guest—Mom said—had believed she was dead and tried to tell Mom this. The impression was fostered by the fact that Fluffy's digestive processes let forth the most foul smells experienced on Earth since all the dead dinosaurs rotted at once.

However, deaf, nearly blind, and possibly a zombie though she might be, there was still one thing that caused Fluffy to spring up in her basket, hiss like a kettle on the boil, and wave a paw with gnarled and yellowed claws in the direction of the perceived threat: me.

"Oh, dear," Mom said. "I'll have to give her Valium again."

I looked at Fluffy's maddened golden eyes peering amid the yellowed fur and sighed. "Yeah."

Ben didn't even say anything—he edged away from the hissing cat and toward the hallway. "Is it all right," he asked, "if I stay on the living room sofa?"

Mom made a clucking sound and followed him. "No, no, no. I'll change the sheets on the guest bed, of course."

Of course. If Ben was in luck, she'd even put a mint on his pillow. Of course the mint might be resting on a note listing the advantages of marrying her daughter, but I was sure Ben could manage. After all, he wore big-boy pants.

I left him to it and, feeling only the slightest bit cowardly, hoofed it up the stairs, one flight to the bedroom floor, then another flight to my bedroom.

I'd colonized the attic when I was twelve or maybe thirteen, with the approval and help of my grandmother, who had convinced Mom that a growing girl needed a room of her own for makeup and stuff, and convinced Dad that I needed more space for my books. What I'd actually wanted, at the time, was to escape the bedroom that had since become the guest room.

Let me explain—the now-guest-room shared a wall with my parents' room. There were certain noises that were unavoidable, and that as a teen I'd become very self-conscious about. By which I mean the sounds of my parents discussing the latest mystery they were reading together, and arguing hotly over the solution.

They could go on till all hours of the morning, and it was starting to affect my performance at school. I would lapse into fitful dreams during math and insist that it was the cook who had poisoned the stew when Mrs. Marplot asked me the result of a quadratic equation.

The attic was finished, in the sense that the walls were plastered and painted. The only place I could stand straight was in the middle, but I spent most of my time in my bedroom either on my bed reading, or at the desk by the window doing my homework, so the fact that I couldn't stand straight hadn't bothered me much. Now, in addition to my bed, there was a little inflatable mattress, which I used whenever E and I had to stay here for some reason.

The only inconvenience, really, I thought, as I set the toothbrush on the side of my desk, was that the nearest toilet was at the foot of the stairs, and it was just a toilet and a sink—what the Victorians had no doubt called a water closet—where I could only close the door while using it because I was short.

The only place to shower was another floor beneath that, next to the kitchen. As a high schooler, I'd showered the night before. I wondered how Ben would fare with his multitude of skin-care products, then decided it was entirely his problem. I really hated to leave him to fend for himself, but there it was. There was always the hope Mom would take one look at the toiletries bag and run screaming into the night.

I realized that I felt very tired, doubtless because of the drive to Denver and the shock of seeing all my personal underthings thrown around. So I went into the built-in closet that took up one of the sloping-roof areas and looked through the drawer for pajamas. I failed to find any, but I found a nightgown that I'd only mostly outgrown, in the sense that it now came to my upper thighs where it had once covered my knees.

I had changed into it and was brushing my hair when someone knocked on the door.

For a horrible moment, as I stammered, "Come in," I imagined it would be Ben. He had come to tell me he couldn't take my parents anymore, and he'd try to persuade me to throw ourselves from one of the attic windows—which in his case would require either greasing or a shoehorn, because the windows were tiny—and shout *Better die free* on our way to the ground.

Instead, it was my mom, bearing a glass of milk and a plate of cookies. I raised my eyebrow at her as she came in, walking stooped, and set the plate and cup of milk on the desk. "I thought you'd need something. Ben said you were on the road all that time . . ."

My first thought of course was that Ben—the rat!—had told my mom about the murder and the break-in. But then Mom sat on the bed in her it's-just-us-girls pose, and I bit my tongue. Oh. That kind of talk. Well, I might as well have the milk and cookies to fortify me, and besides, hell, this would save me from sitting on the bed next to her.

I backed up until my butt was against my desk, and then I sort of pulled myself up to sit on it. The desk was the sturdiest piece of furniture in the house—as sturdy as the house, in fact. It was composed of an oak piece inset in the dormer window and supported by a sort of brick ridge all around. I grabbed a cookie—one of the things Mom has always done well is bake, even if she normally does it with a mystery in one hand, just as she embroiders, quilts, and crochets—and munched it, while looking at Mom.

It occurred to me that I would let her lead into the subject and embarrass herself. Look, I know it is cruel of me, but the thing was that if I had to put up with my parents, then I should derive some satisfaction from it. By the time I was fourteen I had figured out that the only possible satisfaction was amusement.

I sat there, eating my cookies and drinking my milk, while Mom smoothed the bedspread, looked around, and said in a casual tone, "I always thought this was such a pleasant room."

"Mmm," I said. It *was* a pleasant room, surprisingly airy and bright, and I'd enjoyed it, but it was hot as a furnace in summer—forcing me to put in a window air conditioner, which rather diminished the brightness—and ice cold in winter, forcing me to bring up a heater and close the door, which diminished the airiness. However, right now it was pleasant and I was willing to enjoy it. And the show Mom was about to put on.

"You know, Candy," Mom said. "I know that you don't like me to talk about your private life . . ."

I smiled.

This seemed to encourage her. "But you know your father and I always worry about your ending up old and alone . . . after . . . after we're gone." She looked at me with such sympathy that I would have believed it, if not for the fact that I knew any such discussions would have to be sandwiched between arguments over who killed whom in the latest book and that more than likely they would be limited to Mom saying, *I always worry about Candy ending up old and alone.* Then Dad would say, *Who?* Mom would say, *Your daughter, Candyce.* Dad would say, *You know she hates to be called Candy.* And it would all go downhill from there.

"I know that you are concentrating your efforts on being a good mother for little Enoch," Mom went on, caressing the bedspread absently, and almost causing me to say *Who?* in turn. "But you know, you're not getting any younger either, and one day Enoch will be grown and gone . . ." She gave me that piercing *Trust me, I know* look. "And you'll be all alone. Surely you don't intend to be a burden on Enoch . . ."

"Of course not," I said, and smiled reassuringly, resisting an urge to cross the room and pat her hand. In the play we were engaging in, it was, after all, my role to be reassuring. "I'm sure I'll have crashed my car or died of inhaling refinishing fumes long before Enoch leaves the house."

For some reason, this failed to calm her down. She did pause and frown, as if not sure how to answer that, but then she went on with her set role. "The thing is, dear, as I'm sure you know, I always thought your marriage was a mistake."

This was absolutely true, but only because my mother had always had it set in her head that, failing Ben and me coming to terms with our raging love that only Mom saw, I would marry a mystery author. The number of times they'd thrown me at the heads of likely—and unlikely, often visibly married or gay—male authors at conventions was almost embarrassing. And All-ex had established at his first meal in the house that not only didn't he write mysteries, but he also had no intention of ever reading one.

I chewed a cookie and said "Mmmm" again.

"And I know that it's never very exciting, you know . . . to fall in love with one's childhood friends, but I think that you are now mature enough to consider that perhaps it would be better for both you and Ben if you . . . well . . . if you came to terms with the fact that the sort of friendship you have is love, too. If you just . . . made a match, as my mother would say, and settled down." She sighed. "You know your father and I would like to see our grandchildren before we die."

"You see E all the time," I said. Though I would grant they usually saw him for two seconds before he spun off to the back yard in pursuit of Fluffy or on a grand search for bugs.

Mom started, as if she hadn't realized that E was their grandchild, which of course, she hadn't. She thought of E as something that had sort of happened to me. Their grandchild would be little Sherlock, or perhaps little Agatha. "Yes, of course, but . . . our other grandchildren . . ."

"Well, you'll be glad to know I'm seeing someone," I said, though I felt like a complete fool. I knew she would take this to mean that I was dating, though in strict honesty, I was seeing someone. Lots of someones. I wasn't blind. But as she blinked, I couldn't let a good thing lie. Or a good lie rest. "His name is Cas Wolfe and he's a policeman with the Goldport Serious Crimes Unit."

She brightened up, and for just a moment I thought I'd thrown her off the scent and that she would now pursue this idea that I would perhaps marry someone at least remotely connected to crime. But she was a woman on a mission, and I couldn't sway her from it. She frowned a little, clearly trying to control her enthusiasm, then sighed. "I can't help but feel like you keep trying to find substitutes for what is obviously before your eyes, which you refuse to admit . . ."

"Uh . . . You said E would grow up . . . If I want companionship . . . Well, I suppose I could buy a dog . . ."

"Candy, you can be really frustrating sometimes," Mom said, then remembered she was being sweet and kind and concerned about—of all things—my loneliness in old age. "Has it occurred to you that there is a reason that Ben hasn't married yet?"

"Yes, Mom, it has. Ben hasn't married because there's a limited number of states allowing it, and also it's not universally recognized. Besides, he has really bad taste in men. I hope he doesn't marry Les because that man just isn't very tightly wrapped."

Mom sighed and rolled her eyes. "Frankly," she said. "I think you imagine these things. I don't know where you got the idea that Ben is a—a homosexual. I think it's your idea of a joke."

Well, it could come from walking in on him in the music room with the student council president, but I wasn't going to rat out Ben or a poor man who had never done anything to me just to shut Mom up. I was used to this lecture, after all. "Mom . . ."

"No, listen, Candy, I just talked to Ben and he said that he would be willing . . . that is, that he hopes some day you will see how much he loves you!"

"Uh," I said. "He said that?" Because there was a better-than-even chance he'd simply nodded at the wrong time.

"He said that he hopes for the day when you'll realize how pure and true his love is," Mom said triumphantly.

And unfortunately, I was almost sure that she was quoting Ben there. Because that was just the sort of thing he would say. True and pure indeed. The rat fink.

"I see," I said. And in fact I did. I saw that Ben had gotten rid of Mom by sending her to me. Which meant he completely deserved what he had coming to him. "I'll think about it, Mom. I'm really tired now, though. So, if I could sleep . . ."

She took the hint and left, carrying the empty plate and the cup. I went down to the powder room to brush my teeth. Of course, one way to get back at Ben was to tell Mom that I was more than willing to marry him, and that he was the one who had failed to ask me, after all. But that was a dangerous game, because Mom was getting old and desperate to see her pet plan succeed. She was quite likely to book a justice of the peace and get a license and then haul us up in front of him. As amusing as the game was, being married to Ben would be kind of like being married to an older sister, and about as much fun.

By the time I got back to my bedroom, I'd decided on the perfect plan, though. Unless I was badly, completely wrong, Ben was sticking to me like glue on orders from Cas Wolfe. Not just tonight, but from first meeting him. This meant that he would probably find some excuse not to go to work tomorrow, and try to stick to me throughout the day.

First, I had no intention at all of being followed around by the world's most burly advertisement for skin care products, and second . . . and second, he so deserved to be stuck with my parents over breakfast. If he was lucky—very, very lucky—he'd manage to run off before noon. But I doubted it.

I had an alarm clock on one of the bookcases along the wall, next to the bed. I hadn't used it since high school, but it seemed to be in perfect working order. I set it for six a.m., secure in the knowledge that no one else in the house would be up at that hour. Hell, though Ben was an early riser, my parents' nightly plot discussion was likely to keep him up till well past midnight. So at six, he would still be completely passed out. Good. Because I was going to need to steal his car keys.

DIPPED

I WOKE IN GRAY dawn. The light filtering through the window had the peculiar colorless quality of a world not fully awake. I tiptoed out of bed and considered leaving the house without showering, but if I did that, I'd feel like I had bugs crawling all over me all day.

Look, I know it's psychological. People didn't use to wash that often or that well. It was all about washing once or twice in their lives. And they didn't die and their skin didn't flake off. But I'd been conditioned to shower every day, and if I didn't, I felt like I was going to get the black plague or something.

So I showered quickly, taking my clothes with me and changing into them in the bathroom. Before leaving that floor, I tiptoed into Ben's room and noted that Ben still slept like a mummy.

It is inexplicable to me, though I first noted it when I'd gone to wake him in order to go somewhere when we were both very young. Ben rolled himself up in a blanket at night and woke up still rolled in the blanket, perfectly still, face up. There was something vaguely creepy about it, though his mom—who told me that he went to bed like that—seemed to find it endearing.

He was asleep, face up, completely rolled in the upper sheet and blankets. He looked either dead or like he was faking sleep, and I half-expected him to sit up and go, *Got you!* But he didn't. I grabbed the keys he'd put on the bedside table and tiptoed down the stairs. In the garage, I opened the back of his car, took the table, and put it in the back of my car.

Then I tiptoed back into the house, left the keys on the bedside table where he'd left them, went upstairs to grab my own purse and keys, then went back to my car and made my getaway.

I giggled softly to myself while imagining Ben sitting at breakfast with my parents, wondering when I was going to come down. I imagined him having to debate the merits of cozies versus hard-boileds. Unlike All-ex he read mysteries, but he was far more interested in science fiction of the hard science kind. So most of what he would do is make polite noises at Dad until he managed to get away and go wake me up. And when he found I was gone, it would totally serve him right.

Very happy with myself, and very eager to work on the table, I was nonetheless incredibly hungry. I stopped at Good Morning Doughnuts around the corner. There was a police car parked up front, but alas, it was not Cas Wolfe behind the wheel but a blond man with an unruly mane of hair, eating a cruller and drinking a massive cup of coffee. Just as well. Cas Wolfe might be rather upset that I'd given Ben the slip.

I got a chocolate doughnut with Boston cream filling and a cup of hot chocolate. I still had most of both by the time I got home.

To my relief the house looked intact, with no signs of further break-ins. Someone—and I had no idea who—had covered the *Bitch* in a white paint that I assumed to be primer. I didn't think the police would have done that, but perhaps Cas Wolfe had called the landlords. Who knew?

Inside, the writing on the walls had been covered, too. I vaguely remembered the policemen doing that while Ben and I were putting stuff back in my bedroom. I was fairly sure that this wasn't a normal service offered by the law, and wondered if Officer Wolfe had made them do it, and if they'd run down to Shorty Drugs for the paint.

Other than the obvious signs of last night's intrusions, including the unwashed coffee and tea cups in the sink, the house looked perfectly normal, and I started to feel silly for going to spend the night at Mom's. I brought the little table in, locked the door, washed the cups, and put them upside down on a tea towel to dry. Then, carrying the table, I headed out back.

And noticed that something was wrong. Outside the back door, I looked at the shed and saw that the lock I kept on the door was hanging funny, and that the door seemed to be partially open. I had a moment of wondering whether the police had left it unlocked when they'd checked on the shed last night.

Because those little cheap locks weren't exactly hard to open, after all. But I put the table inside, by the back door, just in case. And I grabbed my broom. Then, holding it like a samurai sword, I headed toward the shed.

Closer, I gripped the broomstick tighter, because I could see that the lock was not unlocked but cut through, like with bolt cutters. This was not good. Perhaps someone was looking for the little table.

I pushed the door open with my foot while holding the broomstick at the ready.

My workshop looked empty, and everything seemed to be where it was supposed to, except that there was a funny smell and something felt not right.

I looked around my worktable and saw what looked like a virulently green bundle of rags on the floor. But it wasn't a bundle of rags—it was a human body covered by a hooded green robe that had been thrown over the body. And the body itself, at least the parts of it that I could see, had the same gelatinous look as the one I'd found in the Dumpster.

I think I beat all speed records running back into the house. I don't remember calling Ben's cell phone. I don't remember waiting for him to arrive. I do remember throwing up. And I remember Ben coming into the house—in a suit, for crying out loud—and holding my head as I finished getting rid of the last of the hot chocolate.

I sort of regained my senses sitting at my table as he slid a cup of tea in front of me. He looked stern and serious, and I fully expected him to tell me that was a very stupid thing I'd done, returning to the house without him. I expected him to tell me it could be me out there, dipped in lye and not looking human at all.

Instead, he said, "I've called Officer Wolfe. He's on his way."

"Uh."

"With the body-processing crew."

I took a sip of tea. "I figured," I said, not sure why my voice came out sounding disappointed.

"I'm sure he would come anyway, if he knew you were in distress," Ben said. I gave him a dubious look. I wasn't sure I was in distress. I was, however, sure that Ben, subtly or not, was yanking my chain.

Moments later Officer Wolfe arrived, with his crew, and this time it was hard to even imagine the man had ever taken me to dinner or kissed me. He was very serious, very focused, and almost antagonistic. He asked me again, this time on record, about lye, whether I had access to a lye vat. He asked me about poor Inobart and whether I'd ever felt threatened by him. Threatened. This from the man who had tried to make me feel scared of Inobart. Honestly.

I told him about coming to the house early and why. He gave Ben a narrowed-eye look. "At what time did she leave her parents'?"

Ben shrugged. "I have no idea. Couldn't have been last night, though, because they were awake and discussing who might have killed the . . . er . . . who killed the cop in some mystery or other, until four in the morning."

Four in the morning. I looked at the circles under Ben's eyes and felt strangely guilty.

I wondered if it made any difference and found myself very much hoping that Inobart had died before four in the morning.

"Your neighbors saw someone carrying a bundle to your shed, shortly after we left, they said. Well, your upstairs neighbor. He said he was up and saw some movement in the back of the shed. He was curious, because you'd had police over earlier. Anyway, until we do further exams, we assume that this was when the body was dumped."

"Dumped?"

"Well, there is no lye vat in your shed, so it's unlikely he was immersed right there." He looked like someone with a really bad toothache, I realized. "Is there anything else you want to tell me?"

I shook my head. There were, of course, a lot of things I'd never told him, including about the table in the Dumpster. Oh, and the phone call to Rocky's. But if I started now, he would only get very upset with me.

He dropped into a chair, looking at me from a closer level.. It should have been reassuring, only it wasn't. Somehow seeing his grey eyes up close and personal made it all the more intimidating. "Listen, what I can't understand is why they would put the body here? Do you have any explanation for me? If you're not the killer and someone else is . . ." He paused for a moment. "Then what rational is there to dumping the body in your shed. We've been going on the assumption that you have nothing to do with this, beyond finding that first body in the dDumpster, but now we can't be absolutely sure. You mentioned that Inobart had been harassing a woman, Nell Gwen. Did you know her?"

Rocky's ex-wife? I supposed I did know her. I'd met her, I was sure, at some place or another. Flea market or supplies store or something . . . I squinched my forehead. The problem was that if I had E with me, I was pretty much blinded to everyone around, by the necessity of keeping an eye on my son. Also, frankly, I had a lousy memory for faces, particularly the faces of well-dressed, seemingly successful females. Okay, it was petty of me, but I did tend to make value judgments about people based on that sort of thing. And that kind of female reminded me too much of all the girls in high school who hadn't thought me fashionable enough or composed enough or whatever to be one of them. Which was the impression Nell Gwen projected, at least if she was the person I remembered.

"I met her," I said. "Why? Do you think because Inobart stalked her, he stalked me, too? I'm not the type guys stalk."

Something flashed in his eyes, and for a moment I thought he was going to say something rude, but then he clenched his teeth together, and when he unclenched them it was to say, "No, because she is our first victim. She was the woman found in the Dumpster."

"Oh." The vague memory of an overconfident—pushy—female got overlaid with the image of the body in the Dumpster, and I thought I was going to be sick again, only there was nothing left in my stomach to throw up. I covered my mouth with my hands. For just a moment there was something like pity—or worry—in Cas Wolfe's eyes, but then Officer Wolfe looked stern and serious again, "Look," he said. "You see why I need to know what is going on, and what other contacts you might have had with . . . furniture refinishers. Whatever you want to call them."

I sighed. I didn't want to tell him. But in the game of secrets I was keeping, giving that away was far less important than giving away that I had a table stolen from the scene where the first body was found. A table that, almost for sure, had the handwriting of the first victim on the bottom. A table that might, somehow, be connected to the crime. I shuddered. Fortunately, shuddering was perfectly acceptable in my present circumstances, and I decided I would have to sacrifice my secret phone call. "Well," I said. And sniffled. I hadn't meant to sniffle, but I felt as if my nose were about to drip. "Yesterday, I called Rocky's workshop."

"You what?" he said, in a way that made it sound so personal and particular that it made me jump.

"I called Rocky Mountain Refinishing," I said, trying to be dignified.

"Why on Earth?" Officer Wolfe said, and glanced at Ben, frowning. If he expected Ben to explain the workings of my mind to him, he was more severely deluded than I thought.

"Because I thought, you know, I'd make sure that he had a lye vat . . ."

"Yes?" he asked, and his voice sounded like an adult about to get a child's explanation for a particularly stupid misdeed.

It put my back up, of course, compounding the fact that I'd just realized that I'd have to tell him about the table, if I were to relate the conversation with Rocky's employee verbatim. So I decided he didn't need to know. Okay, fine, so he was a policeman. But last I checked, no one had died and made him God. And besides, it would be no possible good to him to know about the table. And Ben could stop staring at me with that worried expression, too. Besides, if I told him about the table now, he'd probably suspect me. It wouldn't help anyone.

"I called, and his employee answered, and I asked if they had a lye vat and what they used it for." I said. I suspected that if he went to the workshop and really questioned people, he might get a different version of the conversation. But then it would be he said, she said, wouldn't it?

"And what did they say?" he asked, with sort of a curious fascination. It was as though he were asking me, *And how high is the tower you jumped from?*

"I had no idea she had done this," Ben said. "Dyce, are you sure you didn't dream it?"

"Quite," I said. "You were in the shower. And talking to . . . calling Les."

"Oh."

Officer Wolfe gave Ben an *I'm very disappointed in you* look. Ben didn't even notice. He looked like he was deep in thought. Knowing him, he was thinking he should call Les again and possibly wondering why Les hadn't returned his call. Honestly, sometimes I wondered about his sanity.

"And what did Rocky's employee answer, again? I think I missed it," Officer Wolfe said.

"No," I said, impatiently. "You didn't miss it because I didn't tell you about it. Well . . . ," I said, on second thought, "not that there's anything to tell, because he just hung up the phone."

"I see," Officer Wolfe said, staring at me. He closed his notebook and carefully capped his pen. "Ms. Dare," he said, putting the sort of emphasis on the name that seemed to mean that he'd never call me anything else. I'd never be *Dyce* to him, and he'd never take me out again to expensive restaurants, and kiss me by the door. Well, so much the worse. I tried to concentrate on his words and not on the fact that he had very nice lips as he went on. "I would appreciate it if, in the future, you made it a point of not trying to do my investigation for me. I can't say that what you did prompted this death—at least I can't say it until I know a lot more about it. But the fact remains that you have inserted yourself in the middle of a murder investigation, and that your efforts could hurt the work of professionals like me.

"I know that your parents sell mystery books and that those are full of amateurs who solve terrible crimes. But, in my profession, we call such people *corpses*. I would very much prefer if I didn't have to investigate your death next."

The Protection Racket

OFFICER WOLFE STALKED AWAY from me after that. It was very weird because I had the very strong feeling he wanted to shake me. But there was something to the way he hunched his shoulders and to the smoldering intensity of his occasional glances at me that gave me the impression of one of Ben's contained furies.

And the fact that I was noticing Officer Wolfe's broad shoulders and his long legs, and the graceful way he stepped aside to allow his underlings to carry a zipped body bag through the house, meant that I really had issues. Maybe instead of the UPS man, I would become one of those older women who went after college students. There was a young man who often walked by my window without a shirt, even in winter . . .

In contemplation of my impending nymphomania, I sat there as people walked in and out. After a while Officer Wolfe approached and said, ostensibly to Ben, "The forensic teams will be in and out of the shed in the back probably till mid- to late afternoon. You may stay here or, if you have somewhere to be, I'll leave an officer here, and make sure that he locks everything as he leaves. I'll put a new padlock on the door and get the keys to you."

Ben had been looking at his watch now and then.

"You have to go to work, don't you?" I asked him.

Ben shook his head. "I called in and took today and tomorrow off." And I'd swear he was looking at Officer Wolfe and not me as he said that. What? He had been sworn in to the police and his job was to protect me? Gee. I'd always wanted my own personal bodyguard who followed me everywhere, but did he need to be gay and someone I viewed as a sibling?

"Why?" I said.

He shrugged. Another look was exchanged between him and Officer Wolfe, and I hoped that Ben was being paid. Or at least that he got a grope out of it or something. No, wait. I didn't want Ben to grope the policeman—*I* wanted to grope Officer Wolfe. Nymphomania again. Poor UPS guy.

"Come on, Dyce," Ben said. "Let's go grab some lunch. There's no point staying here watching the police go in and out."

Well, he should speak for himself. It was actually lots of fun watching one policeman go in and out, particularly from the back.

I started to say that I was not hungry, and then I realized that the hot chocolate and doughnut had only been borrowed for a brief time. And besides, Ben said, "Come on. I'll take you to Cy's and let you have the banana cherry milkshake."

Not only was I in no state to resist Cy's burgers, but letting me have a banana cherry milkshake, presumably without making fun of me, was a concession indeed, because making fun of my food tastes was one of Ben's joys in life.

I took a deep breath, grabbed my purse, and followed him out to his car. Of course, he was still carrying a reading desk, a vase, and a bust in the back of his car, so—I wasn't stupid—before I left, I grabbed the little table and returned it to its place in the trunk.

Ben didn't say anything until he was driving and well away from the house. Then he said, very quietly, "What did you really talk about to the people at Rocky's?"

"What they used the lye for."

His eyebrows rose. "Dyce . . ."

"Oh, all right. I asked about the table."

"The table in the back?"

"Yes."

"Is that when he hung up?"

"No, that was when I asked about the woman with the frosted blond curls."

"I see," Ben said. I wondered if his having been sworn in as deputy dog would now demand that he tell Officer Wolfe the truth. But I didn't think so. If that were the case, he wouldn't have waited till we were away to grill me. And besides, there were things that were more important than police investigations and, hell, if one of us was going to start talking, both of us could, and despite the pact and the fact that I didn't ask Ben questions about his private life, I knew where quite a lot of the bodies were buried. Largely metaphorically, of course.

We got to Cy's at the end of lunch hour. Apparently having a murder in your house was a real time waster. I didn't remember anything of substance between early morning and now, and I certainly didn't remember anything of importance, or getting anything accomplished. But it was now almost one thirty and the various students and employees of nearby businesses who came to Cy's for lunch had slowed down to a trickle of latecomers.

The burger joint was tiny, and it made much of the fact that it had remained largely unchanged in decades, a fact emphasized by pictures of Elvis and fifties cars on the walls. The counter itself was minuscule, and you could see everything at the back, where they prepared the food. I ordered the double cheeseburger with bacon and mushrooms in butter, and Ben cleared his throat or coughed or something. But true to his word, he said nothing when I ordered a banana-cherry-chocolate milkshake.

He ordered a burger—just a single burger—and . . . get this . . . water. When people were known to drive from Denver for the extra thick milkshakes at Cy's, when the local paper ran articles about Cy's shakes, the man would have water.

As we sat down, I looked at his drink and rolled my eyes. He sighed. "I haven't had time to get to the gym," he said.

Ben lived in fear of his own body. He worked a lot—in fact, it could be said he often was at risk of working to excess. Unfortunately his work was hardly the sort that burned calories. And also, unfortunately, Ben had the example of his father, who was a rather larger version of himself—not fat as such, or rather, yes, fat, but massive, in an imposing and authoritative way that kept his students speechless and cowed. This would not suit Ben, and besides, it would ruin the fit of his clothes. So he starved himself, and he went to the gym for one to two hours a day. That he wasn't planning on exercising seemed interesting enough. "Why don't you go today?" I asked.

"Oh, you know why," he said. And gave me a little grin, as he bit into his burger. "The gym I go to doesn't allow women."

I rolled my eyes at him. "I'm a big girl, Ben. I can look after myself. I don't know what you told Officer Wolfe you'd do—"

"Just make sure you don't get your damn fool ass killed."

"But really, I'm big enough to take care of myself."

"You keep saying that. I don't think you know what those words mean."

I would have made an appropriate response. At least, I was sure I would think of one soon enough, but my mouth was full of cheese-burger-bacon-buttery-mushroom goodness, and as I chewed, Officer Cas Wolfe parked outside and came in.

He looked like a storm gathering—like the sort of afternoon when the clouds are coming in and every radio is hissing warnings and saying that a tornado has been sighted somewhere. As he swung the door open and then shut it behind him, in a tinkle of crashing bells, I expected some background music to stop and the customers in the joint to duck, while the server behind the counter hastily stuck all bottles under the counter. Only, of course, by then Ben and I were the only ones there, sitting at one of the half-dozen tables. And there were no bottles behind the counter.

The worst thing is that as he stood there and glared at me, I could only think he looked good, really good. And hell, even if the music didn't stop, Ben did stop chewing, and his eyes went really large.

Officer Wolfe stepped up to our table, giving the impression of stalking, which took some doing, because all he had to go was three steps. He stood there glowering down at me, and if he thought I was going to stop eating just because he was there, he had another think coming. Hell, Ben could stop because he was eating his plain burger with no mustard or anything, while I was eating good stuff.

Officer Wolfe cleared his throat. "Ms. Dare," he said.

I swallowed the food in my mouth at a leisurely pace. Ben rolled his eyes and made a sound like a suppressed sigh.

After taking a sip of my milkshake, I looked up. "Oh, Officer Wolfe. I hadn't seen you. How may I help you?"

Ben's mouth was hanging open, which someone should tell him was truly unbecoming. Officer Wolfe spoke through clenched teeth, which, frankly, was also unbecoming, but fortunately he was not my responsibility to correct. "If you'd please let me have a word with you outside, Ms. Dare."

"I'd love to, Officer, but as you see I'm having lunch. I'd hate for my burger to get cold." Not the least of which because all the grease in it would congeal, and the effect would be much like taking bites of Crisco.

He should have sighed. If Cas Wolfe were human he would have sighed, or perhaps raised his eyebrows, or something. Clearly, though, he was a robot, because all he did was speak again, still through clenched teeth, "It won't take more than a minute."

I got up. I got up because his eyes were flashing like fiery ice, and frankly, if he was about to start a tornado like a storm god of some forgotten religion, I'd much rather he did it outside, where I'd have more room to duck. Besides, it wasn't fair to Ben to make him face a tornado the day after the fire in his loft.

Daintily, walking in the way Mom and Grandma insisted was *proper for a lady*, something I managed only in moments of stress (which was just as well; otherwise someone might claim that I'd violated truth in advertising), I left the diner. Behind me, Officer Wolfe stormed out in a clash of bells. In my mind, with no rhyme or reason, the words *Next time in fire* flashed.

I thought for a moment of walking all the way to the car, getting behind the wheel, and driving away. But it was Ben's car and the damn man had kept the keys, presumably in his pocket. It was as if he didn't trust me with them.

So instead I walked far enough away from Cy's that the tornado wouldn't take out all the windows in the place, and I looked up at Cas Wolfe with my best good-little-girl expression, which I'd had lots of practice with on various occasions in various principals' offices. Being a woman does have its advantages. If you look innocent and well behaved, there is something—some predisposition—in the brain of males that makes them believe it. They tend to believe it even if you're covered in the blood of your enemies and the knuckles of both your hands are torn from punching out those who richly deserve it. It can't be that men are truly that stupid, or that they don't realize that women can be just as aggressive as men and that women—as a rule—are far less law abiding. Oh, sure, I know, and you know, we've all heard the line sold by various women's organizations, that women are nurturing and naturally peaceful and that without men there would be no war. This is fine and dandy, unless you open a history book. A real history book, not the type that spells *women* with a *Y*. Go ahead, I dare you. Give any woman a position of power and she'll outdo most men in aggressiveness and bloodthirst. Not that this is bad, mind you. I heartily admired quite a few bloody-minded women.

And yet men will go to their graves believing us innocent, soft little creatures who may stray by error but never on purpose. Because men are not—with exceptions—total dolts, one had to assume that it was something in the way the species was designed. It must be evolutionarily good for men to believe that women are sweet, inoffensive, and occasionally, through no fault of their own, capable of going astray.

"What can I do for you, Officer?" I asked, in my best, highest voice—which is not particularly high, because I have a low voice for a woman. What my mom calls a lovely contralto, but causes people on the phone to call me *sir*.

Well, it was a great theory, but Officer Wolfe must have been an evolutionary throwback, stuck in some pathway before men started thinking that all women were sweet and fragile flowers. He glared at me. Actually glared. And then he said, still speaking through his teeth, "To begin with, you can drop the innocent act, Dyce."

If it weren't for the fact that he'd shocked me by calling me *Dyce*, I would probably have pointed out that if he'd accidentally superglued his teeth together, turpentine would dissolve it. But instead, I was so taken aback that I just stammered, "What?"

I wondered if he'd found out about the table, and pretty much decided I would punch him out to keep it. Or perhaps offer to go to dinner with him again. He did have very nice lips, and he danced divinely.

All of which kept me from killing him as he said, "Of all the stupid, idiotic, unthinking . . . females!"

He'd unclenched his teeth. That was the good news. The bad news was that he pronounced *females* as if we were part of some foreign species that he could not have any interest in. Which made me wonder again exactly why Ben was being deputy dog, and it made me fling back, with more heat than I intended, "I thought you liked females."

"Wrong, Dyce. I like *women*. That presupposes there is some sort of brain behind the pretty little face, and the pretty little body and the beautiful curly hair."

Beautiful curly hair? Pretty face? Really? I crossed my arms on my chest. Or rather, just under my chest, pushing it up. Where is it written that I have to fight fair? Never seen it, never read it, don't have to follow it. "And what exactly leads you to believe there isn't a brain?"

"Because if there were a brain, you would realize you are not playing a game with schoolkids. You're a grown-up now. I don't care how much trouble you were as a kid—I've heard stories in this investigation, yeah—but you are a grown-up and responsible woman, for heaven's sake. You are a . . . a mother!"

"Yes, people often call me that."

His gaze smoldered in my general direction. "I just bet they do," he said. "Stay out of this investigation, do you understand? Stay out of it. You don't know how dangerous this murderer is. You don't know how bad it could get." He stopped in the middle of the words, and he did something like hiccup. "It could be you out there in that shed, Dyce, damn it. It could be you looking like Jell-O and . . ."

"And I fail to see where it would be any of your business. I told Ben I'm a grown woman. It makes some sense for him to forget that because he knew me when I was very young. It makes no sense at all for you. So please stop treating me as though I were very young or very stupid. You have no right."

"Oh, I have every right," he said. If his eyes could actually shoot rays, the look he gave me could have cut diamonds. "And as for your not being that young, good. Because I keep thinking I would love to take you over my knee."

I chose to ignore that. I'd left a man because he had slapped me, but the thought of Officer Wolfe taking me over his—admittedly shapely—knee didn't evoke feelings of anger and fighting. It evoked quite different feelings, which I pushed to the back of my mind as I asked, "What right? Who has given you the right to look after me?"

He didn't answer. He glared at me, and I thought either he was going to grab me and turn me over his knee right there, in front of the entire diner—which admittedly at that moment was the two employees and Ben, but still way too many people—or he was going to turn and stalk away.

He did neither.

Suddenly there were hands around my waist. Two hands. One on either side. Large hands, strong. They lifted me effortlessly and so abruptly that I didn't even think of kicking him in the crotch—and normally that was sort of my reflex thought. Instead, I allowed him to take the three steps that separated him from the door of a red SUV.

It wouldn't, at that point, have surprised me if he'd opened the door, flung me inside, and driven off with me to the equivalent of a caveman's abode, where he would keep me tending the fire and having the babies while he hunted mammoth. By then I was so confused, I might have let him.

But he just put me down with my back to the SUV. With his hands on my waist, I was thoroughly trapped, and then he bent down and . . . kissed me. Said like that, it seems like all too simple a thing. It was anything but simple. His mouth captured mine. His tongue broached my lips like a victorious army breaking through a city's wall. His teeth scraped against mine as he pressed closer, demanded more, as though he could by the simple act of kissing me blend with me, become one with me.

I fought back. Me, I'm never one to stay passive in the face of naked aggression. Or even clothed aggression. I kissed back as hard as I was being kissed, my tongue fighting its way into his mouth, my hands clenching as hard on his shoulders as his were clenching on my waist.

I don't know how long it lasted. I know my head grew dizzy and my knees became lax, but it was probably due to the impossibility of breathing freely like this. At last the choice of ending the kiss or dying

146

presented itself, and I considered dying, because it was much easier, but he must have had more self-preservation instinct than I—mammoth hunters had to, after all—because he broke off.

I stared up at him, slowly closed my mouth, and swallowed to regain composure. The word came to my mouth and I said it, sounding much like my mother when she saw something impressive. "Well!" I said. Of course, I meant *Wow*, but I'd be damned if I was going to let him know that.

He wiped his mouth with the back of his hand, as if his lips were wet, or as if he had to wipe away the kiss, as if I had forced it on him, which I bloody well hadn't. He swallowed, too, and it was the same sort of swallowing you do to reassure yourself that your body is still yours and that there is nothing strange about you, not a single solitary thing.

"You," he said, as if he'd thought deeply on this subject, "are the world's most infuriating woman."

"Unlikely," I said. "And besides, how would you know? It's not like you know every other woman in the world. There might be some girl in the next block who is considerably more infuriating than I am, and you just never met her."

He looked like he was going to either argue the point or kiss me again, but he shook his head. "You're going to drive me insane. I bet this is what all these crimes are about. You drove some poor sap insane, and he's out there dipping people into lye and not waiting till they melt down, oh, no, just throwing them somewhere you'll run into them. It's probably a cry for help."

There was no way to dignify that with an answer, and I didn't try. He stepped back. "Look, I don't want you to get killed. It's very important to me that you don't get killed. I have the hardest time finding a girl who is presentable and can swing dance with me. Okay?"

"Okay," I said. Of course I had no intention of getting killed, but if he didn't realize that by ordering me to stay out of the investigation, he had just ensured that I would in fact investigate as much as I could, then the man had about Ben's level of knowledge of women. No, lower. Ben would know exactly what I planned. Which, of course, was going to be an issue, as he might very well have some idea what had happened out here.

As if to reinforce this concern, Cas said (after that kiss, I felt like I could think of him as Cas), "Don't give Colm too much trouble, okay? I've asked him to keep you from getting killed, and he's trying to."

"Oh, he's trying all right," I said. Of course, I would have to find a way to get rid of Ben for a few minutes or hours. But I had no intention of letting Cas—or Ben—know that. Instead I nodded. "Look, I will not get killed, and I think you're blowing the whole thing out of proportion. Maybe, yeah, maybe—perhaps—they put the body in the shed because I called. Or perhaps, it was something else completely different. Remember that Janet said that Nell Gwen had put in a restraining order against Inobart? But you said you couldn't find it? Well, perhaps it was someone else stalking her. Perhaps this person is obsessed with women in the refinishing business. Perhaps that's why he put Inobart in my shed."

He looked worried. "You realize you're not setting my mind at rest about your safety?"

"Well . . . perhaps not," I said. Setting people's minds at rest didn't seem to be one of my specialties. Just look what I'd done to Mom. "But chances are my phone call didn't ruin anything."

"It also didn't solve anything," Cas said. "I'll go talk to people at that workshop today, and we're looking through the victim's house." He must have guessed how badly I wanted to ask him to come along, because he sighed and said, "If I tell you anything I find, will you promise me not to try to investigate on your own? Can I trust you if I tell you stuff?"

I nodded.

"Well, good, then. I'll take you out . . . tomorrow?"

"I have E tomorrow," I said.

A sane man would have grimaced, but we'd already established that Cas Wolfe was not a sane man. He smiled. "Okay, then. We can't dance, or at least not swing dance, but we can go somewhere they'll be okay with him. The High Times, maybe."

The High Times was not—as it sounded—a head shop, but a steakhouse specializing in western fare. It was also a place of choice for families. Although it did have a dancing area—and a country band that played boot-stomping, partner-swinging favorites—it was as likely to be occupied by toddlers as by adults. And the other attractions of the place—a gigantic swing mounted from the roof beams, able to hold ten or twelve people at once; a mechanical bull set on very low indeed, so that it was almost just a rocking bull; and a two-story-tall slide—made it a favorite of kids of all ages.

I would have said no. I swear I would have. I was strong enough to. Yes, I was. But the thing is that E wouldn't have to have pancakes for dinner. And besides, he'd never been to the High Times, and it seemed like just the sort of place he would love. It would be unfair to deny him the fun.

So I said, "All right," and I meant it, at least as far as he could trust me with anything he told me, and I went back inside in a subdued mood.

Ben was standing by the counter. He came back to the table and set my half-eaten burger in front of me. "I got them to nuke it warmer," he said. "Otherwise, just looking at it would clog your arteries."

I thanked him, hoping he wouldn't say anything about Cas Wolfe, which was sort of like praying that this time the sea wouldn't be salty or the water wouldn't be wet.

He cleared his throat. "Of course, you know, the heat coming from that kiss should have warmed it enough, but . . ."

I didn't say anything, just took a bite of my burger and chewed. He looked terribly amused. But as I finished the burger and drank my considerably melted milkshake, he grew serious. "If you don't mind," he said, "I'd like to swing by the symphony and see if I can talk to Les."

Oh, there were things I would mind less. Like, say, putting my head in a lit oven. "What?"

"I know, I know," Ben said, proving that he clearly didn't. "But I do need to talk to him. We've had this huge misunderstanding. Just completely blown out of proportion. I need to talk to him."

"Oh, fine," I said. "But what would he be doing at the symphony on a Monday afternoon?"

"There's a classics for schoolchildren program," he said. "It runs till just about three, so if we go now, we can talk to him as he gets out. Come on. I promise not to embarrass you."

There was a promise he couldn't keep. He was already embarrassing me. But because I needed time to think how to give him the slip, this might do as well as anything else.

BROKEN LINKS

THE SYMPHONY IN GOLDPORT is housed in a fine turn-of-the-century building at the very edge of town. To understand why it's at the edge of town, one needs to know how and when Goldport was built, or at least how it became a town worthy of the name.

There were legends of Native American camps in this region, and in fact our town hall was decorated with the usual nineteenth-century paintings of noble savage communing with civilizing newcomer. Muskets and feathers and the occasional turkey.

It might all be true, but I suspected not. I suspected yeah, some native hunters might have camped here on the way across the mountains, but I very much doubted that any particular significance had been attached to the area, much less that it was considered sacred ground. And I would bet good money that the wild turkey had never roamed the Goldport area in multitudes. At least if one were to believe that the largest tree in the region when colonizers arrived was scrub oak.

At any rate, after the turkey-native-colonizer time, Goldport had been a little struggling settlement of half-a-dozen cabins belonging to one family—the Goldport family. And then the gold rush had hit.

People had hastened to settle in Goldport. Newly made millionaires commissioned gingerbreaded mansions to rival anything in the East. The—mostly immigrant—workforce imported to put up the buildings and be servants and such had settled in smaller workingman Victorians.

At the height of the gold rush, there had been illusions that Goldport in its full glory would eclipse Denver. Because of this, and because it was expected that the city would continue growing toward the West, one of the gold rush nouveaux riches had built . . . well, I supposed an opera house, though to my knowledge, at least after the end of the nineteenth century, no opera had been performed there.

The failure of the gold mines that supported Goldport had put an abrupt end to the city's expansion. The city had been prevented from turning into a ghost town only because the Tasty Treats pet food plant had moved in, giving employment to all the blue-collar workers. And then in the early twentieth century the University of Colorado at Goldport had opened up. Since then Goldport, with its skilled workforce, had become something of a tech center, a miniature—very miniature—Silicon Valley.

However, the development, when it had come, had gone to the north and east, extending in suburbs and neat subdivisions.

The symphony remained stranded on the edge of town, a huge building that looked like someone had taken a tour of Europe and brought back a blurred memory of what impressed him most. To begin with, the building was set in the middle of a wide lawn, which in the Colorado climate was brown ninety percent of the time and overgrown with weeds the rest of it.

Approach was made through a narrow path in the middle, which was in turn flanked by several statues of tritons and water nymphs, which, judging by the bone-dry pools around them, were meant to be fountains of some sort. Of course there was no water. I imagined the statues looked a little startled, as if they were thinking, *Wait a minute there, where did the ocean go? It was here just a minute ago.*

Up from that was a huge staircase with towering columns supporting a portico that was entirely too small for the number and the size of the columns. Mind you, it all looked very impressive at night, with the front doors open and light spilling out. And during the holiday season when the entire thing—statues and all—was festooned in lights and the struggling nonlawn mercifully covered in snow, it could be downright romantic.

In the few months between Ben returning to Goldport and taking up with Les, I'd come to the symphony with him often. Ben had a season ticket and his local contacts were still shaky, or perhaps he thought I needed some time out or some fun, because that was right after my divorce. And at night, one could really get caught up in the atmosphere. During the day, it wasn't nearly as impressive.

The fact that instead of climbing the stairs we took the little path to the side to go in through a side entrance made it even less impressive. Of course, the side also had statues of bare-breasted females, supporting vases above their heads that I suppose were meant to have profuse greenery growing out of them. The city had really made an effort there—at least for the level of effort that Goldport normally put into public beautification—and when the real plants had failed, they'd stuck in sprigs of what looked like artificial ivy. Which was a really good idea, except that no one dusted them and—Goldport being the dustiest city ever, because of all the drought—by now they looked as brown as the lawn, so that the poor nymphs seemed to be lamenting the state of vegetation in the area and hefting their vases to show the level to which the horror had climbed. Of course, their male counterparts on the other side of the building just looked angry with the situation, like *Come on, guys, let's dump these plants and go get a beer.*

The door to which Ben walked was small and set unobtrusively between two distressed nymphs. It, too, was distressed in the sense that the paint was all blistered and flaking. For once not a sign of neglect. Having grown up in Goldport, I knew that Mom and Dad had to paint their house every couple of years because the sun was so strong up here, and only made stronger by reflecting off snow.

On the other hand, once Ben opened the door—and yes, it was unlocked—the interior was exactly what I remembered from my symphony nights, only smaller. The front door led to a great domed entrance, much like the Orthodox churches the architect must have seen on his grand tour of Europe. The back door led to a corridor with a ceiling like the interior half of a cylinder, curving smoothly around.

Both were gilded, and both painted with the sort of frescoes that wouldn't be found near an Orthodox church much less in it. I remembered spending time in the front entrance during intermission, staring up at a scene of debauched orgy that involved not only fauns, nymphs, and every Roman god, but also cute little cherubs and the occasional African animal, none of them in the combinations you'd expect. And meanwhile, all the well-dressed people swirling around me never looked up. It wasn't so much like they didn't know what was up there. They did. But they were ignoring it as hard as they could.

Entering through the side, I looked up and found that the orgy was going on there, too. "Ben, is that elephant . . . ?"

He didn't even look up, but nodded and said, "Probably," as he headed down the hall like a man on a mission. He turned to another hallway on the left and stopped. In front of a door was a man wearing the most flashy uniform I'd seen in a long time. Oh, he was clearly supposed to be private security of some sort, but he wore silvery-blue pants with silver piping and a jacket whose cut and fit wouldn't be out of place in the armies of Prussia. On the jacket was a huge, glittering badge. The man was almost as wide as he was tall, which meant he wouldn't pass the fitness requirements for any security force, and he wasn't wearing a gun, so I assumed that no one had decided to arrest the symphony performers. Which wouldn't be deserved, because most of the time they were pretty good, Les notwithstanding. Now, if he were to arrest the architect who'd designed the building, that would be justified, but of course the coward had probably died long ago.

Ben stopped short and looked at the man.

"May I help you, sir?" the man asked.

"Yes." Ben drew himself up and managed to look as if he were wearing a uniform at least as shiny and official as the guard's. "I would like to go in. I must speak to a friend of mine."

"And your friend's name is . . . ," the guard said, looking suspicious. Because people normally don't look suspicious of Ben, and because frankly the chance of anyone lying to get in and see one of our local performers was about like the chance of someone trying to steal all your Monopoly money, I started to get an awful sense of how this was going to go.

If Ben also did, he didn't show it, but then Ben at the best of times showed very little to any official person. "Les Howard, please?"

The guard stood straighter, which meant his height gained maybe two inches over his width. "You wouldn't be Mr. Ben Colm?" he asked.

Yup. I'd guessed right.

"Yes, my name is Benedict Colm, but . . ."

"Mr. Howard said you were stalking him and that under no circumstances was I to allow you in."

I must have snorted at the idea of Ben stalking anyone, because the security guard looked at me, and while I was trying to put on my most innocent expression, I missed Ben's look. I don't know if he was angry or appalled. All I know is that when he spoke again, he was perfectly calm, "I see. Would you please see if Mr. Peter Milano is in there and if I may speak with him?"

The guard looked dubious, as though Ben might be some sort of all-purpose stalker, out to harass every performer, but at length he went inside and closed the door carefully behind him. I heard talking, then footsteps approaching the door, then more talking, then what sounded like a muffled laugh. I assumed that Peter Milano—whoever the hell he was—had been called to the door and also that either he found Ben's predicament funny or the guard did.

Then the door opened and I expected to see the guard come out. Instead . . .

Well, my first thought was that Ben could do worse than stalk Peter Milano. And if he wasn't, I'd like an explanation of why not. Okay, Milano wasn't as cute as Cas Wolfe, but that was a matter of personal preference. I prefer my men not to look like they'd left one of the frescoes on the ceiling and somehow exchanged a toga for a tux. Though he seemed to be at least forty—judging from the eyes and the touch of white at the temples—he looked both decorative enough to have been a Greek god in a past life, and also just the slightest bit decadent, as if he'd spent the last hundred years watching the world's most unlikely orgy. It was all there—the slightly overlong curly hair, the Greco-Roman nose, the intense gaze, and the amused smile twisting his sensuous-looking lips.

The look he gave Ben managed to combine both pity and amusement. He shook his head, even as the security guard came out and resumed his place at the door. Without speaking, Milano gestured with his head to indicate, I suppose, that they should move a little away from the guard. Because neither of them was paying any attention to me, I slid along with them.

"Ben, Ben, Ben . . . what is it now?" Milano asked. "What have you done to the unstable one, my darling?" The voice had just the faintest bit of a British accent, which made the *my darling* feel perfectly natural. He was also, I realized, more than likely one of what Ben generally called *my people*. Meaning his, not mine. At least I couldn't imagine any straight male looking at Ben and calling him *darling*, particularly not with that intonation that implied he was a young and sweet thing.

"It's Les," Ben said, as if he hadn't understood who the *unstable one* might be. Or more likely pretending not to understand. "There's been a terrible misunderstanding and I must talk to him."

Milano's eyebrows rose. "A misunderstanding?"

"Yeah . . . he did something stupid with . . . with the stove fan." Yeah, that's what Les had done something stupid with. "And he's probably afraid I'm mad at him over it. Would you tell him I'm not?"

Pity won out over amusement in Milano's eyes. He sighed. "Ben, he's not afraid of anything. He's furious at you. He says you're playing around on him. He did this whole drama for everyone in the symphony, complete with much in the way of tears."

"Playing around?" Ben said. "Would this be at poker or bridge?"

Milano shrugged. He leaned against the wall in a pose that was both boneless and gracefully calculated. "Look, I'm not going to give you my opinion of this relationship, right? And I'm not going to say anything about Les, because, you know, we have a deal and all." Just how many people did Ben have a deal with? "But my advice to you would be to let the unstable one have room to cool off and think about things. You know what he's like when he gets in these moods."

Ben opened his mouth as if to protest, then snapped it shut. "Yeah. Artistic temperament."

Milano looked up and the amusement was back, playing across the dark eyes. "Right," he said. "That's what it is." He shrugged. "Let's just say that we did *Peter and the Wolf* for the kiddies and Les did the most unstable, shaky, watery wolf to ever run the prairie, right? Not a good time to talk to him. Not unless you relish the idea of being screamed at in front of the entire Goldport Symphony."

Ben wouldn't relish the idea of being screamed at in front of a group of his closest and dearest friends. In fact, his reaction to being screamed at was normally to wheel about and leave. Which, unless I was much mistaken, had caused this whole problem with Les to begin with. Les looked like the type who would like to set up a good screaming match now and then.

"Uh . . . but I have to talk to him," Ben said. "He's blowing all this out of proportion. And I have no idea where he came up with the idea that I was . . . that there is anyone else."

Milano muttered something out of which the words *chrome* and *pipe* emerged, but I wasn't about to even imagine what it might mean.

"That's not . . . ," Ben said, as he turned a shade of red slightly lighter than his hair.

Milano raised an eyebrow. "Fine, but look, it really won't do you any good to talk to him now. How about you wait a couple of days, let him cool down, and then maybe he'll listen when he's talked to? Maybe."

Ben sighed. He rubbed his forehead. "Yeah. Okay," he said. And we turned to go. I noted he hadn't so much as introduced me to his friend, which I would have been upset about, only of course, Ben was thinking about Les. As for me, I was thinking of the whole conversation.

It was clear that Peter Milano was Ben's friend, even if Ben had never mentioned him to me. Not that it was a big deal. Ben didn't exactly give me a detailed account of his entire life. But all the same, it felt a little strange. So, as we were halfway down the hallway, I said, "Peter Milano is one of your people, right?"

"Yeah," Ben said, without looking at me.

"Old flame?"

"What? Not . . . no."

Okay. If Ben was going to be outraged at the idea, then he definitely needed mental help. I mean, he had eyes, and just comparing Les with . . . An idea occurred to me. "He has someone?"

"Who?"

"Milano?"

"Why do you care?" Ben said looking at me, and frowning as if he suspected I was going to start chasing the man. I was about to tell him that yes, of course, he was much preferable to the UPS guy.

"Just curious."

Normally this would have brought a snippy reply from Ben or perhaps a question about what exactly my curiosity entailed, but now he shrugged and continued walking. Until we were almost at the back door, and then he stopped. "Wait here," he said. "I forgot to tell Peter something to tell Les."

"Uh. He said Les wasn't disposed to listen—"

I was talking to Ben's back as he wheeled around, saying, "Yeah, but this might make all the difference!"

I stood in the middle of the hallway, imagining what would make all the difference in *that* relationship at this point. I thought the only thing would be *Honey, I won over fifty million in the lottery*, but I was probably doing Les an injustice.

I heard the rumble of Ben's voice from the side hallway and the tones of the security guard answering him. It went on for a while. I looked at the ceiling. Yes, the elephant was doing exactly what I thought he was. And with a cherub, no less. Though I had no idea what the faun a little to the side was up to. I suspected I didn't want to know. The nymph to the right of them didn't want to know, either. She was fainting. Although that might be caused by what the creature with the bottom half of an emu—

While my eyes, and most of my mind, were absorbed in this sort of artistic contemplation, the rest of my mind seemed to have been thinking furiously. I say *seemed* because I was not conscious of any of this until—with sudden force—the idea presented itself to my mind that I was very close to Michael Manson's—aka Charity Jewel's—workshop. And that Ben was otherwise occupied.

I looked down at my feet. I was wearing sneakers. If I ran, and took alleyways, Ben would never see me go. And he probably wouldn't have any idea where I had gone. And I could ask Mike about Rocky's ex-wife and poor Inobart and all. Mike might not know much about it, but Charity Jewel was, after all, a gossip, and they happened to share a head.

Walking carefully, mindful of the conversation still coming from the side hallway, I opened the door, closed it very slowly, and slipped onto the walkway amid the parched lawn.

Right. I'd assume I had five minutes and get the heck out of here.

Devil with a Blue Dress On

I RAN DOWN ONE alley, up another, and across yet another, up to the squat old brick warehouse where Michael Manson had his workshop. He had taken over what had probably been an abandoned building.

The front of it had the sort of slide-down metal doors such buildings usually have, but all the times I'd been there, it had been wide open—even when the snow was blowing outside.

Now on this mild spring day, not only was it open, but my first feeling was that the workshop was full of people, from the sound of wood being scraped, nailed, and sawn, and the smell of wood and various varnishes.

Manson's work had one distinguishing characteristic—though he might refinish the occasional piece, what he mostly did was build reproductions by period techniques so that, except for the age of the wood, his work was indistinguishable from the real thing. Rumor had it—though I'd never asked—that he held a doctorate in history and had used his knowledge to develop his methods of working with wood.

He had once told me in a casual meeting that he'd lived for a time in a school bus in the mountains of West Virginia. He admitted to being functionally unsuited for business life as such—for going to an office or even working full time in a workshop. But this business he could manage, partly because it was creative and partly because it was very well paid. He personally built two to four pieces a year, and that was enough to get him money to live on. The rest of his business came from selling pieces built by his interns, who, for the greater part, came from history courses at the nearby university.

Now, as my vision and senses resolved, I realized that there were five people in the workshop, all young, two men and three women. The women wore their hair pulled back in scarves, as I did when I was working around heavy solvents or with wood that might snag it. They wore very bright coveralls, which gave them the look of children in a playhouse.

The nearest young man, wearing a red coverall, was applying a coat of something that looked homemade (from the fact that it was in a glass jar and had a deep amber color like none I'd ever seen from commercial products) on a boxlike piece that might have been a bedside table.

He had a light turned on across from him and was looking across the piece, probably to check for dry spots. Without looking away from his work, he said, "May I help you?"

"I would like to see—" I started.

"Dyce!"

I looked up. Miss Charity Jewel was standing a few feet away. To understand the glory that was Miss Charity Jewel, you first had to understand that Charlie Michael Manson was an ex-Marine who towered to six foot five in his stocking feet and who had one of those naturally craggy faces that looked carved out of granite with a blunt chisel. He wasn't so much ugly as incredibly masculine, from his heavy brow, to his aquiline nose, to the square chin that sported a permanent five o'clock shadow. He had long, wavy black hair, which he wore tied back.

Miss Charity Jewel, however, wore *her* hair loose down her back, which would have been fine if Michael had ever heard of hair care products or clipping one's split ends. I'm sure that he used curlers for his female persona, but his hair remained scraggly and ratty, rather like the tresses of a hippie leftover.

As for Miss Jewel's makeup, let's just say that if Michael was wearing the style of makeup he'd seen on his mom or his ex-wife, neither of them were good women.

She had blue-green eye shadow caked on her eyelids. Her use of foundation and blush and mascara made televangelists' wives look discreetly made up and almost clean-faced. And none of the powder and paint managed to disguise the distinctly masculine features or completely erase the five o'clock shadow. Despite all this, Michael was so convinced that he passed as female that no one was willing to disabuse him.

Miss Jewel was grinning at me, her painted lips curled in definitive welcome, showing overlarge and nicotine-stained teeth. She extended both callused hands to me. There was a large silver ring on her thumb. "Darling," she said, making me think of Peter Milano greeting Ben, only in this case there was a good deal more camp in the mix.

"Hi," I said.

"How nice of you to pay me a visit," Miss Jewel said.

"Oh, yes, I was in the neighborhood."

Her unfeminine features sharpened. "Have you heard about Inobart?"

I wondered if I'd be violating police confidence by telling her that Inobart had been found dead in my workshop, then decided that I was doing enough to show Ben and Cas Wolfe that they couldn't control me. I didn't need to potentially drive them both nuts by babbling about possibly secret police stuff. "Uh . . . I saw him in Denver yesterday," I said.

"How is he looking?"

I bit my tongue on *gelatinous*, but I shouldn't have bothered. Miss Jewel went on, rapidly, "You see, the last time I saw him, he was so sadly low on his meds. Oh, my dear, he was practically raving out of his mind. He was talking about how he was having an affair with Nell. You know Nell, of course? Nell Gwen?"

I wanted to give him a prize for mentioning two people recently turned to Jell-O within five minutes of my coming in. Of course, that in itself might be suspicious. "I'm not sure. I think I met her, once or twice."

"Well . . . she had a big fight with Rocky, you know, about six months ago. Over his workshop, you know. Oh, would you like to see the new wardrobe I'm making? An order from one of the house-staging firms for the Parade of Homes."

I nodded. Miss Jewel led the way, wearing stilettos and fishnet stockings, I noted. Her heels were at least five inches high and probably six. It was a miracle that she could actually walk in those. I'd tried once, in Mom's high heels and . . . it had not ended well. After they removed the cast from my leg, I'd vowed never to go near anything that tall again, unless it was for a circus act and someone was paying me big money.

We walked across the workshop, with Manson unerringly avoiding stepping on fallen pieces of wood or tools left on the floor. He put a hand out to restrain me as I was about to accidentally kick a jar full of yellowish fluid. "Joan, dear," he called in an unconvincing falsetto, "are you actually leaving this lacquer around to dry, or is that just a fun side effect?"

As the girl in pink coveralls and a blue head scarf came running, red-faced, to retrieve the jar, he said, "Always, always, always cap your jars, children." He walked away with the most unconvincing hip swing I'd ever seen. I suppose I should say *she*, because Michael was very much convinced that no one could tell that he wasn't female when he was in drag. But the truth was that he was just so strongly male—and fairly clueless male—even in female attire, that it became impossible to maintain any kind of belief in Charity Jewel for long.

He led me around several planks stacked against a workbench to look at a huge, carved cupboard, the kind that I believe the Germans call a *Schrank*. It looked like a massive wardrobe, but had carvings and fretting all over the top and on the doors, too. "What do you think?" he asked, then, seemingly in the same breath, "Would you like some coffee?"

"I wouldn't want to give trouble," I said.

"Oh, no trouble," he said, and called across the workshop, "Jason!" A green-coveralled figure popped up like a jack-in-the-box. "Get me a coffee and one for my friend Dyce." He'd completely forgotten his Charity Jewel voice, and the bellowing was very much Mike. "How do you take your coffee, Dyce?"

"Two sugars," I said. "And about three tablespoons of cream."

The green overalls scurried across the workshop to a door at the back, and I thought it must be good to have lackeys. Which, of course, I did not tell Mike. Instead, I said, "You have a lot of interns."

"Well . . . ," he said, as if this were a difficult thing to explain and he had to warm up to it and think about it for a while. "I have more orders than I can fulfill, and I figure I can get the interns to help me build more and then, you know, after that, they can set up their own businesses."

"You're not afraid they'll saturate the area with accurate antique reproductions?"

He gave me one of those *You're cute when you're dense* looks that males sometimes give females. It was very annoying when given to any female by any male, but it was absolutely infuriating when given to me by a man wearing a blue minidress, fishnet stockings, and stiletto heels. I repressed an urge to glare at him and was saved by the bell, or rather by the coffee fetcher arriving, out of breath, carrying two foam cups. He handed them to us, and when I'd taken a sip of the coffee, I recovered my composure.

"Nah," Mike said, finally answering my question. "You see, it's like this—each of these pieces, this one, for instance, sells for around sixty thousand dollars. So you see, the thing is, there never was a market in Goldport for it. The clients come from all over the country and sometimes even from Europe. There are few of them, but not that few, and I couldn't keep up with their demand if I worked twenty-four hours a day, seven days a week, which I have no intention of doing. So ... my interns are welcome to set up shops themselves ..."

I looked at the cupboard again. I could not doubt it took a lot of work to do with the hand tools I'd seen strewn about the place. But still ... sixty thousand dollars was a lot of pancakes. "How ... how long does it take you to do it ..."

"About two, three months," he said. And gave me a look. Now, despite his sartorial ways, I'd been assured—more than once—that Mike was strictly hetero. In fact, Ben had reassured me of this when he met him. However, there is nothing—nothing—in the world quite as creepy as being given the *Come on, baby, I'd be good for you* by a tall, decidedly masculine man wearing women's clothes.

I said the first thing that crossed my mind, entirely off topic. "What do you think of lye vats?"

He gave me a sly look out of his heavily mascaraed eyes. "Uh ... they're ... vats. And they're full of lye." He seemed to realize what had made me uncomfortable, and I think it amused him.

"Oh," I said. "Some people think it's unethical to use lye on furniture. That it ... burns the fibers and ..."

"Kills the spirit of the tree?" he asked indulgently. "Oh, come on, only Inobart believes that stuff. And if I were you I'd be careful about listening to him too attentively, because he will then think you have a crush on him. He's plagued Nell something awful and has managed to convince himself that it's *Rocky* who is plaguing her."

"And he isn't?"

Mike gave a little laugh that tried to be Miss Jewel, but fell ever so slightly short of the mark, so that instead of sounding high-pitched and ladylike, it sounded like the cackle of the mad villain in the scene where he laughs about taking control of the world. "Dear! There was never any doubt that Nell and Rocky belong together. I mean, if you see them ..."

Of course the problem was that I couldn't remember seeing them together, but I wasn't about to admit to that. Instead I said, "So, they're reconciling."

"Oh, yes, foregone conclusion."

"But I'd heard that the problem was that Rocky ... didn't give her enough responsibility at the workshop?"

"Well...," Mike said. "I suppose that his employees will have to learn to take orders from a woman. Yeah, I know that young men can be very temperamental, but my interns do fairly well taking orders from me."

161

I looked right up at his heavily made-up chin, through which the five o'clock shadow still showed. "Some young men are more tolerant than others."

He nodded enthusiastically and sipped his coffee. "So, what do you say?" he asked. "You can intern for six months, learn to do this . . ."

"I can't," I said, before thinking of a reason. The fact was that anticipating more tête-à-têtes with Mike in his Miss Jewel persona was more than heart and mind could stand. But as he looked back at me, I realized I needed a reason, and it couldn't be, *It's not that you're a transvestite. I mean, I could live with that. It's that you are such an unconvincing transvestite and you hit on me while in unconvincing drag. That's what makes it impossible. I'd either burst out laughing or hit you with a manual planer or a period crowbar or something.* I couldn't say that and I didn't know what to say, but fortunately my subconscious must have been working very fast and for once to a purpose. "I have E," I said. "My son."

Mike looked startled. "Oh, I thought . . ."

"You thought?"

"I thought your ex-husband had gotten full custody?"

I almost spit out the last mouthful of coffee. Instead I swallowed hastily and said, "Why would you think that?"

He looked genuinely confused. "Don't know. Heard it somewhere. Something about some incidents at your house, and your ex having asked for and gotten full custody. And I mean, you're here without the kid . . ."

"Yeah. No. It's his three days with his father, this week." My mind was spinning fast. What did he mean, he'd "heard"? I didn't think that Mike ran in the same circles as All-ex, but then . . .

But then All-ex's Michelle worked at the university. And the interns were mostly university students. That could be where the rumor had come from, couldn't it?

Where and how would it have originated? Could it be that All-ex was actually behind the murders, as part of a plan to persuade the court to give him full custody of E?

I don't remember what I said or what I told Mike, but I found myself walking outside the workshop.

I was half-aware that by now Ben was very likely to have realized I was missing. I headed down the alley and toward the street, hoping he would find me. I wanted to go home, which was at the other end of Goldport. I took out my cell and hit Ben's number. Nothing. The battery was dead.

Out of the alley, roaring, came a nineteen fifties red Thunderbird convertible. I jumped and knit myself with the wall. The Thunderbird screeched to a halt about twenty feet from me and backed up slowly.

I found myself looking into Miss Charity Jewel's face. "Hi, Dyce. Wanna ride?"

"Uh . . ."

"I'll take you home. Get on in."

Various things flashed through my mind, including that this man, who thought he was a woman, who thought she was a man—no wonder Ben burst into Lolla every time I mentioned Michael Manson—might be a murderer. The next time anyone saw me, I might be a gelatinous mess on my workshop floor. On the other hand . . .

On the other hand, if Miss Charity Jewel had done it, she would have left something behind—mascara or a lipstick, or . . . something. No lipstick scrawled on the Dumpster's side, so it was not Miss Charity Jewel, I guessed.

"Uh . . . ," I said, thinking only that he might give me more detail on exactly where he'd heard rumors about All-ex and E. "Sure."

He reached over and opened the door for me, and I slid in onto the creamy white seat.

"Isn't she lovely?" he asked. "I got someone to restore her for me!"

"She's beautiful," I said, as he started the car up again and drove down the alley with an abandon that belied the pristine condition of the cherry-red fenders.

"Yeah, I *love* her," he said, falling completely out of his Miss Jewel voice. "Hey, you're still living on Quicksilver, aren't you?"

"Yeah . . ." I had no idea he knew where I lived, and for some reason it made me a little uncomfortable.

"Do you mind if I swing by Sixteenth Street on the way?" he said. "I have to drop by Rocky's, because he wanted to consult me about this dresser he got."

"Uh," I said. Well, if he was going to kill me and dismember me or immerse me in a lye vat, he wasn't going to bother explaining, was he?

On the other hand . . . now I knew for certain that Rocky's had a lye vat. I looked sideways at Michael Manson. I was sure if push came to shove I could push harder than him. He was wearing stilettos. How hard could it be to tip him over? All the same, it was with a cold feeling in my stomach that I said, "Yeah, that's all right."

LYE, LADY, LYE

I SOON REALIZED THAT—JUST as with his speech and his mode of walking—the car was being driven, alternately, by Miss Jewel and
Michael Manson. Or at least, as the voice deepened and became more
masculine, he would drive more carefully and actively avoid hitting the
walls on either side. On the other hand, when the voice went up and
it was Miss Jewel behind the wheel, the car careened down the roads
with a will and traffic signals were viewed as helpful suggestions, but
by no means hard-and-fast rules.

Closing my eyes as we crossed an intersection without even slowing
down for the red light, I wondered if Miss Jewel drove like that because
it was Mike's perception of how women drove, or if perhaps Miss Jewel
was the inner and freer version of Mike who simply couldn't be bogged
down with *could*s and *should*s.

I know quite well it was fruitless to think about it, but it was ever
so much more relaxing than worrying about what was happening out
there. I kept telling myself that the car was not dented or scraped or
anything, and therefore Mike and/or Miss Jewel couldn't be that bad
a driver. On the other hand, as much money as he made from his
workshop, perhaps he was, in fact, just getting the dents pulled and the
paint fixed whenever needed.

Not a comforting thought, and frankly I couldn't hear a word he was
saying as he careened this way and that, his voice and driving mode
changing pitch. I closed my eyes and thought about praying.

At long last, we stopped. After I made sure we hadn't stopped because Miss Jewel had gotten lost and Mike was trying to figure out
directions, I opened one eye. Yep. We were stationary and in front of a

big-as-life sign that read *Rocky Mountain Refinishing*. I opened the other eye.

I'd been by Rocky's lots of times. As a rule, in fact, I came by once a week on the day I knew they did their culling. But I drove in the back, through the alley, where the Dumpster was and where they left the various pieces of furniture they were discarding.

From the back, Rocky's was a forbidding brick building, with a ratty lawn and a cement walkway. The door was tiny and there were industrial-looking windows covered in grime very high up on the façade.

From the front, which I supposed I had driven past countless times without slowing down to notice, Rocky Mountain Refinishing looked like an office, with broad glass doors and a pleasant woman—just discernible through the glass—sitting at a desk.

As I followed Miss Jewel, who stepped through the glass doors with the unerring confidence of someone who comes up a full head taller than anyone around herself, I thought the place looked like the receiving area of a classy dry cleaner's, from the checkered white-and-black tile floor, to the desk and the woman with a computer and a stack of claim tickets, to the potted plastic plant sitting beside the desk.

She looked up with a practiced smile and started what must have been a practiced spiel, "Welcome to Rocky Mountain Refinishing," she said. "How may I . . . oh."

That it took her that long to recognize Miss Jewel or realize we weren't there on normal business was witness to either her lack of brain or her boredom. It seemed, though, that she knew Miss Jewel because she said, "Rocky is out back," and then looked at me, as if I were her last hope that this was a business transaction, which I had to counter by saying, "I'm with him . . . er . . . her . . . er . . ."

The receptionist nodded, looking appropriately sympathetic, and gestured us to a door behind the plastic plant. Miss Jewel didn't notice, as she was already headed that way, clopping along in a way that should have been impossible for someone in those high heels. I thought that the world had lost a great stilts dancer when Mike had decided to be a TV instead.

He was still present enough in Miss Jewel, though, and held old-fashioned-enough principles that he held the door till I was through it, admitting me to . . . a place like none I'd seen before.

I'd been wondering if Rocky's actual refinishing work took place elsewhere altogether or if perhaps there was a workshop at another location and this was just the offices. Because from what I could see of the lay of the land, the only possible windows providing ventilation to a refinishing room at the back of the building would have to be on the side. I had no idea if there were windows on the side, because I'd never walked the narrow space between Rocky's and the two buildings on either side.

Now my question was answered. Yes, there were windows, large windows, fairly high up—probably to avoid break-ins and people trying to huff the chemicals. They were open, and there were fans above, circulating the air. But more than that, there was something I'd never seen before. It was as if the ventilating hood above my stove had a family and this were its parent, at least ten times larger, making a sound like a controlled hurricane, as it sucked air up.

I stared at it, mouth dropping open, as I stepped out of the way so Miss Jewel could come fully in and close the door. I vaguely heard her say, "Rocky, you bastard," and then I looked down and around me. The workshop looked exactly like hell, I thought, if hell were run like a hospital. Wherever I looked there was some noisy or smelly process going on.

There was indeed a lye vat, in a corner, or at least I assumed that was what the large cement-exterior tank was—I had no clue what the interior was. A pimply young man was fishing in it with what looked like a gigantic version of salad tongs. As I watched, he brought up a door. He must be stronger than he looked, I thought, as he then dipped the door in another tank, which I assumed was vinegar to neutralize the lye. I realized that the tongs weren't exactly being held by him, but by a sort of robot arm, which he was guiding. Nifty.

There were other machines at work close by. One of them seemed to be slathering a large wood piece in some fluid, then moving along to scrape paint off the surface, then repeating. I wondered if there was some sort of control on it, or if someone just kept an eye out. Because it seemed to me all too possible that the scraping could be overdone. I thought of how much Rocky did and put out for sale every week and thought, well, some shoddiness might be understandable. Besides, who was I to criticize someone who did a hundred times better than I did?

Somewhere farther along, something that looked like a fully mechanized version of the crevice sander that Ben had given me was sanding the indentations on the piecrust top of a table.

There seemed to be only three people in the place. Rocky was in a full argument with Mike, from the sound of it. (It was Mike, not Miss Jewel, judging by the bellowing tones.) Puzzled, because I was sure that Mike had said Rocky had asked him to come by, I wandered around, bewildered by the noise. Maybe Rocky had asked *Miss Jewel* to drop by, not Mike. I didn't think Mike was a split personality as such. He couldn't be. If he were, Miss Jewel would be far more convincing.

I rounded the corner of a place where what looked like gingerbreading from a Victorian's façade was being painted by a spray robotic arm, and almost ran full on into a small many-drawered cabinet being given personal attention by a woman who appeared to be around my age.

Like me, and like the young people at Mike's workshop, she favored bright-colored denim coveralls—hers in a cheery hot pink—and her hair was caught back in a scarf of the same color. The little armoire had every single drawer out, and she was lovingly staining them a rich oak color.

She looked up at me—she was kneeling—at the same time I looked down at her, and I suspect mirrored my surprised look, though I couldn't have said why I was surprised except that at this point I expected a robot rather than a human.

The girl cleared her throat. "The application forms are up front," she said, speaking just slightly louder than normal, to be heard above the roar of the exhaust hood above and the various whirrs, cracks, and chirps of the little robots all around.

"Applications?" I asked, probably screaming louder than I should have.

"You're not here to apply?" she asked. "To work?"

"Oh. No. I'm with him," I pointed vaguely in the direction from which Mike's voice came. "Or her . . . or . . ."

She smiled at me, a fellow female smile, full of solidarity. "Oh, that's a him, no matter how much makeup he wears. The weird thing is that Mike is a perfect gentleman, but Miss Jewel is like an octopus." She shuddered delicately. "Hands everywhere."

I nodded. "That's just so wrong."

"Tell me about it," she said.

I feared she might think *I'm with him* was more permanent or something, so I said, "He's just giving me a ride home, because I was walking and . . . it's kind of far. And then, trying to change the subject from Mike and his peculiaritiesI'm Dyce. Dyce Dare."

"Oh," she said, and looked startled for just a moment. "You're the girl that . . . that does furniture refinishing."

Considering where we were and what was going on all around us this seemed like a very small distinction, but I nodded.

Into the silence caused by my momentary awkwardness came Mike's voice, loud. "Look, I'm not saying that Nick is a bad refinisher, but you have to stop letting him cull the estate stuff for you. It was a Sheraton chair, I tell you, with a lyre back."

Rocky answered something back that couldn't be readily understood, and Mike roared back, "Are you calling me stupid? It's not that hard to recognize a Sheraton, man."

The girl looked concerned, stopped her staining, and looked at the source of the noise.

"Are they going to come to blows?" I said.

She glanced at me. "What? Oh, no. They're friends. They went to high school together. Were on the football team. Rocky finds . . . Mike's *thing* bewildering, but they're still friends. Yeah, they always yell at each other, but it doesn't mean anything, you know?"

I knew. Or at least I knew men like that.

"I'm Tiffany, by the way," she said. "Tiff. I . . . I was just concerned because Rocky . . . well, you know, he's a very busy man, very successful. He can't do everything."

Of course he couldn't; that's why he had robots. In my mind I saw Rocky as a science fiction villain, standing there, arms outstretched, ordering his mechanical legions to attack me and . . . and what? Dip me in lye? Sand me? Who knew? Though if he were really a supervillain, he'd probably have them hold me while he told me his plans to conquer the world.

But Tiff clearly didn't know of my own thoughts, because she looked like she was still following the conversation—which meant that she must be able to hear better than I could. Obviously she was sympathetic to Rocky's plight, whatever that might be. "He's a very busy man. I mean, it's not just the work as such. We do refinishing of exterior pieces of buildings for renovators, including, you know . . . All Saints, downtown? Yeah, we refinished all the woodwork there. And . . . commercial buildings and all. We are the go-to for wood refinishing. And Rocky can't do it all. He just can't . . ."

Of course he couldn't, and to banish the mental image of robots whirring around All Saints, and also to try to do something that resembled investigating murders, I said, "I bet he misses Nell's help a lot."

She jumped a little, which could be of course because by now it was widely known that Nell had been murdered. At least I assumed it was. I hadn't had time to look in the paper, but I assumed it was there. Tiff looked down and really seemed to concentrate on the staining as she said, "I was never sure that Nell was very good for Rocky. All she ever wanted to do was manage the workshop, and instead of pitching in, she kept telling Rocky what he was supposed to do."

"But I thought they were about to reconcile," I said.

"Well . . ." She shrugged. "Men are like that, aren't they?"

I thought of Ben calling Les. "Oh yeah."

Once more we shared a look of female understanding. And then she said, "But yeah, we miss her. I mean, even a supervising pair of eyes was better than nothing. She got most of the machines in, you know? A huge investment but very helpful. But her real issue was Nick, because . . . like Mike, she thought sometimes he put valuable pieces outside. The thing is, you know, we have so much work that the occasional loss of a few hundred dollars is not that big a deal."

I didn't know, though I hoped someday to be in a state in which a few hundred dollars wouldn't make a big difference.

"And Nick has been doing the work for five years. He came straight here from high school and in a way, I think he's like a son to Rocky. At any rate, Rocky is very loyal, you know?"

I looked across the workshop where the loyal Rocky was gesticulating violently at Miss Jewel. He didn't look so much loyal as aggrieved and perhaps volatile. He was a big man with red hair and beard. Red beard. Wasn't that a pirate or something who was supposed to have killed many wives? Judging by Tiff's softened gaze, whenever she looked at her boss, she might be the next victim. I shivered and wished Mike would hurry up.

"But it still was a terrible way to go," Tiff said. "I mean, immersed in lye. Oh, I know they say she was probably already dead or out cold and that it would have been quick, because lye dissolves a human in like . . . what . . . twenty minutes? But it's still terrible."

Amen sister, and at that, she hadn't seen the body. I shivered again and felt nauseated. "Perhaps I should start walking," I said. "If Mike is going to be—"

At that moment, as if summoned by my words, Miss Jewel called out, "Come on, Dyce. Our work here is done."

Because that statement was normally preceded by the words *confusion, chaos, destruction* I wondered what Miss Jewel considered her work. But I didn't want to know, truly. I just wanted to get out of Rocky's in one relatively solid piece.

I mean, perhaps Rocky was one of those men who didn't kill outside marriage, but why count on it?

MASCULINE WILES

I CLOSED MY EYES in the car, of course, and opened them again only when I realized we had stopped for long enough that we must have arrived. In addition, I heard Miss Jewel—oh, it had been her driving the last ten minutes, for sure—get out of the car and the click, click of her heels walking.

I opened one eye, not without trepidation, because after all, Miss Jewel might be more than a guy in killer outfits, she might be a killer in girls' outfits. But we were in my driveway, facing the unlovable dilapidated hulk of the Edwardian mansion with its chipped blue paint and the big white primer patch where *Bitch* had been written.

My relief lasted about two seconds. Maybe less. Before Miss Jewel's impeccably manicured hand had opened my door, I realized that there were three cars in the driveway. Three. Mine and Ben's and . . . another, which I couldn't identify. It wasn't All-ex's and that was probably to the good, because surely he'd be more than a little upset to see me arrive with a guy dressed as a woman. Heaven only knows what he would think of my proclivities then.

But it was still a car, which wasn't a good thing. And for that matter, neither was the fact that Ben was there. I was hoping he'd gotten so wrapped up in stuff with Les that he would completely forget I'd given him the slip. Failing that, that he would realize it only after I was home safe and sound. Then I could have lied and told him I had taken a taxi home.

The forlorn hope that he wouldn't notice that I'd arrived, and therefore wouldn't know how I'd arrived, was lost as I saw the front curtain twitch aside and someone at Ben-height peek out. Followed by another person at Ben-height.

Oh, Archons of Athens! as Dad would say. I clenched my teeth as I got out of the car and faced the house. I was so preoccupied with what awaited me inside that I didn't realize that Miss Jewel, instead of stepping away, stepped closer.

Before I had time to do more than recoil slightly away from the painted, five-o'clock-shadowed face about an inch from mine, she brought it closer. Lipsticked lips touched mine, and as my mind thought, *Oh, ew*, I felt a manicured hand touch my rear.

Several responses were available to me, including backing up and screaming or perhaps hauling out and slapping him/her. Only at that point I wasn't thinking of how normal people would react. I was more preoccupied with an overwhelming sensation of *ew* and the fact that up close and personal, Mike smelled of equal parts of old tobacco and new makeup. Which didn't help.

My knee rose. He was way above me, but my legs were proportionately long and his very short. The skirt of the blue dress first rose, then caught and tore under the violent impact. And then my kneecap hit something soft and something not so soft full on. I stepped full force on the nearest stiletto-heeled foot, ducked under the arm raised between me and the door, and ran hell-bent for leather toward the steps to the front porch.

I was vaguely aware of a hoarse moan behind me and a bewildered, "What was that for?" but I didn't care. I had my key out and was about to open my door . . .

And the door opened. I was faced with a wall of male disapproval. Ben stood on the right, looking pale and serious—very serious—and at a great risk of turning into granite. To the left, at about the same height even if a lighter build, stood Officer Wolfe. Somehow he was no longer looking like a Cas. Both of them crossed their arms on their chests, and both of them stepped back to allow me in.

The resemblance ended there. While Ben looked like he had removed himself to some unreachable polar region, Officer Wolfe looked . . . like a man who was trying to appear stern while fighting hard not to crack up.

Like all generals facing a tough battle, I chose the weaker point on the wall and gave the policeman my best *It wasn't my fault* look. This look had stopped working on Ben some sixteen years ago. He'd said that although one should never attribute to malice what could be easily attributed to stupidity, he knew I wasn't stupid, and so that left malice and a total lack of self-preservation instinct.

Officer Wolfe didn't react with sympathy, but perhaps that was too much to ask for, at least depending on what Ben had told him—which at this point was probably that I'd been born to hang—but he did smile and shake his head. "Is that how you normally react to kisses, Ms. Dare?"

"No," Ben said sourly. "Only when she doesn't have a chair handy."

Both Officer Wolfe and I turned to him surprised, Wolfe probably thinking the resentment was personal. I knew better, as I was remembering the incident in question.

"New Year's Eve seven years ago," Ben said. "She hit some poor guy over the head with a chair. He was drunk. We had a hell of a time convincing the EMTs that he'd tripped and hit the chair just right."

"I see," Officer Wolfe said appreciatively. "So felonious assault is a specialty."

"He had already tried to drag a woman into a bedroom," I said. "Besides, he was fine. Well, he still has that thing with his left eye, but he's okay. And he doesn't get drunk now. Or attack women."

For some reason this made Wolfe smile as he stepped farther back. Ben gave him a betrayed look, as if—I thought—they'd agreed they wouldn't smile and that neither of them would give me a chance to charm them. Which just went to show that Ben did not get straight men and the "cute little thing" effect. Having been born small and relatively inoffensive-looking was my best asset.

"Very well," Officer Wolfe said, recovering his composure and clearly remembering their pact. Ben walked behind me to close the door. I'd heard Mike start up his car, but all the same, I felt a little odd as the door closed. There went my one avenue of escape. I was now trapped here with these two hulking males. And it wasn't like I could hit Ben on the head with a chair. Well, I could, but first I'd need a ladder to reach it, and second, annoying though he was, I kind of liked him. I kind of liked Cas Wolfe, too. At least he didn't wear lipstick to kiss me.

Remembering the lipstick, I rubbed my lips on my sleeve, which brought another smile to Officer Wolfe's eyes. It didn't touch his lips this time, but it looked wicked. As though he took great joy in my discomfiture.

Grandma had always told me to beware of the big bad wolf. She never told me he'd be wearing a policeman's uniform. "Mr. Colm called me and said that you had disappeared," he said. "He drove all over for two hours trying to find you."

Gee, if they were accomplices, you'd think that he would try to call him Ben, not Mr. Colm. Perhaps the clothes intimidated him. I opened my mouth to say something along those lines, but then I noticed that

Ben was turned away from us, and that his right hand was climbing up to rub the middle of his forehead. Right. I was many kinds of bitch, as the person who had spray-painted the outside of my house had so kindly pointed out, but it was no part of my mission to hurt Ben. Besides, I realized with a pang, it probably was truly low—by any description—to have left him and disappeared while he was trying to check on Les's issues.

I opened my hands full on and looked at Officer Wolfe with my best innocent look, coupled with genuine embarrassment and guilt. "Look, I didn't mean to disappear. Ben went back in to ask his friend something and I . . ." And I realized I couldn't possibly tell the truth, not without seriously upsetting Ben and making him feel like a fool. "I walked outside to get some air. And then Michael Manson stopped by, and he asked if I wanted a ride home."

Ben turned around, and from the way his eyes looked, he had the mother of all headaches forming. "And you thought you would go for a joyride with him for three hours?" he asked.

"No!" I said. The fact that I'd never intended to joyride with him or anyone else was probably a good thing. "No, you see . . . I got in the car and he told me he had to stop for a few minutes, and then he—"

"And you couldn't have gotten out of the car?" Ben said skeptically.

"Not the way he was driving. Or rather, she. When his voice goes up, his driving . . . I think he ran fifteen red lights between the symphony and Rocky's, I swear."

"Oh, yeah, Michael Manson has a list of traffic citations too big to transcribe," Officer Wolfe said. "In fact, his license might be suspended right now, not that that ever stops him."

"*Rocky's?*" Ben asked, displaying his uncanny ability to zero in on the part I didn't really want him to hear.

I sighed. "That's where he went. But . . . you know . . . it's okay. I mean, what could he do, what with Rocky right there, and his employees, too? Besides, I'm not married to Rocky."

Ben opened his mouth, then closed it. Both his hands went up and this time massaged at his temples.

Officer Wolfe looked me over appreciatively. "So you went to Rocky's . . . Anything interesting?"

"No! I wasn't investigating," I said. Which of course was true and also a lie. The thing is that I'd been so determined to get out and investigate because they'd told me I couldn't. But now I realized that the whole thing wasn't just about me. Oh, it was about me, too, undoubtedly, or at least there had to be some reason poor Inobart's remains had been left in my workshop, but the fact of the matter was that my actions affected the innocent, too. Like Ben. The last thing he needed, on top of whatever crap Les was giving him, was to have me go nuts on him, too. Poor man. Perhaps his bad taste extended to friends as well as to lovers. "Look, Ben," I said. "I'm several kinds of idiot, but I honestly didn't mean to worry you." I reached out and touched his arm, which when he was in this mood was at best risky, as it might make him withdraw more. But it might also make him come down to Earth and realize I was still Dyce. Stupid, yeah, and okay, maybe he was right and I attracted trouble like muck attracted pigs, but honestly, I hadn't meant to hurt him.

No, the truth of it is that I hadn't thought of him at all. "I thought you'd be busy," I said. "You know . . . with . . . the other issue." I wasn't sure that Officer Wolfe knew of Ben's current domestic troubles, and at any rate, it wasn't any of his business.

Ben looked at me and sighed. "I know. Sometimes I just want to shake you."

I nodded. Hell, sometimes I wanted to shake myself. Only if I did, trouble would just shed off me, like water off a recently washed dog, and land on everyone else.

"I called you. Must have been a dozen times," he said.

"I tried calling you, too. But my phone wasn't working."

There were many things he could have said, including that I was an idiot, and that my habit of not charging my phone drove him bananas. All true, of course. Just as it was true that he had the right to be absolutely furious, and to leave and not to talk to me for a month or perhaps for life. As far as I knew he was involved in this murder investigation only because he was my friend.

But then, this was Ben, known far and wide for giving everyone a second chance, including idiot Les and me. He just looked after broken-winged birds, was all. Probably because he'd first had to look after his many siblings. I didn't like to think that I was in the same category as Les, but I undoubtedly was. Ben took a deep breath. "Oh, damn it, Dyce. I finally came back and I thought I'd find you dead, and what the hell would I tell your parents?"

"That I died by murder?" I said, then regretted it and explained. "I'm more worried about upsetting you than them."

This got me a pale smile. "I know that, too. Damn it, Dyce."

"Yes, I know," I said. Then I looked at Officer Wolfe. "I'm sorry we troubled you. As you see, I was being an idiot. I never thought that Ben would be so concerned when he noticed I was gone, which probably means that . . . well, I'm an idiot."

Cas Wolfe had an expression much like that of Tiff back at Rocky's place. He looked concerned and amused and soft all at once. I hoped the soft was for me, and then I hoped it wasn't, because, really, did I have the time for emotional involvement right now? Look how I treated my friends. Gee, no wonder All-ex had gone nuts while married to me.

"It's all right," he said at length. "It's my day off, and I wasn't doing much of anything." He looked at Ben, then back at me. "Tell you what . . . I think Mr. Colm could use some time by himself for a while." And then, looking at Ben, not at me, "Do you mind if I take her out for dinner?"

My, what big teeth you have! I thought. I remembered him kissing me, and my knees went wobbly. Only the fact that I was being passed—as a charge—between the two of them made me buck up again. Right. They viewed me as a load of trouble, which admittedly I was. But that didn't make me feel better about it.

On the other hand, considering how stupid I'd just been, I suspected I owed it to Ben to give him some Dyce-free time. I touched his arm again. "There's aspirin in the medicine cabinet."

This managed to elicit an almost normal smile. "Thanks," he said. "We'll talk when you get back."

THE BETTER TO EAT YOU WITH

"DIFFERENT CAR," I SAID, remembering vaguely that he'd been driving a massive red SUV. This was a small white SUV. Yes, that was my level of interest in cars. Kind of like my interest in clothes. They were things that served a purpose. I noted, however, that the inside of the car was clean and neat, with immaculate gray leather seats.

"My car," he said, getting behind the wheel. "When I'm on duty I usually just grab whichever of the force's cars is available."

"Oh." To be honest, my grandmother couldn't have warned me that this very good-looking wolf would be wearing a police uniform, because he wasn't. Unless the uniform was mental. Because what he was wearing was an open-at-the-neck polo in a gray that exactly matched his eyes, and a pair of snug jeans. Mind you, for the area we lived in, this counted almost as overdressed for a casual evening.

He smiled at me. "How do you feel about diners?"

"Uh."

"That good, uh? So what do you like, Chinese? Hungarian? German?"

"Hungarian, *really*?"

"The European Kitchen around the corner. Oh, oops. It's pretty much a diner."

I got the feeling he was toying with me and shook my head. "I don't have anything against diners," I said. "I have just never been asked what I think about them. Though as far as I can tell, the European Kitchen . . . uh . . ." I'd walked by the place two or three times. If it was a diner, it didn't impress me as such. Actually it didn't impress me as much of anything except maybe a restaurant run by people who had no idea what made for an appealing eating place. It was small and square and, most of the time, empty. It had all of a half-a-dozen tables, and they were covered in red-and-white tablecloths.

He smiled at me. "It's not that great. But I wanted to throw my exotic card down, to mitigate the fact that I mentioned diners . . ."

"But I don't have anything against diners," I said. "As long as I don't have to eat pancakes. I make those better than they do."

He gave me a look as if asking what was with the pancakes. He could go on wanting to know. "I have lots of practice," I said.

"I see."

"But you don't have to buy me dinner," I said.

"I know," he said, meekly. "But if I try to steal it, people get upset and I'd be likely to lose my job. You wouldn't want that, would you?"

"Uh, of course not," I said, rallying. "If that happened, you wouldn't be able to take me out dancing."

He looked at me, and his eyes sparkled almost blue. "We can't have that," he said. "So, have you eaten at the George?"

"Weirdly, no," I said. "I don't eat out much. See, the money . . ."

"Ah, but if you don't mind diners—or even if you do—you must go to the George at least once. We get people coming from all over the country to eat there."

I was fairly sure he was joking, but he winked at me and started the car. "It's really very good. Truly. And not pricey for what it is. And since you live just blocks away, you have to go there."

"Uh," I said.

He gave me a quick look. "Well, if you want to go somewhere else . . ."

"No. I just . . ." I shrugged. "To my knowledge it's the only diner that Ben will frequent. From his comments, I always assumed he had a crush on the owner."

Wolfe smiled. "Probably. I really have no idea, but I suspect he's good-looking. At least his girlfriend is a five-alarm fire waiting to happen. She's the other owner."

"Oh." Typical of Ben, he'd never mentioned there was also a female owner.

"My friend Rafiel goes there all the time, too. But I don't think it's because he's interested in Tom, the guy who owns it. Now, Kyrie, his girlfriend, I wouldn't say anything." He shrugged. "Mind you, they'd both be equally out of luck. Tom and Kyrie are a nice couple. I think you'll like them."

I didn't think I'd have any choice, though looking at a cute couple cooing and billing didn't count as fun, but I didn't want to tell Cas Wolfe that, because he might decide I was jealous of people who had relationships. Which, damn it, I was. But there would be time for that when E got married or ran away from home, whichever came first.

We drove a short distance and parked at the back, in the spacious parking lot between the bed-and-breakfast next door and the George.

Then we walked around the building to the front entrance.

The George was a dumpy building—one floor, and a short floor at that. I had no idea what it was actually built of, but it was covered in stucco and indifferently painted white. The front door was aluminum and it tinkled as you opened it—because of the bells tied behind it.

When I'd grown up, the George—then called the Athens—was not a place where anyone ate willingly. There were reports of cockroaches the size of tables, and food poisoning was a given if you even looked into the place.

But since the name and ownership change, it, like the area it was in, had become gentrified. It retained enough of its ... essential dinerness to make it interesting or perhaps curious to the suburbanites who came here to eat. They wanted authentic and working class, and the George hadn't prettified to the point where it lost that. Someone always wrote all the specials on the window with colored markers every morning, and inside there was a cozy atmosphere of booths and then larger tables in the little glassed-in porch next to the main diner. Then there was the long, polished aluminum counter, with single stools—also of polished aluminum—for single diners.

"They put all new vinyl in the booths," Wolfe said. "And replaced the tables in the extension." He waved toward the porch. "And Tom is a fantastic cook. Also, they hired this baker, recently, Laura ... Her bread and cakes are to die for."

In front of us was a sign saying, *It will be our pleasure to seat you.*

Within moments, a young woman came up. Her name tag said *Kyrie*, and I realized what my escort meant by a five-alarm fire waiting to happen. As far as her looks went, she could be Native American, Italian, Greek, or any mingling of any dozen things. However, the things had mixed very nicely, and I'm sure that she was a great part of the reason for the success of the diner.

It hurt a little to think that Cas Wolfe thought she was attractive, but it hurt more that she had just slightly wavy hair, which she had cut in layers, then dyed, so that her hair looked like a tapestry in earth tones, with the pattern shifting every time she moved. I'd kill for hair like that. The only time I'd dyed my hair ... It didn't end well.

DIPPED STRIPPED AND DEAD

She led us to the booth in the corner, even though it had a sign over it that said it was for four or more people. It also had, right overhead, a painting of St. George slaying the dragon. I'm sure it was a fine painting and it looked old, but I sat with my back to it all the same. The only red I wanted to see while eating was ketchup.

Officer Wolfe sat across from me. The proprietress took our order for drinks—two iced teas—and smiled when I asked her if she should give us the biggest booth. "I can always put groups in the tables in the extension," she said. "But this is the quietest booth."

Quietest booth. I looked across the table at Cas Wolfe studying his menu. "Do you come here often?"

He looked over his menu. "Only when there's a pretty woman involved in a case I'm investigating."

"Officer Wolfe, I—" I started, not sure at all what I was going to tell him, except that I wasn't looking to date, couldn't date. And if it was information he wanted, I'd give it to him without his having to beat around the bush and pretend to court me. I'd only not told where I'd gone exactly because after all, Ben would have been even more upset.

"Call me *Cas*. Or *Castor*, though that always makes people ask if my middle name is *Oil*."

"I . . . don't know you that well."

"Well enough," he said. "Read your menu. You'll need to order."

I read my menu. It was very cute, having the name of the food, and then underneath it the diner lingo for it. Clearly, though, they'd run out of diner lingo, because I didn't believe that there was any such thing as Armageddon Steak, even if it was squid steak. "Really," I said. "In Colorado?" It was the second time I had come across them. Was there some secret squid mine around here?

"It's fresh," Kyrie said, materializing in front of our booth. "We get it flown in. Tom does it with a garlic marinade. It's very popular."

It was also, according to the menu notation, low in fat. "All right," I said. "I'll try it." As I said so, I looked toward the grill, where a dark-haired man was working with the spatula. He had a bandanna tied around his head pirate style, I suppose because of health regulations, but his hair fell in a ponytail as long as his girlfriend's. I couldn't get up to verify Ben's assertion that the young man had the best-looking ass in the tristate area. Besides, I didn't know where the competition was or who had judged it. But I was willing to take Ben's word for it.

After Cas ordered steak, rare—"No, I mean, get the cow, bring it near the grill, let it get scared of the flames, then cut the steak and put it on my plate"—and fries, Kyrie went away, and he turned to me. "Now suppose you tell me what really happened this afternoon."

I told him. To the best of my ability, though I can't say I remembered everything. Only of course, I avoided all mention of the tea table, because I wasn't stupid, and besides I still intended to keep that table. As far as I was concerned, if someone was going to put gelatined corpses in my workshop, I was going to get something out of it.

He listened to it all with an appraising look, then raised an eyebrow. "You really are something else, you know that."

I shrugged. "Compared to what?"

He didn't say anything as our meal was put in front of us. I really am not qualified to judge food. I mean, it wasn't pancakes, so it seemed pretty good to me. But I can say that it was a pleasant experience I wouldn't mind repeating. The salad was fresh and crisp, the Greek dressing perfectly balanced, and the squid steak tender and flavorful. And the gentleman across from me was amused at my adventures—though I hadn't yet decided whether that was good or bad.

At the end of the meal, he got up to pay, and I followed him. While he was paying, I stood in the little entrance area, which had a few copies of local papers, including college papers.

I grabbed yesterday's copy of the local paper—the *Weekly Inquirer*, which was, of course, daily—more or less so that I wouldn't have to look at Cas Wolfe as he paid. Because, see, I was wondering, after all the looks he'd given me during dinner, whether he had the intention of kissing me again. And I didn't want him to feel I was either expecting it or dreading it. Particularly because I had no clue how I felt. All of which was very weird, because, of course, I knew that I couldn't possibly date until E was much, much older. I mean, it was bad enough he had to cope with All-ex's Michelle without my further confusing him.

It wasn't even a matter of my remarrying. That by itself might be fine. It was the dating leading up to it. If I dated a succession of men I didn't marry, how would that make E feel? He was bound to be confused. Now if I could marry someone compatible without dating . . . but that was like the lion and the goats again.

I looked through the paper and stopped suddenly on the fifth page, which was the crime report. There was only a very small paragraph mentioning a body found in a Dumpster, identified as local resident Nell Gwen. Something about the report bothered me, but it wasn't until I got in the car to be driven back—tragically still unkissed—that I realized what it was.

"Uh," I said. "Have you gone over to Rocky's and interrogated them yet?" I asked.

He shook his head. "No. We talked to Rocky himself, but we asked him not to talk to his workers or . . . well, anyone." He looked at me. "What is going on in your head?"

I shook my head and decided that the last thing I wanted to tell him was what was going on in there. Besides the fact that he was taking his sweet time to kiss me again—which frankly I wouldn't tell him unless he drove rusty nails into my fingers, and even then, I might hold out—I did not intend to tell him I was wondering how and when Tiff had found out about the circumstances of the murder. Instead, I said, "No. I was just wondering what Rocky was doing . . . I mean, has he been married many times?"

"Three."

"And?"

"All to the same woman."

"Oh." I said. Well, there went a lovely theory. "Unless he changed all their names, so you thought it was the same woman?" I asked, as we pulled into my driveway. Okay, that sounded as stupid as suspecting small, slight, and definitely nice Tiff. Maybe actually more stupid.

He grinned as he got out and walked around to open the car door. Then he suddenly leaned in, said, "Don't get that complicated," and kissed me.

It was worth the wait.

In the Still of the Night

I CAME INTO THE house, half-expecting to find Ben hastily scurrying back from the letter opening. But he wasn't there, and the light was off. I was about to turn it on when, my eyes having adapted, I realized that Ben *was* there. He was on the sofa, wrapped in one of my extra blankets, in his usual mummy position, except for an arm thrown over his eyes.

I considered waking him up to discuss the crime, because, you see, I was wondering: Did Tiffany find out from Rocky that Nell Gwen had been put in lye? And if not, how did she know? I still didn't think she was the murderer, but I also couldn't make heads or tails of anyone else being the murderer. I mean, if Rocky had killed his wife, why would he tell Tiff? And if he hadn't, why would he tell her how the body was found, once the police had asked him not to?

But I remembered that Ben had told me my parents had kept him up till four a.m. and then he had gotten up early to come looking for me. And then there had been . . . poor Inobart and all. I could see that Ben needed to sleep, and I'd already been too inconsiderate of his comfort and well-being.

I very much doubted I was going to be able to sleep while this stuff was on my mind. And I wanted to work on the tea table. But I hated going to the workshop after dark at the best of times, and these weren't the best of times. I could imagine being out there in the dark, fumbling for the light switch by the door . . .

I shivered. It was impossible to shake the feeling that out of the dark a hand would emerge, a gelatinous and distorted hand, swathed in a bright green polyester robe.

But even as I shivered, I realized that if I didn't go back now, soon I would be unable to use the workshop at all. First I would be afraid of going out there at night, and then I'd become unable to go during the day, and given time and my active imagination, it was quite possible the day would come when I'd be afraid to go near anything made of wood, night or day. I'd imagine poor Inobart's spirit reaching out to touch the wood, or perhaps to protect the wood from me.

Imagine was the operative word. The thing was that Ben was right here on the sofa, his car out front, should anyone look. And the killer had already put a corpse in my workshop once; surely he—or she—wouldn't do it again. Plus, the police had been in and out all day. In fact, before they left, they had put a new padlock on the workshop door, and Cas had given Ben and me the keys. I could go in, I thought, and take the padlock off and padlock myself from the inside. Then no one could come in and do anything to me.

Satisfied with this compromise, I grabbed Ben's car keys from his briefcase which was on the floor next to his head. I went outside, opened the car, and came back in, carrying the table.

On my way through the living room, I noted today's newspaper by Ben's side, but I didn't have the time to stop and read. Instead, I went all the way out back, carrying my padlock key. I unlocked the workshop, which didn't look spooky at all and in fact looked far cleaner than it had been in a long, long time. I supposed it was the effect of all those little crime-scene vacuums that the police had brought.

I set the tea table down while I padlocked the door on the inside, very glad that this was possible.

I opened the windows, turned on the fan, and went to work. I know I'd planned on using the heat gun, but the problem with that was that the heat gun also could cause stains and burns on the piece, and I wanted this one as good as possible. I started working with a layer of paint at a time, swathing it in my turpentine-mineral-spirits-corn starch. I'd do a small area at a time—the area I could scrape off once softened before it dried and hardened again. Before I started scraping, I'd put the mixture on another patch, so that my only relatively idle time was the time the first mixture was taking effect. I used that time to assemble drawers of my in-pieces dresser.

I don't know how long I worked, but I'd gotten one of the corners down to the wood, which was indeed cherry, and the other side to the last layer, white paint. I despise people who paint good furniture in white paint, but it seems to be almost as common a sin as painting in metallic or green.

By the time I'd gotten that much done, I was exhausted and re-membered that I, too, had been up very early. Which was not a good thing. With a sudden shock I realized that if Ben woke up and I wasn't in the house, and he called Cas and was told I had been dropped off hours before, he might get worried.

I unlocked the padlock and pushed on the door. Nothing hap-pened. I thought the door was just stuck, but as I pushed harder, I heard steps walk away.

Damn. Someone had locked me in. Someone had locked me in the shed where a corpse had been found. Someone might, even now, be going to get gasoline to pour around the workshop and set a match . . .

I put my shoulder to the door and pushed, hard. Nothing hap-pened. I was wondering what tools I could use, thinking I probably could pry parts of the door off with the crow bar, but then I wouldn't be able to lock .

Okay. I'd try once more, with brute force, and then consider the crowbar.

I ran at the door and kicked it hard on one of the reinforcement crosspieces.

It flew open and I went forward, propelled by my own momentum, to stop against a nearby tree, hands forward. I turned around. The workshop looked completely innocuous with the light on. I didn't see a chain or a padlock, or any hint there had been one on the outside.

A shiver went through me. The ghost of Inobart had come back and . . . But then I saw a stick on the ground, next to the two rings I normally padlocked. It was broken through.

I took a deep breath. Not Inobart. Completely unrelated. Obvi-ously, one of the college students who passed by late at night, the same ones who often left empty beer bottles or cigarette butts on this path, had done this. Probably not even with malice, just one of those absentminded things. There was a stick, and there was a loop it went through.

And I'd gotten myself all worked up, imagining that someone had locked me in. Which only went to prove that I had way too much imagination and used it in a stupid manner

Still . . . I didn't feel quite up to leaving the tea table. I wiped it clean of all traces of chemicals, grabbed it by the legs, set it down, put the padlock on the door, walked to my back door, opened it, and went in.

I set the tea table in the powder room, in such a way that it didn't block access to the toilet, should Ben wake up in the middle of the night. He was still asleep in the same position on the sofa.

I went back to my bedroom, closed the door, undressed, put on the long T-shirt I used for a nightshirt, and went to the bathroom to brush my teeth.

The day had been so long and I was so tired that I actually started brushing my teeth before something struck me as not being quite right. I looked up. There on the mirror, written in bright red lipstick, were the words *Come back* and an imprint of lips, as if someone had put on lipstick, then kissed the mirror.

I stared at it a long time. Michael. It had to be Michael Manson. It just had to. And what had been bothering me about Tiff knowing that the body had been dipped in lye suddenly made all the sense in the world. Of course, Michael had told her. She had intimated that Miss Charity Jewel wanted to . . . get cozy with her.

It all made perfect sense, and for a moment I contemplated getting up and going back to Manson's place and . . .

Then I came to my senses. The clock on the shelf in the bathroom said it was three a.m., and I was dog tired.

Of course, Cas had given me his phone number. I could call him and ask him to drop in on Miss Jewel. But again, it was the middle of the night. How happy would he be to be called? I would call him first thing tomorrow.

I was about to go to bed on this resolution when a terrible fear took hold. What if Michael Manson was *still* in the house? Worse, what if he had done something to Ben? When I was a teen with a great appetite for blood and gore, I'd read pirate stories, and there was a scene that had stayed with me—a pirate attack where they'd killed a woman with a wire by cutting her head off, so that it looked like she was asleep. I was fairly sure this was impossible, but what if it wasn't?

I walked back out to the living room and turned the light on.

Ben jumped, and his head stayed remarkably attached. He blinked, then looked at me. "Dyce?" he said. "What on Earth?" He rubbed his eyes. "How long have I been asleep? When did you come in?"

"A while back. I was just going to sleep, but I thought you might be dead. Pirates, you know, might have cut your head off with a fine wire." I realized what I had said. "I mean, not pirates, but I read . . ."

A smile twitched at the corners of his lips. He shook his head. "Not so I know. Have you checked on E?"

"What?"

"E. Your ex dropped him off . . . right after you left to go to dinner. Well, actually the wife did. They brought him back a day early. Your ex was upset . . ."

I wasn't ready for this. And I wasn't ready to do anything before making sure E was all right. There had been someone in the house, I was sure of it, unless Ben had taken to writing on the mirror with lipstick, and that was too strange even for him.

"E's in his crib?"

Ben nodded. " I read him Allingham and he fell asleep, and then I came out here. I didn't realize I'd dropped off. I know he's as likely as not to climb out and go running off."

Oh, please, no. My heart beating somewhere near my throat, I made it all the way to E's room. His crib was full of stuffed animals, and I didn't see him.

I turned the light on, conscious of Ben behind me.

A little head rose from amid the stuffed animals. "Bah!" he said.

"Hi, monkey," Ben said.

I waved E down. "Go back to sleep."

Ben and I walked back to the living room. "Sorry I woke you," I said.

"No, sorry I fell asleep while babysitting. I didn't mean to. I guess work isn't as riveting as usual. How did the date go?"

I shrugged. "It wasn't a date."

He grinned at me, the shameless grin of someone who didn't believe a word I said. "So, no kiss?"

"Oh, there was a kiss."

He grinned wider. "Date. Second. Or third? There was that kiss in the parking lot."

"Benedict Colm, don't make me throw things at you. Why did Alex bring—send E back?"

"Apparently E got hold of a baseball that your ex had gotten at a Rockies game and had signed by the team members or whatever, and he tried to flush it down the toilet. And when your ex yelled at him, because he had to call the plumber and pay him full price, E started saying, *Oh, holy you-know-what*, and wouldn't stop. So the new wife brought him back."

I leaned against the door frame. "Oh, good." And bad. E had been in the house while a killer roamed around. And it was my stupid fault, too, for leaving the back door unlocked when I went out to the workshop. I had done it in case I needed to come in quickly to ask Ben's help. And instead, I left my baby and my friend at the mercy of some unknown fiend. I wasn't about to admit it to Ben—what he didn't know wouldn't hurt him—or make him angry at me again.

"And bad," Ben said. "I *have* to go to work tomorrow morning. I have a meeting with a client who is driving in from the mountains. I have to stay at the office for as long as it takes. I can come back afterward, but . . ."

"It's okay," I said. "I just won't work on furniture tomorrow."

"No. That's not it. If someone . . ."

"Oh, that," I said. "Don't worry. I think there's a good chance the killer will be identified by tomorrow morning."

He gave me a dubious look. "I wish I had your confidence." But he didn't ask me why I thought that, which was good.

Before going to bed, I cleaned the mirror, to keep Ben from being startled when he tried to take a shower in the morning.

In the Cool Morning Light

AND IN THE MORNING I found that I wasn't so sure that the writing on the mirror had been Michael Manson's doing. I woke up late—nine a.m.—and Ben had gone to work. He'd left his stuff—which I guess he must have reclaimed from my parents'—all around the house. Toiletries in the bathroom, his clothes carefully hung in the normally empty coat closet beside the living room sofa, a morning paper on the table.

His used teapot and teacup were washed and drying on the drying board when I carted E in, moments after waking him up, and gave him cereal and milk from the supplies that Ben had left in the pantry and refrigerator.

"Bah?" E said.

I was starting to suspect that *Bah* was his name for Ben. "He's not here," I said. "He had to go to work."

"Work? Oh, holy fuck?"

"Hardly," I told him. "And you shouldn't say those words."

"No?"

"No."

"Daddy anggggggy."

"Yes, I imagine. They're very bad words."

E gurgled laughter, and I decided it truly was better not to poke around and find out what the laughter meant. I wondered what exactly the marks of the Antichrist were supposed to be. I had looked him over

DIPPED STRIPPED AND DEAD

from head to toe at birth, and I was fairly sure there was no triple six anywhere, but perhaps there was something else I was supposed to look for.

Instead, I made sure that all the doors were locked and went to shower, leaving the bathroom door open so I could hear any sounds from the house. In the bathroom I discovered that a lipstick tube in the trash had come from the little ziplock bag where I kept all my makeup. It was a singularly weird color. My mother-in-law had given it to me for Christmas the last year of my marriage, and I'd always wondered if she meant something by choosing that peculiar shade of red.

There were no sounds other than E eating the cereal and—as I approached the kitchen, after dressing—pouring the remaining milk onto the floor.

I cleaned up the milk while thinking. Come on. It had to be Michael Manson. Who else would leave the message in lipstick?

But the message saying *Come back* and, more important, the kiss seemed oddly out of kilter. I remembered what I'd done to Michael before running into the house . . .

Now, if I'd found a drawing of someone's kneecap, that might have come from Michael. Though my kneecap had imprinted on something other than his mind's eye, I was sure. But . . . a kiss?

A kiss was right up there with my knifed table and the hanged monkey. Stuff that didn't seem at all related to the two bodies dipped in lye. So we'd have to go on the assumption that there were two crazy people running amok in Goldport. One was a homicidal maniac and the other one was . . . just a maniac.

That assumption bothered me because it was a violation of Occam's razor, which said the simplest solution that covered all facts was the truth. Only I couldn't find a solution that covered all the facts . . . not even if I stitched it around, cozylike.

I made tea and sat down to drink it while E explored the windowsills for bugs. I got the newspaper from the living room. Today's newspaper, which meant that Ben must have bought it before he left.

I looked in the crime blotter page, and there was still nothing about Nell, and of course nothing yet about Inobart . . .

I drank my tea. Then I fetched my notepad and one of my flat yellow pencils and sat down to list everything that had happened, starting with the corpse in the Dumpster and ending with my getting locked in the workshop.

There were two separate sets of events here. There had to be. I noted down the table, the inscription on the bottom of the table, calling Rocky's, finding Inobart. All of those were part of one set. The locking of the workshop might be, or not. But because there had been the lipstick inscription at the same time, probably it belonged with the other set, which started with Ben arriving at my house with a dented car and a scratch on his face and proceeded through his car tires getting slashed, the monkey getting hanged, the multiple *Bitch*es being painted on and in my house, and most recently the inscription on the mirror. If I added in the situation at Ben's apartment, it became clear that maybe, just maybe, a certain more-than-a-little-unstable musician might be involved: Les. Les, who thought that Ben was playing around on him, an idea that was perfectly insane, because Ben's life was work and home.

Then it hit me. The other major part of Ben's life was—visiting me. And Ben had a picture of himself and E in his wallet.

I paused, contemplating the enormity of Les's insanity. It was perfectly all right for my parents to think that Ben was really straight and in love with me, but surely Les knew better? What would be the purpose of the elaborate deception, if Ben were carrying on with me?

There was no logic to it, but then the stuff that had been done around my house was not the work of a rational mind. And frankly, when it came to sexual affairs, men were often less than rational. Perhaps Les had convinced himself that Ben was having doubts about his sexual orientation . . .

I could call Les. But I didn't think I'd get an answer any more than Ben had. Or I could . . .

I pulled the phone book to me and looked down the *M* columns. There was one Milano. Peter Milano. Which was of course a lucky thing, because if he had a partner, the listing might very well have been under his partner's name.

The phone rang twice and was answered by a distinctly cheery male voice. "Hi there."

Well, and double to you, with a scoop of ice cream. Aloud I said, "May I speak with Peter Milano?"

"Sure. Who do I tell him is calling?"

"Dyce Dare," I said, and then, remembering that Peter had never been introduced to me, "on behalf of Ben Colm."

"Oh," the voice said. And after a pause. "All right."

I had the feeling of someone unfolding out of a comfy chair, and the sense more than auditory clues that a cup of coffee was being set down. Then I heard "Peter!" followed by more indistinct sounds and a graver male voice responding.

Moments later, a half-awake-sounding man said, "Hello . . . ?"

"This is Dyce Dare," I said. "I'm Benedict Colm's—"

"Quasi little sister. Yeah. Heard of you. What's wrong?"

I realized the poor man had probably been performing till late—if Les had come by here, he'd come after a performance—and that I had just wakened him relatively early.

"Well . . . I don't know if it's a question you can answer, but Ben is in a meeting and I don't think he knows. I mean, he knows he's in a meeting, but he doesn't know about what I'm calling about because even if you told him, he wouldn't believe it. And Les wouldn't answer me even if I asked, so . . ."

"Yes?" the voice asked, with just a hint of mischief.

Oh. "Uh . . . when you said that Les Howard suspected that Ben was having an affair with someone . . . he didn't by any chance think it was me?" The absurdity of it hit me, even as I said it. I felt a blush climb up. Now Peter Milano was going to think I believed myself so irresistible that even gay men lusted after me.

But my answer was a delighted cackle, followed by the word, "Zonkers."

"I'm sorry, it's just that . . ."

"Oh, not you, honey. Les is zonkers. He *must* have drama, and he has the temper of a prima donna. It goes with his largely imaginary artistic talent. Yeah, that's exactly what he believes about you and Ben. He also thinks your son is Ben's and that's why Ben likes him and has a picture with him. He thinks that's why your son is blond."

"But . . . my ex-husband is blond!"

"Yeah, I told you he was zonkers. We've always suspected it. You know, Les is one of those musicians who thinks himself above mere mortal beings? He came from somewhere out east, acting like he was God's gift to Colorado music. And he can't take a joke. Of course his attitude incited the brass section. Which, you know, are pranksters in every symphony I've ever been in. So they started pranking him, and instead of laughing and going along with it, he got oh-so-offended. He said they were jealous of his talent. And then the brass section got tired of his airs, and they put a whoopee cushion on his seat during a recording session . . . Well—. . . Instead of realizing he was being an ass, he punched the trombone player. Fortunately he's a bantamweight, but then he went after the guy's instrument, and . . . we had a hell of a time calming everyone down and keeping the cops out of it. I thought maybe Les would calm down then. But no, he got . . . strange. No, stranger. This thing about Ben and you is about the strangest. I told Ben he's well off without Les, and that he should change his locks, but Ben, you know . . . tries to parent the world, and Les is really such a . . . helpless idiot, beneath all his aggression . . ."

I sighed. "Ben . . . ," I tried to explain, "doesn't like it when things don't turn out the way he planned."

"I know that. I've known Ben for ten years."

Oh.

"Tell him I said to change his locks. Then make sure he does it. He's more likely to listen to you than to anyone else. Sooner or later, Les is going to have a full-blown breakdown, and he's a violent son of a bitch who will hurt somebody. Ben doesn't want it to be to him. Trust me."

I trusted him. Decadent Roman gods knew insanity when they saw it. And a Roman god who worked under the sort of ceilings the symphony sported would be an expert in it. I thanked him and hung up. So . . . even though the evidence was circumstantial and the timing for that tire slashing must have been very tight indeed, it was highly probable that the nonmurder insanity was the result of Les having gotten a truly weird hair . . .

As for the murder . . . I went back into the bathroom and read the inscription on the bottom of the table.

Now that I knew what it was likely to say, it seemed very clear. It said *Botched* and *Nell Gwen found in alley*. And then the description. So this was one of the pieces that Nick in Rocky's workshop had put out in the alley . . . and Nell Gwen had found it. And guessed its worth . . . and . . .

I caught E in the process of eating a fly, made him spit it out and wiped his lips and hand with a baby wipe, then took him to the bedroom and put clothes on him.

"Bah?" he said hopefully, as I was tying his sneakers.

"No," I said. "We're going to see if Mommy is right about who the murderer is this time."

"Oh, holy fuck!"

"Precisely."

Once More into the Lye Vat, My Friends

I 'VE BEEN CALLED RECKLESS at various times in my life. Which isn't exactly the truth. I didn't just go charging into Rocky's workshop, demanding to talk to Tiff. No. I did the prudent and rational thing. Before going into Rocky Mountain Refinishing, I called Officer Wolfe, and got his answering machine.

Clearing my throat, I told him the name of the killer—or who I suspected to be the killer— and I told him I was going to talk to someone to confirm it. Then I called Ben's cell and told him the same.

Then I picked E up and went in to talk to Tiffany. I breezed past the receptionist, who recognized me as having been there before.

Tiffany was alone in the machine-filled room, which meant I was in luck. She was fine-sanding what looked like a coffee table and looked up when I approached. "Oh, hi," she said. "Rocky isn't here. He went to deliver some stuff."

"That's okay," I said. "I wanted to talk to you."

"Me?" she said, looking much like the third dancer on the left in the chorus line, when told she must fill in for the main actress. "Oooh. What do you need?"

"I . . ." I hesitated. There are ways of telling things and ways of telling things, and you don't outright come out and ask someone if she's an accomplice in a murder. "I know how Nell Gwen died."

She let her sandpaper drop and went pale. "Look, Rocky didn't mean to," she said. "Honest. It's just he gets these tempers, and he pushed

193

her, and she must have hit her head or something and died, so he threw her in the lye vat. Only, as I told Nick, the police would suspect Rocky first, because, you know, he's the ex-husband. They were reconciling and all, but who would believe that? So I told Nick they'd analyze the lye vat when she disappeared, and there's chemicals, you know . . ."

"Rocky?" I said. This wasn't in the script at all. "Rocky did it?"

"Oh yeah," she said. "He told me that Rocky had done it, and then threw the body in the vat and left."

He. My twelfth-grade English teacher used to rant on about unclear antecedents. Clearly Tiff had never studied with her. "He?"

"Nick. When I came in, I found Nick all distraught, and Nell was in the vat. So I told him about how the police might find—traces—and Rocky . . . well, we're both very fond of Rocky. So I helped Nick get the body out—it was *awful*—and he put it in the Dumpster. We never thought she would be identified, you know? It was an accidental death. You're not going to feel the need to tell anyone, are you?"

"No! She can't say anything!" a male voice said, and I turned. It was the pimply young man I'd seen fishing stuff from the vat with the assistance of a robot arm. Damn. He must have been somewhere. Somewhere like a break room, because he was carrying two cups of coffee.

Before I could recover from my surprise, he dropped the cups of coffee. They shattered on the floor, spraying my ankles with hot coffee. This might have been because he was shaking like a willow tree. Despite that, he reached over and grabbed E.

I jumped after him, holding onto E.

Nick—I assumed that's who he was—backed toward the steps to the lye vat. He was still shaking, and he looked close to tears. "She's not going to say anything, or . . . or we throw her kid in the lye vat."

My heart jumped. I was holding onto E's chubby little arm. Nick was holding him around the middle. I wasn't sure if I was more scared that Nick would do what he was threatening or manage to throw him in the lye vat, as that he'd let E go and E would run into one of the saws or worse. "Yes," I said. "I mean, no. I won't say anything. I promise. Honest."

Tiffany was looking from one to the other of us. "Don't be silly, Nick," she said. "Of course, she wouldn't say anything. She knows it was an accident. There's no reason to destroy Rocky's life over an accident."

I was fairly sure that Tiffany had a brain somewhere. Possibly in a bottle of formaldehyde in her dresser drawer. "Does Rocky usually come in Saturday mornings?" I asked.

"Well . . . no, it's a big selling day and he had that thing with All Saints . . ." She paused. I could hear a dime drop behind her eyes. "I never saw . . . uh." She stared at Nick with wide-open eyes. "If Nell came in to talk to you about . . ."

"It's all lies," Nick said. His eyes were wild. "I never killed her. Why would I kill her?"

"Because she knew you had put a valuable piece out in the alley," I said. Then I went with a wild hunch. "A colonial tea table worth at least five thousand dollars. You were putting pieces like that out back regularly, for your accomplices to pick up, weren't you? You were getting kickbacks, weren't you? No one would be stupid enough to discard a piece like that table." I remembered that some of the pieces in the alley behind Rocky's were always set apart from the others. I'd always been hesitant about them, because it wasn't clear if they were discards. "Who were your accomplices? The trash men? Did they give the pieces to a refinisher in Denver? Or resell them as they were? How much did you make? How upset were you when Nell tweaked to it?"

"No. *No!* It's just she argued and argued and argued. She said it was theft, and she said . . . she said I'd go to jail. And I . . . ," Nick said. He shook his head. "I pushed her. People don't die from falling over! They don't die even if they hit their heads. I've fallen dozens of times. It's a lie. I didn't kill her!" Now he was crying.

He took a deep breath. "I have to stop you from telling more lies. Either you go right up that ladder and jump into the lye, or I throw your kid in."

The chances of his doing that were slim. On the other hand, the chances of his dropping E, considering the state he was in, were very high.

I looked up the steps to the lye vat. Sometimes you just have to throw the gasoline at the grill and hope none of the flames hit you.

"All right," I said, "but you hold on to my son." I let go of E's arm, and Nick held him in his arms. I started up the steps slowly.

"No," Tiff said. "I know you did it, Nick. I don't think she's making up lies. I will—"

"You'll just have to jump in the lye vat after her," Nick said, his voice breaking. "If you're going to tell lies, you'll have to jump in the lye, too. Because otherwise I'll have to kill the kid, and you don't want his death on your conscience."

Tiff looked anguished.

"Come on, up the steps with you, too," he said. E whined. Nick was holding him too tightly, I could tell.

195

I should have been terrified, but mostly I was annoyed, not at his causing Nell's death but at his bungling the cover-up and now his obvious meltdown, which had led him to the bizarre idea that killing me and Tiffany and whoever else would solve his problems.

Whoever else . . . "Why did you kill Inobart?" I asked.

"Nell had told him she was going to confront me. He guessed I'd killed Nell—which I didn't, but he said I did. He was going to tell Rocky about everything. Besides," he said, "I put him in your shed because you'd called that morning and you needed to get the message to stop asking questions. I don't want to have to kill anyone else."

I stepped up and up and up, calculating my height. Steps are wonderful things. When a man stands right next to them, it's perfectly possible to stand at the same height as his head and . . . kick.

Nick made an odd sound and fell. Tiffany screamed. E, who had been kicking with increasing frenzy, pulled away from the falling Nick and ran off, straight toward a saw.

"No, E," I yelled.

"Oh, holy—"

"Enoch Dare Mahr, stop right this minute," a voice called out.

E stopped. I couldn't really believe it was Ben, even if the voice was his. But E turned around, inches from the saw, and said, "Bah!" with every look of delight.

Ben came forward to hold his hand. "Right. Now get away from the dangerous stuff. And Dyce, come down those steps."

"Tiff," she said, starting down ahead of me.

"You were in a meeting!"

"Yeah, but it ended happily and quickly and I was on the way to your house when I got your message. I didn't grab it in time, but then . . ." He shrugged.

"Woof!" E called out. And in fact, Officer Wolfe was coming through the workshop, avoiding various automated refinishers.

He waved at E, which, considering he looked very worried, was a feat in itself. "Dyce? What has been going on here?"

"Well," Tiff said, as we both reached terra firma and I started toward Officer Cas Wolfe Hotstuff. "I thought that Rocky had killed his wife, only it turned out that Nick did it and then blamed Rocky, so that I would help him hide the crime, so that no one would find out that he was putting valuable pieces out in the alley and he wouldn't lose his job."

"Dyce?"

"What she said," I said, as I reached the safe haven of Cas Wolfe's arms, and he put them around me. It felt very warm, very safe. "Other than all those unclear antecedents."

"And Nick is—" Cas said.

"Oh my God, no!" Ben yelled. We all turned, in time to see Nick, with a loud cry, dive into the lye vat.

WHO'S AFRAID

"You DIDN'T GET INTO trouble at all for letting the suspect kill himself?" I asked.

Cas shrugged. "I had witnesses to the whole thing. Although one of them isn't exactly impartial. Tiff is madly in love with Rocky, you know?"

"I figured. Maybe now that Nell is not around he'll notice that."

"He probably will. He will see the convenience of marrying his only remaining employee. He was totally unaware of all of it, you know. Theft, murder, hatred, love, all of it."

"Men often are." Then I realized I was talking to two men and blushed. "I mean—"

"Yeah, like I was unaware of the table. Let me tell you, it was harder to work around that, as evidence, than to explain Nick's suicide. Fortunately the chair that we found in the Dumpster also had a note on the bottom. It appears to be a Hepplewhite and quite valuable.

"So I didn't need to confiscate the table. I asked Rocky and he said you can keep it. I think he's grateful to you, you know, for clearing the whole thing up. He says you can come by and have first look at his discards before he puts them at the curb in the future.

"But next time, if you have something that might even remotely be involved in a crime . . . just tell me the truth, all right? I'll do what I can."

"But why did Nick get rid of the furniture?" I asked.

"Some of this is guesswork, but it seems that after he and Tiff got rid of the body, Nick drove Nell's car back to her house, so no one would know she'd been to the workshop. Then he had to get rid of the furniture Nell had confronted him with. He was afraid of passing

198

it on to his contacts because of the inscriptions. He couldn't sand them away, because it would have been obvious. And our experts said there's something about not erasing writing?"

"Well, if he sanded the bottom, people likely would think he was hiding the seal of a manufacturer, like Michael Manson's," I said. "Something that would have shown that the piece was not antique. So he couldn't get much for them. And if he didn't sand the bottom, then sooner or later someone who knew Nell's handwriting might come across the pieces. Refinishers don't sand off writing. It's part of the history of the piece." "Right," Cas said. "So as far as we can figure, he walked back to the workshop, got his own car, then got the furniture and discarded it with the body."

"But if he was just going to throw it away, why didn't he sand the bottoms?" I said.

"My guess is that from the moment that he realized Nell was dead, he stopped thinking clearlyHhe was running scared," Cas said. "Otherwise, he would have used a different Dumpster. And if he'd done that, we might never have known what happened. We got his accomplices, by the way. It was the trash men and a guy in Denver who then refinished the pieces and resold them."

The three of us—Ben, Cas, and I—were sitting around my kitchen table having tea. This had necessitated my getting one of the folding chairs from the closet. Cas insisted on using it. I'd been just about to sit down with Ben, trying to make sense of the events of the day before, when Cas had come in unexpectedly. At least it was unexpectedly for me, though Ben didn't look quite as surprised as he should have been.

"So, your loft is all fixed?" I asked Ben. He had removed his things from my bathroom and living room just minutes ago and put them in the back of his car.

"Yeah. It will take me months to replace the vases. Years, maybe. But the rest is fine."

"And you changed the locks?" I said.

"Yeah," he said.

"Good. I'd prefer that Les not kill you."

He looked startled, as if this possibility had never crossed his mind. "Dyce, he didn't even destroy any of my stuff when he broke in here. Only my tires, and that was because he was really angry when, you know, E interrupted the phone call. Okay, and he did damage the loft, but most of that, like the vases, he did before I left. Other than that, he went after your things. Out of jealousy."

Ben continued. "Les was . . . a little afraid of me, I think. And at the same time, he was convinced I didn't love him, because he could never make me mad. He couldn't make me lash out." He shook his head. "I don't lash out! You know that. Much less at someone smaller than me. Besides, I thought I must have done something terrible to make him go around the bend. It took a long conversation with my friend Peter for me to realize how around the bend Les was when he wasn't around me . . ." He shrugged. "But I wouldn't worry. He's joined a symphony in . . . well, I couldn't read the word properly, but it looked like Belize. Or it might have been Brazil. Or . . . ," he said, thoughtfully, "maybe Berlin."

"Read . . . ?"

"He sent me a letter telling me I had driven him from his native land. You'd think he was joining the Foreign Legion."

Cas laughed. "Well, next time, file a complaint, okay? If I'd known what was going on . . ."

"Yeah, yeah," Ben said. "But see, I thought it was my fault. Dyce keeps saying that one day she'll put a hatchet in my head. Either that or pink panties."

"Pink . . ."

"It's a very long story."

But the funny thing was that Cas Wolfe didn't seem to be put off by our stories. He might ask what was behind them, but he didn't pout and sulk because he didn't understand them at first.

"And I'm not going to tell it now," Ben said. "Because you guys have reservations."

"We have what?" I said, and I'm afraid my voice squeaked.

"Reservations. I called Ben first, because I wanted to be sure he could babysit."

"But we were going to the restaurant with E and then the crime got solved and you had to do a report and . . ."

"And tonight we're going somewhere nice," Cas said, firmly. "Where we can dance. There's this place that just opened up. They have a jazz band."

"Oh," I said, blushing. "Okay." I looked over at Ben. "If you don't mind . . ."

"I don't mind the babysitting," he said, giving me a disdainful once-over. " But—Dyce Chocolat Dare, you're *not* going out to a place with a jazz band to dance in jeans and a stained T-shirt!"

About Elise Hyatt

Elise Hyatt is the pen name of Sarah A. Hoyt, who also writes as Sarah D'Almeida. She writes historical novels, fantasy, science fiction, historical mystery, and mystery. In fact, it's safer to assume no genre is safe from her.

Her Science Fiction novel, Darkship Thieves, received the Prometheus Award.

Her Fantasy Novel, Uncharted, co-written with Kevin J. Anderson won the Dragon Award.

Sarah was born in Portugal and lives in Colorado. She shares her domicile with four cats, two sons and a husband. When not writing, she's usually ruining the household by buying history books, sprucing up the surroundings by refinishing the furniture, or otherwise getting into trouble.

Also By Elyse Hyatt

Or at least, also by Sarah A. Hoyt, who is the person behind Elise Hyatt. If you read urban fantasy, you might want to check out the shifter series, which borrows the setting and some characters from Daring Finds.

www.ingramcontent.com/pod-product-compliance
Lightning Source LLC
Chambersburg PA
CBHW031110260626
47172CB00001B/303